FEB   2016

Love Is Power, or Something Like That

Blackass

A Novel

A. IGONI BARRETT

Graywolf Press

First published in 2015 by Chatto & Windus, an imprint of Vintage/Penguin Random House UK, London

This publication is made possible, in part, by the voters of Minnesota through a Minnesota State Arts Board Operating Support grant, thanks to a legislative appropriation from the arts and cultural heritage fund, and through grants from the National Endowment for the Arts and the Wells Fargo Foundation Minnesota. Significant support has also been provided by Target, the McKnight Foundation, the Amazon Literary Partnership, and other generous contributions from foundations, corporations, and individuals. To these organizations and individuals we offer our heartfelt thanks.

ART WORKS.
arts.gov

MINNESOTA
STATE ARTS BOARD

CLEAN
WATER
LAND &
LEGACY
AMENDMENT

WELLS
FARGO

TARGET.

Published by Graywolf Press
250 Third Avenue North, Suite 600
Minneapolis, Minnesota 55401

www.graywolfpress.org

Published in the United States of America

ISBN 978-1-55597-733-7

2 4 6 8 9 7 5 3 1
First Graywolf Printing, 2016

Library of Congress Control Number: 2015953593

Cover design: Kyle G. Hunter

Cover art: istockphoto.com

To Carlton Lindsay Barrett

O gbodo ridin (don't be stupid)

O gbodo suegbe (don't be slow)

O gbodo ya mugun l'Eko (don't allow
yourself to be taken for a fool)

—Words on the plinth of the *Agba Meta* (Three Elders)
statue at the entrance to Lagos

FURO WARIBOKO

"And now?' Gregor asked himself,
looking around in the darkness.'

—Franz Kafka, *The Metamorphosis*

Furo Wariboko awoke this morning to find that dreams can lose their way and turn up on the wrong side of sleep. He was lying nude in bed, and when he raised his head a fraction he could see his alabaster belly, and his pale legs beyond, covered with fuzz that glinted bronze in the cold daylight pouring in through the open window. He sat up with a sudden motion that swilled the panic in his stomach and spilled his hands into his lap. He stared at his hands, the pink life lines in his palms, the shellfish-coloured cuticles, the network of blue veins that ran from knuckle to wrist, more veins than he had ever noticed before. His hands were not black but white . . . same as his legs, his belly, all of him. He clenched his fists, squeezed his eyes shut, and sank on to the bed. Outside, a bird chirruped short piercing cries, like mocking laughter.

When he opened his eyes again the air was silent, the bird was flown. Turning on his side, his gaze roved the familiar corners of his bedroom and rested on his going-out shoes, their brown leather polished to a dull lustre, placed at attention beside the door. His blue T.M. Lewin shirt and his favourite black cotton trousers (which he had stayed awake till after midnight, when power returned, to iron) were hanging from the chair at his desk. His plastic folder, packed tight with documents, was on the desk. He stared at the folder till his eyeballs itched with dryness, and then he rolled to the bed's edge and blinked at the screen of his BlackBerry lying on the floor. He grimaced with relief: the alarm hadn't gone off: he had sixteen minutes until it rang at eight. On account of Lagos traffic he planned to leave the house at half past eight. A bath, get dressed, eat breakfast, and then he would be off.

Furo heaved on to his back and fixed his gaze on the white ceiling squares festooned with fragments of old cobwebs. He tried to corral his thoughts into the path of logic, but his efforts were brushed aside by his panicked heartbeats. Through the window and far away he heard the unruffled buzz of traffic, the whale honks of trailers, the urgent beeping of a reversing Coaster bus, the same school bus that arrived every weekday around this time. The accustomed sounds of Monday morning. It appeared a normal day for everyone else, and that thought brought Furo no succour, it only confirmed what he already knew, that he was alone in this lingering dream. But what he knew did not explain the how, the why, or the why today. I shouldn't have stayed up late, he said to himself, no wonder I had such nightmares – I, who never dream! He tried to remember what he had dreamed of, but all he recalled was climbing into bed with the same dread he had slept with since he received the email notifying him of his job interview.

He was startled back to alertness by his phone alarm. He reached forwards to turn it off, then pushed his legs off the bed, and sat at the edge with his feet pressed into the rug. The pallor of his feet was stark against the rug's crimson. He was white, full oyibo, no doubt about it – and, with his knees swinging, the flesh of his thighs jiggling, his mind following these bone-and-flesh motions for bewildered seconds before moving its attention to other details of his physiology, he began to comprehend the extent of his transformation. He stilled his knees and, calming himself with a deep suck of air, raised his hand to his cramped neck. As he massaged, his mouth hung open and gastric gasses washed over his tongue in quiet hiccups.

Then, without telltale footsteps, three knocks sounded on the bedroom door. Furo caught his breath and glared, thinking, I locked it, didn't I? I hope I locked it! 'Furo,' his mother called, tapping again. 'Are you awake?' The handle turned. The door was locked.

'I'm awake!' Furo cried out. The relief in his voice made it sound strange to his ears, but otherwise it was his, unchanged. 'Good morning, Mummy.'

'Morning, dear,' his mother said, and rattled the handle. 'Come and open the door.'

'I'm not dressed, I'm getting ready,' Furo said in a rush, and bit his lip at the quaver in his voice. But his mother it seemed had noticed nothing abnormal. 'I'm off to work,' she said. 'Remember, today is Monday, traffic will be bad. You should leave soon.'

'Yes, Mummy.'

'Your father's awake. I asked him to drop you off.'

'OK, Mummy.'

'I've told Tekena to fix you breakfast, but you know how your sister is, she won't get out of bed unless she's dragged. Remind her before you enter the bathroom.'

'Let her sleep. I can take care of myself.'

In the ensuing silence, the back of Furo's neck ached, the hairs on his arms prickled, and he moved his hands to his groin, cupped it from view. When his mother spoke again, her tone sounded like it came from a troubled place.

'Don't worry too much, ehn. Just do your best at the interview. If that job is yours, I'm sure you'll get it. Everything will be OK.'

'Thank you, Mummy,' Furo said. 'Have a good day.'

At the sound of the front door closing, Furo raised both hands to stroke the sweat from his bristled scalp, and after dropping his hands to the bed to dry them, he tried to focus his mind on the problems that swelled before him. His father and his sister were obstacles he had to elude. Another hurdle was money. He had no money, not a kobo on him. He'd planned to ask his mother for the bus fare to the interview, but even if he'd dared to speak about it through the closed door, his father's offer of a ride had quashed any chances of that succeeding. (It was impossible to accept, absurd to even think it, but there it was before his eyes, this skin colour that others were born into but he, Furo, had awoken to.) There was his sister, and he could try borrowing from her, but how to collect the money without facing her? No, too risky – he would have to walk. There was no time to eat, to bathe, to take chances. He had to leave now. There was no more denying what he was experiencing at this moment: he, Furo, son of a mother who knew his voice, was now a white man.

Furo rose from the bed, pattered across the cold floor tiles to the bedroom door and grabbed his towel from the hook. With the towel he scrubbed his armpits, wiped the sweat from his torso and back, rubbed down his legs, and then he straightened up and turned, turned, kept turning, his eyes scanning the room. A sachet of pure water lay on his desk. Beside it, the hand mirror. His gaze moved to the bed with its rumpled sheet, and the louvred window above it, the dust-clogged mosquito netting that sieved the morning light, the old rainwater blotches on the window ledge: every-thing familiar, as it should be. His eyelashes were stiff with sleep crust, and his breath stank of last night's meal: noodles and fried egg garnished with raw onions. He ran his tongue along his crud-caked teeth. A large, reddish-brown cockroach emerged at that instant from under the bed and, waving its antennae furiously, skittered across the floor and into the darkened wardrobe. Furo stopped turning, strode to the desk, grabbed the hand mirror, and with a quick glance at his face, he flung it after the cockroach. Picking up the water sachet, he tore open the edge, and after rubbing his teeth and tongue with a finger, he squirted water into his mouth, gargled, and swallowed. He squeezed the last drops of water on to the towel, mopped his face with it and cleaned the crust from his eyes, then put on his clothes.

Getting from his bedroom to the front door was easy. There was no one about – his father and his sister were still in their bedrooms – and he reached the front door in a soft-stepping dash. Getting to the gate was easier. He sprinted across the yard, shoe heels smacking the concrete. He breathed a sigh as the gate swung closed behind him, and then reached into his trouser pocket for his BlackBerry to check the time, but his pocket was empty, he had left the phone behind. He hesitated a moment, and then, with a brusque shake of his head, he stuck his plastic folder under his arm and set off at a trot for his job interview.

The first person Furo met was the stocky Adamawa man who had the monopoly on garbage collection in the quarter of Egbeda where Furo lived. He was pushing his garbage cart down Furo's street, and he drummed the cart's side with a hooked metal rod to announce his presence to the gated houses. But on catching sight of Furo, the rod slipped from his grasp and dangled on a string from the cart's handle, and then he averted his gaze to the shambles in the cart's bed, but kept on advancing, his steps growing slower, the cart trundling before him with its bold stench. Furo usually delivered the house garbage to him, and they had bantered several times over the haphazard costing of his seller's market service, so Furo, out of habit, greeted him as they drew abreast, and at once regretted the appearance of his voice. The man's silence only sharpened the bite of Furo's blunder. They pulled past each other, and Furo reached the bend in the road before casting back a nervous, salt-pillar look. The cart was abandoned in the middle of the street, and the man stood several paces in front of it, one hand shading his eyes and the other slapping at blowflies, and stared at Furo with festering intensity.

On the next street Furo approached the Isoko woman who ran a buka in front of a tenement building for navy personnel and their families. She was frying hunks of pork in a cauldron of seething oil that straddled a coal fire. Her naked toddler – a girl, her round tight belly accentuated by strings of coloured plastic beads looped around her waist – sat on the ground a short distance from the fire. The child played with fistfuls of charred wood chippings and coconut shell; she babbled to herself – or her imaginary friend – through popping bubbles of spit. As Furo drew near, she looked up with fat-cheeked wonder and caught her breath. He was expecting it, but when the howl came it startled him nonetheless. Hearing the rush of the mother's footsteps, he glanced around to see her picking up the child, and after turning back, he heard her say with a laugh, 'No fear, no cry again, my pikin. No be ojuju, nah oyibo man.'

And so it went: stares followed him everywhere. Pedestrians stopped and stared, or stared as they walked. Motorists slowed their cars and stared, and on occasion honked their horns to draw his face so they could stare into it. School-bound children hushed their mates and poked their fingers in his direction, wrapper-clad women paused in their front-yard duties and gazed after him, and stick-chewing men leaned over balcony railings to peer down at him. As he passed by the corner store where his mother got her emergency groceries, a hubbub of voices burst out, and when he looked over he saw the attendants, Peace, Tope and Eze, crowded in the doorway, gawping at him. A radio jingle – *Mortein! Kills insects dead!* – blared from the barbershop where he got a shave every weekend and his hair cut every month, and when he hurried past the front, Osaze, the Bini barber, who was bent over a smouldering pile of hair, froze in that position, only his head moving through thickening smoke as he followed Furo with his eyes.

No one had called out his name. He'd passed houses he wasn't a stranger to, and he'd been stared at by several people he knew, people whom he had lived beside for many years, joked with, been rude to, borrowed money from – and yet no one had recognised him.

Lagos, they say, is a city of twenty million people. Certainly no less than fifteen million. The economic capital of Nigeria and its most cosmopolitan city, Lagos hosts the highest numbers of foreigners in the country. Construction workers from China mainly; restaurateurs, hoteliers and import dealers from India and the Middle East; tailors, drivers, domestics and technicians from West and Central Africa; expat employees of Western multinationals and global bureaucracies; sojourning journalists and religious crusaders; few exchange scholars; fewer tourists. In some parts of the city it is not unusual to see a white person walking the streets on a sunny day. Ikoyi, Victoria Island, and Lekki Peninsula. That's where oyibos – light-skinned people – live, work, play, and are buried. In private cemeteries. In Apapa, Oshodi, Ikeja, and other business districts of Lagos, the sight of a white man passing through in a chauffeured car is by no means a rarity. But if in traffic his car were bumped by another motorist and he came down to demand insurance details, it is likely that a Lagos-sized crowd would gather to stare, drawn by this curious display of courage. As for the outlying – economically as well as geographically – areas of Lagos, places such as Agege, Egbeda, Ikorodu: a good number of the inhabitants of these neighbourhoods have never held a conversation with an oyibo, never considered white people as anything more or less than historical opportunists or gullible victims, never seen red hair, green eyes, or pink nipples except on screen and on paper. And so an oyibo strolling down their street is an incidence of some thrill. Not quite the excitement decibels of seeing a celebrity, but close.

One anxious step after another and Furo finally reached the stretch of roadside marked out by collective memory – the script on the metal signpost had since rusted away – as Egbeda Bus Stop. It was mid-June, the flood-bearing rains had arrived, and the road drainage, which was clogged with market litter, was undergoing expansion by the municipal authorities. Half of the sidewalk was dug up, the excavated soil heaped on the other half, and these hillocks of red mud had been colonised for commerce, turned into a stage for stalls, kiosks, display cases, impromptu drama. In this road-side market stood food sellers with huge pots of steaming food, fish sellers with open basins of live catfish and dead crayfish, hawkers with wooden trays of factory-line snacks, iceboxes of mineral sodas, and armloads of pirated music CDs, Nollywood VCDs, telenovela DVDs. Then there was the noise, the raw sound of money, of haggling and wheedling and haranguing, the rise and rise of voices against the roar of traffic. The bus stop was crowded with heads and limbs in a swirl of motion, and jostling for space on the motorway were all types of vehicles, from rusted pushcarts to candy-coloured mopeds to sauropod-sized freight trucks, all of them vying with pedestrians for right of way.

Lone white face in a sea of black, Furo learned fast. To walk with his shoulders up and his steps steady. To keep his gaze lowered and his face blank. To ignore the fixed stares, the pointed whispers, the blatant curiosity. And he learnt how it felt to be seen as a freak: exposed to wonder, invisible to comprehension.

About two hours into his trek, just as he sighted in the skyline the straggly multi-storey buildings of Computer Village, Furo realised he had misjudged the distance. His interview was at Kudirat Abiola Way, on the other side of Ikeja, at least an hour's walk from Computer Village. A long way still to go. His face smarted from the sun's heat, the underarms of his shirt were moist with sweat, and thinking of the road he had to cover, he pulled out his handkerchief and scrubbed his face. The cambric came away browned with grime. He fisted the handkerchief into a wad, adjusted the folder under his arm, and quickened his pace. He hadn't come this far to be defeated. This was the time to find a solution. But first he had to find out the time.

He picked the nearest person in front of him, a young lady in a tank top and tight jeans, and slowing his steps as he drew up to her, he said, 'Excuse me.' The lady glanced around without stopping, her expression puzzled, but as Furo raised his hand in greeting, she halted and turned to face him. 'Sorry to bother you,' he said to her, and when she gave a smile of accommodation, he asked: 'Can you please tell me the time?'

She glanced at her wrist. 'It's twelve past ten.'

'Ah,' Furo said, blowing out his cheeks. 'Thank you very much.'

The lady waited as he mopped his neck with his handkerchief. She seemed oblivious to the attention they attracted from passersby. After he folded the handkerchief and put it away, she said, 'How come you speak like a Nigerian? Have you lived here long?'

'Yes,' Furo answered.

She made no move to continue on her way, and as Furo tried to step backwards so he could go around her, she reached out and grabbed his elbow. His muscles tensed at her touch, and he resisted at first as she tugged his arm, but then he realised she was only guiding him out of the path of a motorcycle that was bearing down the sidewalk from behind. 'That's interesting, that your accent is so Nigerian,' she said when the danger was past. She released his arm. 'Where are you from?' she asked.

'I'm Nigerian.'

She squawked with laughter. Astonished faces turned to gawk, and seeing Furo's embarrassment, she caught herself. 'Sorry for laughing. But how is it possible that you're Nigerian?'

Furo's eyes lingered on her face. Her smile showed small white teeth and health-shined gums, and the dimples in her cheeks were signifiers of a merry disposition. Any other day, in a less pressing position, in his old skin, he would have asked her name. But there was no need for that, as she now offered, 'My name is Ekemini,' to which he responded, 'I'm Furo.'

Her face pulled a look of doubt. 'As in, *Furo*? Isn't that a Niger Delta name?'

'Yes.' Furo cast an impatient glance past her. 'Actually, I'm in a—' He fell silent, distracted by the idea forming in his head.

'Yes?' Ekemini prompted.

'Hurry,' Furo said. 'I'm in a hurry.' He lifted his shoulders in a shrug. 'I'm going for a job interview that starts at eleven, but I just realised there's no way I can make it in time.'

'Oh no, that's bad,' Ekemini said, and checked her wristwatch. 'Where's the interview?'

'It's here in Ikeja, near Ogba side. Kudirat Abiola Way.'

'What!' Ekemini cried, and grasped Furo's arm again, this time in excitement. 'But that's not far from here. If you take a bike you'll get there in twenty, twenty-five minutes max. But you have to go now.' Dragging him along, she crossed to the sidewalk's edge. As she raised her hand to flag down a motorcycle, Furo spoke.

'That's the problem. I don't have money on me.'

'No money?' Her tone was startled. 'I see.' She freed his arm and drew away from him. Her eyes glinted with suspicion, and it seemed clear to Furo that any moment she would mutter something rude and whirl away, convinced he was some sort of confidence trickster. To forestall this, Furo took the offensive. 'Yes, no money, that's why I'm walking.' His confidence mounted along with her curiosity. 'It's not like I chose to trek to my interview, you know,' he said, and held her gaze. Settling deeper into character, he softened his tone: 'I was attacked by robbers this morning. They took my car, my wallet . . . and my phone. I was lucky to get away with my documents.' He tapped the folder under his arm.

In the silence that followed, Furo and Ekemini were jostled together by a flash wave of pedestrians. With her chest pressed against him and her breath in his face, Furo almost regretted lying to her. But he had no choice, he told himself, no choice at all. 'I'm sorry,' Ekemini now said to him, and after pulling back from his body, she continued, 'So what will you do? Do you need to call someone?' She reached into her handbag. 'Here, you can use my phone.'

'I've called already. My people will meet me at the interview venue.'

'Oh yes, of course – your interview. You really must get going.' She waited a beat, and then spoke in a rush, her tone embarrassed. 'Can I give you some money for the bike fare?'

Furo's grin was truthful. 'That would be nice of you. It's just a loan, of course.'

Ekemini pulled a thousand naira note out of her handbag, and her face was pleased as she handed it over. 'Thank you, thank you,' Furo said, tucking the note in his breast pocket. He opened his folder, took out a pen, passed it to her and said, 'Can I have your number? I'll call you tomorrow so we can meet. To return the money.' He watched with growing impatience as she wrote down three sets of numbers on the back of a business card. After she passed the card to him, he swivelled to face the curb, held his arm aloft, and a swarm of motorcycles shrieked towards him. He climbed aboard the first to arrive and, blocking out the shouted banter from the disappointed riders, gave the man directions. After the okada jumped forwards and weaved into the rush of traffic, Furo turned sideways in his seat to wave goodbye to Ekemini. He got a shock when he saw her running along the sidewalk after him with a raised arm and her face twisted with effort. 'Your pen! You forgot your pen!' she shouted against the wind, and the rider heard her and slowed, but Furo leaned forwards, said in his ear: 'Abeg keep going.'

Arriving at the interview venue, Furo realised with a sinking feeling that even if he had walked over he would still have got there on time. Through the grilled gate – from which hung a white signboard announcing in green block letters: HABA! NIGERIA LTD – he could see a mass of people standing in single file in the bright sunlight, all dressed in formal clothes, all clutching folders, briefcases, shoulder bags. It was obvious who they were, why they were there, what they were dressed up for. He had heard of them. He had seen their faces under newspaper banners that screamed '50% *Youth Unemployment in Nigeria!*' He was one of them. And yet, despite his own desperation for a job, despite the worst scenarios he had conjured up in the days since he got his interview invitation, he had never imagined that so many people would turn up for the same job he wanted. As far as he knew there was only one position on offer. And for that at least forty people were standing in line.

After he paid the okada rider and collected eight hundred naira in change, Furo hurried to the gate to find it unlocked. Inside the compound stood a whitewashed, gable-roofed, two-storey vintage building with a residential aura. The expansive compound was unpaved, the red clay soil spotted with clumps of weed, and several cars were parked close to the building. By the back fence, a Mikano generator squatted on concrete pilings. The only other structure in the compound was the yellow-painted gatehouse, which Furo approached. News in Hausa blasted at full volume from a small radio perched in a rocking chair facing the doorway, and even before Furo stuck his head in, his nose was greeted by the smell of incense. He saw a wooden table on which was balanced the incense stick, smoke spiralling from its tip, the floor beneath it sprinkled with ash. Prominent in the room was a longbow and quiver of arrows, and there were clothes hanging from nails in the walls, as well as a kerosene stove, cooking utensils, and other domestic trappings. The gatehouse looked lived-in, but there was no one there.

Rather than wait for the guard's return to enquire about a process that seemed apparent, Furo decided to join the queue. Stares he expected, and got as he approached the waiting group, and when he stopped behind the last person in line, the long row of heads began all at once to chatter. Furo dropped his eyes to his shoes, powdered with dust from his trek, and shut his ears to the grumblings. He had as much right as anyone to be here. He had probably suffered the most to get to this place, and all for a chance to be treated the same as everyone. He, too, needed a job, and come anything, despite everything, he would stand his ground. He ignored the rising voices.

'I'm talking to you!'

A sharp-toed pair of shoes – oxblood leather finely cracked, the uppers lopsided from long wear, black laces untidily knotted – appeared in Furo's line of sight. He raised his head.

'Yes, you, don't act as if you didn't hear me. Or you don't like black people?'

Tall man, lean and dark, with a round small head from which his cheekbones stuck out. In the corners of his mouth white flecks of saliva showed.

'I don't understand,' Furo said, and took a step backwards.

The man barked with laughter, a false laugh, showering spittle. Furo gave a start as he was strafed in the face; he fought the urge to raise his hand as a shield. Scattered titters drifted along the queue, and when he stole a look, a gang of eyes confronted him.

'My elder brother lives in Poland.' The man stared at Furo as if awaiting a reply. Furo took another step backwards. 'Where are you going?' The man's tone was surprised, and striding forwards to close the gap between them, he crowded Furo with his height and sun-beaten odour. 'Didn't you hear what I said?' he demanded, his Adam's apple jumping.

Furo managed in a calm voice, 'What does that have to do with me?'

Sadness suffused the man's face. 'Your people have refused to give me a visa. I've applied four times. My brother is getting tired of inviting me.'

'I'm not from Poland,' Furo said.

'Did I say you were from Poland?' At Furo's silence, the man added in a softened tone, 'You came for the job interview?'

Furo's nod set off a flurry of exclamations from the queue. The person ahead in line, a Deeper Life-looking woman – hair banished into a scarf, no earrings on, and dressed in a polyester skirt suit of baggy cut – glared at him with fuck-you intensity. The animosity in the air was so noxious that for an instant he thought of leaving. For an instant only. He needed the job more than he feared a lynching. Lucky then that he didn't have to face his convictions, because the tension eased when the mob leader – *this idiot who wants to get me in trouble*, Furo thought with a flash of hatred – raised his voice: 'It's a nonsense job anyway.' He turned his attention back to Furo. 'You have to go inside and write down your name, then collect a number from Tosin, the woman at the front desk. She will call you in by your number.'

Relief flooded Furo's guts. 'Thank you,' he said quickly,

and then stood waiting, uncertain of how to take his leave. He wondered if he should shake hands to show his gratitude and dispense the man's assumptions about his feelings towards black people, but the handshake it turned out wasn't needed, as the man seemed to have forgotten the grudge he held. He grinned at Furo, placed a hand on his shoulder in a gesture of affability, then bent his face close and said, 'I like you. You don't talk through your nose like other oyibo.'

Furo forced a smile. His face itched from the flying spittle.

'Black and white, we are all brothers,' the man continued. 'We should support each other, you know, like Bob Marley, one love.' He held up his free hand with the middle and index fingers entwined, and waved these under Furo's nose. 'We should be like one. I plan to marry oyibo when I reach your country. My brother's wife is oyibo. She's the one inviting me—'

Furo interrupted him. 'I have to go and put my name down.'

'Yes, go and write your name,' the man agreed, and nodded vigorously, but did not release his grip on Furo's shoulder. 'You will get the job, for sure. Me and you have plenty things to talk about.' His eyes bored into Furo's, and his face hardened, shed its friendliness, twisted into a scowl. 'Watch out for Obata!'

The vehemence of his words spattered Furo with spit, and this time he couldn't help it, he raised a hand to wipe his face before muttering, 'OK, thanks.' He shrugged off the man's hold, drew away from him, and ran the gauntlet of hostile faces towards the building entrance.

The receptionist smiled at Furo from her chair. The push-button phone on her desk had started ringing as Furo entered, but she ignored it. She gave him her full attention.

'Are you Tosin?' Furo asked.

'Yes, I am. How may I help you, sir?'

'Someone told me to come in here and collect a number from you.'

The puzzled expression that leapt into the oval of Tosin's face was quickly replaced by a smile of apology. 'I'm sorry about the mix up,' she said. 'You must have spoken to one of the applicants. We're interviewing for a vacancy.' She flipped open the visitors notepad on her desk and picked up a biro. 'Who are you here to see?'

The phone had fallen silent, but the air vibrated with anticipation of its next ring. The Haba!-branded clock on the wall above Tosin's head pointed to nine minutes past eleven.

Furo said, 'I'm here for the eleven o'clock interview. I'm really sorry I'm late, but I've been here – I've been outside for the past fifteen minutes. My name is Furo Wariboko.'

Tosin's eyes widened. 'You mean the interview for the salesperson job?'

'Yes,' Furo said.

The biro slipped from Tosin's fingers, clattered on the desk, and as if to complete her embarrassment, it evaded her scrabbling hands and rolled to the floor. She was bending to pick it up when the phone rang. She jerked upright in her seat, snatched the receiver from its cradle, and pressed it to her ear. Her eyes avoided Furo all through her low-voiced conversation, and by the time she replaced the receiver, she had regained composure. 'OK,' she said with a light clap of her hands, and rising to her feet, she looked at Furo. 'Please come with me.'

He followed her up a staircase that ended in a hallway lined on one side with doors. Each door was fitted with a copper-coloured plaque announcing function. SALES.

MARKETING. IT. LAVATORY. The last office, the door closing the hallway, bore a plaque that read, AYO ABU ARINZE. Tosin halted in front of the second-to-last door. HUMAN RESOURCES.

'Yes?' a surly voice responded to her knock, and she cracked the door open. 'I've brought one of the candidates for the salesperson job. I think you—' A cough cut off her words, followed by the abrupt clatter of cutlery. The man spoke, his angry words slurring through a mouthful of food. 'But I told you to wait! Is something wrong with your ears?' Tosin shot back, 'Just stop there, Obata, I don't have time for your rudeness this morning.' Throwing open the door, she waved Furo in. As he stepped forwards there was a gasp, and the man seated behind the desk leapt to his feet and spilled his plate of stewed beans. '*See now!*' he snarled, staring down at his shirt, and then he looked up at Furo and stammered out, 'My apologies, sir, but . . . surely . . .' he swung his gaze to Tosin and a furious note entered his voice, 'you've made a mistake!'

'No mistake,' Tosin replied, her tone impassive. 'His name is Furo Wariboko and he's here for the salesperson job.' Without another word, she pulled the door shut behind her.

Obata was still on his feet, one hand gripping the desk and the other his plate. His mouth hung open, and in his face irritation and disbelief mixed like the mess of beans in his cheeks. He noticed the direction of Furo's gaze, and closed his mouth, then bent down and pushed his plate under the desk. Straightening back up, he swiped his hand across his lips. With the same hand he jabbed a finger at Furo and said in a voice gruff with challenge, '*You are Furo Wariboko?*'

Furo nodded yes. In the wall behind Obata an ancient

air conditioner hummed, rattled, regained its rhythm, and dripped water into an empty paint tub placed underneath.

'That's impossible!' Obata burst out, and dropped into his seat. 'I saw that CV with my own eyes, I have it here.' He swept his hands through the papers on his desk, plucked up two stapled sheets, held them close to his face and ran his finger along the script. 'See here, it says that Wariboko is Nigerian! And . . . and . . . attended Ambrose Alli University!' He flung down the résumé and glared at Furo. 'Come on, you – a white Nigerian? That is just not possible!'

'But it's my CV—'

Obata cut him off with a shout. 'I say that is not possible!'

Despite the chill in the room, Furo felt his palms grow moist with heat, and he resisted the urge to wipe them against his trousers. His eyes roamed the walls, the ceiling . . . on the ceiling above Obata's head, a tiny green moth was flinging itself against the glow of the fluorescent tube, over and over again. Obata's breathing sounded like beating wings.

'I say that is not possible!' Obata repeated.

In a cowed voice, Furo started, 'Excuse me, sir,' but Obata interposed with a raised arm and flattened hand. 'Hold on,' he said, and took his own advice. Arranging his features into a parody of calmness, he inhaled deeply and exhaled through his mouth. 'Listen carefully before you say anything,' he said. 'I don't know what your mission is, but I advise you to give it up. We're a respectable company. You can't just walk in here and tell me some cock-and-bull story. I will investigate everything to the very last! Secondary school, university, even youth service, all those places have records. I will personally contact the registrar at Ekpoma—' He picked up the résumé and waved it at Furo. 'So just think very well before you talk.'

As Obata spoke, Furo began to see that he had no past

as he was and no future as he had been. His folder of documents now felt useful only as fuel for Obata's anger. He had no hope of getting this job, any job at all, not as long as his own credentials proved him a liar. He felt bone-tired, hope-weary. He had wasted his efforts chasing after the same thing he was running from. There was nothing left to do but turn back home. It was time to face his family with the truth.

And yet he said, his voice shaking with conviction, 'I am Furo Wariboko.'

Fury contorted Obata's face. 'Look here,' he said in a voice as deep as a shout in a well, 'do I look like a fool?' He stood up and strode around the desk towards Furo. The résumé, folded in his hand, was raised above his head as if to swat an insect. 'Do I look stupid?'

The squeak of hinges stopped Obata in his tracks, and after he lowered his arm, Furo looked around. Standing in the doorway was a man of average height. His frail shoulders, slim arms, and small feet – which were laced up in blue canvas sneakers – gave him the look of a bully's punching bag. But his forceful features put the lie to first impressions: bushy eyebrows set in a straight line over big-balled eyes, his forehead broad and high-domed. Between wide nose and pointed chin, a thin-lipped, stubborn mouth. And an aura of power that he wore as lightly as his stonewashed jeans and green-striped batakari.

Obata found his tongue. 'Good morning, Arinze,' he said in a civil tone. The man nodded acknowledgement, and striding into the office, he held out his hand to Furo. His grip was strong. 'I'm Ayo Abu Arinze,' he said.

'Good morning, sir,' Furo dipped his head in respect.

'Please, call me Abu,' Arinze said with a quick smile.

Breaking the handshake, he turned to Obata. 'I thought I heard shouting.'

Unease flickered in Obata's face. 'It's just a small matter, a misunderstanding,' he said, and cleared his throat. 'I'm handling it.'

Arinze nibbled on his bottom lip, and stared steadily at Obata, a speculative light in his eyes. 'What happened to your shirt?'

Obata glanced down, and began brushing off his shirt with his left hand. 'I spilled some food,' he muttered without looking up.

Arinze turned back to Furo. 'If you don't mind my asking, why are you here?'

'I came for the job interview.'

With a lift of his eyebrows, Arinze asked, 'The salesperson job?'

'Yes, sir.'

'So what's the problem?' Arinze's gaze was directed at Obata.

'This man is lying. He's an impersonator. He claims his name is Wariboko!' Obata's tone was affronted. He drew closer to Arinze and extended the résumé to him. 'See the CV he sent.'

Arinze scanned the sheets in silence, and then he said, 'Mr Wariboko?'

'Yes,' Furo answered.

'What's your date of birth?'

'Sixth of May, 1979.'

'Your secondary school?'

'Baptist High School.'

'Where?'

Furo stared at Arinze. 'I don't understand.'

'What town is the school in?'

'Oh,' Furo said, relief washing through his voice. 'Port Harcourt.'

'What are your hobbies?'

Furo thought a moment. 'Swimming, travelling and reading.'

'And your mother's maiden name?'

'Osagiede.'

'That's not what it says here.'

Furo's brow creased in perplexity; he raised his hand to massage his nape. 'My mother's maiden name is not on my CV,' he said at last.

'It's not,' Arinze agreed, and lowered the résumé. He spoke to Obata. 'I would like to interview Mr Wariboko myself. Is that OK?'

The stain on Obata's shirt rose and fell with his breathing. 'I guess,' he said, and averting his face, he added tonelessly, 'What about the others? Do you still want me to interview them?'

'By all means do,' Arinze said. 'We still need a salesperson.' He walked to the door, pulled it open, and stood to one side. 'After you, Mr Wariboko. Let's finish this in my office.'

The stuffiness of Human Resources had left its impression on Furo's mind. So much so that when Arinze opened the door to his office, Furo, disoriented by the burst of daylight that lit up the room like a terrarium, hesitated so long on the threshold that Arinze touched his elbow to urge him forwards. Leading Furo to a glass-top desk the size of a ping-pong table, Arinze said, 'Please have a seat,' and inclined his head at two soft-leather chairs arranged in front. 'Coffee?' he asked after Furo was seated, but Furo shook his head no. While Furo cast furtive glances at the room's decor – the window ledges decorated with a plethora of bric-a-brac, the white walls adorned with colour-splashed paintings and brooding masks and a samurai sword in its wooden sheath: ornaments announcing a moneyed, well-travelled life – Arinze strode to the coffee table beside the open French windows and poured a mug of coffee, its woodlands aroma rising with clouds of steam. Returning to the desk, he set down the mug and sank into his swivel chair. A shellacked bookcase covered the wall behind the desk from floor to ceiling. To Furo's bemused gaze it seemed about to topple from the weight of books.

'Mr Wariboko,' Arinze began, and rested his elbows on the desk with his hands cupping his mug. He pinned Furo under the force of his stare. 'I'll be frank with you – we need a man like you on the team.' He paused for his meaning to sink in, and then said, 'I'm about to offer you a job. But first of all, I need you to answer three questions. And I expect the truth.'

'Yes, sir,' Furo responded in a too-loud voice. He struggled to keep a straight face, tried not to grin with pleasure, and failed. His mouth felt full of teeth.

'Another thing,' Arinze said, smiling back. 'Please don't call me "sir".' He took a sip from his mug, set it down, and rubbed his palms. 'First question. Is your name really—' he glanced down at the résumé on his desk, 'Furo Wariboko?'

'Yes,' Furo said fiercely. 'Yes, it is.'

Arinze gave a slight shrug as he spoke his next words. 'Second question then. Do you have any ID that confirms you're Nigerian? Like a passport or driving license?'

'I don't,' Furo said, relieved it was the truth, and as Arinze watched him in silence, he added, 'Actually, I have an old passport, but I left it in a place I can't go back to.'

Arinze took a long drink of coffee. 'We can't risk any

25

allegations of illegally employing a foreigner, so you'll need to get a passport before you start with us. Is that OK?'

'Yes,' Furo answered. He hadn't the faintest idea of how to go about getting a passport, but his joy would not be spoiled by a predicament in his future. A future that hadn't existed just minutes before. A strong breeze from the open French windows fanned his excitement, gave him the courage to ask, 'And your third question?'

Sip, replace mug, and rub hands together. Arinze was a creature of methodical action, Furo could tell. Already he felt his heart filling with respect for the man he would soon call boss.

'When was the last time you read a book?'

At this question, Furo's heart skipped, and he strained to keep his disappointment from showing. The truth had served him thus far in answering Arinze's questions, but the truth this time was inimical to him. And what was the truth? He read newspapers for job announcements. And on his smartphone he read Facebook and Twitter, blogs and news websites, ephemera of the World Wide Web . . . and not forgetting the countless rejection emails from all the companies he had applied to for jobs. The whole truth and nothing else was that he'd read no books since 2007, not since he got the pain in his neck from studying for his final examinations.

Furo had dreaded this question ever since he saw the newspaper advert announcing a salesperson position with a company that sold business books. He had applied for the job despite his misgivings, after first altering his résumé to add 'reading' to his hobbies, and he was ecstatic when he received the email inviting him for an interview. It was only his second invitation in three-plus years of submitting job applications. On the same day he got the email, he decided on the book he would use as his cover. I love *Things Fall Apart*, he'd planned to say, it teaches us about our culture, where we as Africans are coming from. But in fact he chose that book because he was forced to read it in junior secondary and still remembered the storyline. Even the opening line: *Okonkwo was well known throughout the nine villages and even beyond.* And in his head the voice of Mr Zikiye, his English Literature teacher, still droned: *The white man in this book is a symbol of progress. Okonkwo fought against the white man and lost. Progress always wins, that's why it's progress. Now tear out a sheet of paper, you have a test.*

The test that now faced him was as difficult as any he'd encountered in school. He was almost certain he wouldn't get the job if he spoke the truth. For how could he, when the last book he'd read was a biochemistry textbook for his BIC 406 exam? But if he told a lie and was caught out by Arinze, forget the almost, he was certain he would lose the job. Suddenly oppressed by a full bladder, Furo wriggled his sweating toes in his shoes, and soon began to think not only of what to answer but also of how to explain why it took him so long to answer. When Arinze's chair squeaked, Furo looked up, his thoughts in a whirligig, his body tensed for disappointment. He saw Arinze put down his mug, and after rubbing his hands together, he heard him say:

'But will you read the books we sell?'

'Oh yes, I will!' Furo responded, his voice cracking with eagerness. 'I promise I will.'

'Good man,' Arinze said. 'So let's get down to details. The position I'm offering you is Marketing Executive. You'll be my point man, my big gun, the person I send out to bring in important clients. It's high-level marketing – you'll have to dress formally for meetings. The company will provide you with an official car and a driver. How does that sound so far?'

Speechless, Furo nodded, and Arinze continued.

'The marketing office is empty, so you'll have it to yourself. Do you own a laptop?'

Furo shook his head no.

'But you know how to use one?'

He nodded yes.

'It's company policy that all employees must own their own laptops. We'll buy you one, but you'll have to pay back from your salary over six months. Is that OK?'

'Yes.'

'Perfect. Now your salary. Executive pay at Haba! starts at eighty thousand a month. That's what you'll earn at first. But you'll also get a percentage on your sales. For sales of up to five hundred books, you get two point five per cent. For sales of five hundred to a thousand, you get . . .'

While Arinze reeled off percentages, Furo was calculating his good fortune in decimals. This offer of employment was the first he'd ever got, and a salary of eighty thousand naira was eighty thousand times better than nothing. It was also fifty thousand more than he'd expected, as the vacancy he'd applied for, the salesperson job, paid thirty thousand naira. Even better, this position came with a car and driver, free transportation, meaning more money for him. With all that money in his hands he wouldn't need anyone. He could feed himself, buy new clothes, start his life for real, and still have enough left over to save towards renting an apartment. Eighty thousand naira wasn't just money, it was freedom. For the first time since waking that morning, Furo had no doubts about the path to take.

Arinze had fallen silent, and now Furo could ask the question burning his tongue.

'When do I start?'

Arinze reached for his open laptop, then tapped the keypad and stared at the screen, his eyes reflecting the plasma glow. 'Today's the eighteenth,' he said. 'How about the first Monday in July? That's July second. You can start then.'

'I'll be here,' Furo said. And in a voice hoarsened by emotion: 'Thank you.' On impulse he jumped to his feet and stretched his hand across the desk, and his eyes, catching a movement, swung to the glass below. He was still staring at the white face staring back at him when Arinze took his hand. 'I like that, a businesslike approach to business,' he said, nodding with approval. 'I have a strong feeling I made the right decision. I'm looking forward to you proving me right.' He walked round the table, placed his hand on Furo's shoulder, steered him to the door, and threw it open. 'Go well, Mr Wariboko.'

When the mind is at rest the body shouts its demands. Furo Wariboko, back on the streets of Lagos, now realised how hungry he was. Weak with it, his head aching, stomach juices churning, his breath reeking with it. He considered his choices. He had eight hundred naira left over from the money he'd borrowed from Ekemini, and that amount would just about cover a meal at Mr Biggs, the cheapest of the fast food chains. He was reluctant to spend everything. Thus far he had refused to pop his jubilant mood by thinking about where to go next, where to sleep tonight, but somewhere behind the wall of his mind he knew there was no going back.

No choice then. He had to eat in a roadside buka.

The roadway by which he strolled was jammed with traffic, cars crawled along at a pace that turned the drivers' faces tight with frustration, okadas tore through gaps that even the bravest hawkers hesitated to enter, and petrol fumes from overheated engines thickened the air. Like oases on a desert caravan route, child vulcanisers and apprentice mechanics loitered in roadside lean-tos that offered scant shelter from today's sunshine and tomorrow's rainstorms. Exhausted vehicles dotted the roadside, some with bonnets opened to let out steam from gasping radiators. A riot of honking assailed the ears: short warning honks, long angry honks, continuous harrying honks: a language as universal as a scream. But in Lagos, overused. The clamour was deafening.

'*Oyibo!*' a female voice yelled from across the roadway, and Furo, startled out of his fascination with the automotive babel, glanced over. Vivid in her Fanta-bright shirt and white gloves, a traffic warden sat on a tyre under the shade of a neem tree. She was eating a peeled orange that was gripped in her right hand, and when she saw she had Furo's attention, she grinned and gave him a left-handed wave. Furo moved his gaze along. Beside the neem tree, outside the shadows cast by its leaves, stood a three-legged easel blackboard. Scrawled on its surface in pink chalk were the words FOOD IS READY. Furo reached his decision before he realised he'd reached it, and stepping on to the asphalt, he dodged between trapped bumpers and strode across to the buka, a wood-and-zinc shed backed against a concrete fence and hung on the front and sides with grimy, once-white lace curtains. As he parted the front curtain, he heard the traffic warden exclaim, 'Where this oyibo man dey go?' and from the corner of his eye he saw her jump to her feet and fling away her suck-shrivelled orange. He ducked into the buka.

A middle-aged woman with a red hairpiece styled in a bob sat on a bar stool behind a table laden with aluminium

pots. Four benches were arranged in front of the table. A
man dressed like a construction labourer – blue denim shirt
faded grey on the shoulders, mud-spattered jeans scissored
off at the knees, and yellow rubber boots – sat astride one
of the benches, and in front of him was a sweating bottle of
Pepsi, a steaming bowl of okra soup, and three wraps of cold
fufu, one opened. The fermented whiff of cassava meal mixed
with the aroma of boiled okra and smoked panla fish made
Furo lightheaded, and he sat down quickly. After placing his
folder on the same bench he straddled, he looked up to catch
the food seller staring at him, as was the labourer, his hand
stilled in his soup-smeared fufu.

'Do you have egusi soup?' Furo said to the food seller, but
she stared on in silence. He raised his voice. 'Madam – do
you have egusi soup?'

The labourer recovered first. 'Answer am, e dey ask you
question!' he said to the food seller in a biting tone. He
seemed angered by the reflection he saw in her face.

'Yes,' the woman said. She rose from the bar stool and made
a clattering show of opening pot lids to check the contents.
Then, as if unable to stop herself, she looked up at Furo and
said in a rush: 'Abeg, no vex, but you be albino?'

'Open your eye, woman,' the labourer said. 'No be albino.'

The woman ignored the labourer, she kept her questioning
gaze on Furo, and so he shook his head no. 'I'm not an albino,'
he confirmed.

'Ewoo!' the woman exclaimed. 'You be oyibo true-true.'

The woman fell silent, but her thoughts played across her
features, changed her expression from wonder one moment to
glee the next. The labourer resumed eating, his face soured
with scorn. Seeing as the woman made no move to serve him,
Furo asked with a touch of asperity, 'Do you have eba?' The

woman caught the note in his voice, and she beamed a smile at him as if to say, *What can you do, you white man, you barking puppy*, but she said nothing, she nodded yes. 'Give me three wraps of eba with egusi soup,' Furo said.

The woman placed the eba on a steel plate, and then picked up a soup bowl and her serving ladle. 'How many meat?' she asked, and Furo held up one finger. But when she set the food and a bowlful of water before him, he saw two chunks of meat mixed with the shredded vegetable of his soup. He glanced up in surprise to meet the woman's wide smile. 'I give you extra meat,' she said, her voice lowered, conspiratorial, but still overheard by the labourer. At his loud sniff of derision her smile slipped, she shot him the evil eye, and then returned her gaze to Furo with a smile that shone even brighter.

The stiff smile Furo shot back strained his jaw. He was grateful for the extra piece of meat, but he was also wary of the woman's reason for giving it; he didn't want to be drawn into conversation about himself on account of the gift, and so he said nothing. In the silence opened up by the missing thank you, the food seller beat the air with her expectant breath, and then, coming to see the futility of waiting, she shuffled her feet on the hard-packed dirt floor. As she moved from Furo's side, he bent forwards and rinsed his hands in the bowl of water, then began to eat, his hand moving swiftly from eba to soup to mouth.

'Hah!' the woman exclaimed from her new spot behind him. 'See how oyibo dey chop eba. This one nah full Nigerian o.'

The labourer had had enough. 'You this olofofo woman, I been think sey you get sense,' he said. 'As you old reach, why you dey behave like small pikin? You never see oyibo before?'

'Why you insult me?' said the woman. Her voice bubbled with outrage.

'Who insult you?'

'So you no insult me?'

The labourer clicked his tongue in irritation. 'Leave me abeg. Make I finish my food.'

'I no blame you sha. Nah your mama I blame. She no train you well.'

'No carry my mama enter this talk o,' the labourer said. He rose to his feet and pointed his finger at the food seller. Long strings of okra soup dripped from his hand on to the bench.

'Hah!' the food seller cried with a sharp clap of her hands. 'You dey point me finger?'

The labourer's courage didn't falter and neither did his rude finger. 'And so?' he asked the woman in a taunting tone. 'Wetin you fit do?'

He shouldn't have asked. Not of a woman who made a living off dealing with hungry men. And especially not of a woman who wore red hair. Furo steeled himself for the explosion.

'Dirty Yoruba rat!'

'Old Igbo mumu.'

'Bastard son of kobo-kobo ashewo!'

'Useless illiterate woman.'

'Thunder fire you! See your flat head like Sapele dodo!'

It was now a roaring quarrel. The woman's curses were more colourful, her delivery more dramatic, and her well of invention ran deeper. The man's voice was louder. Their yells vied for supremacy with each other and also with the horn blares of the traffic outside, which muffled their words doubtless for passersby, but not for the person trapped between them. Furo rushed through his meal, eager to make his escape before a crowd collected. After he cleaned out the soup bowl with his fingers, he washed both hands, rubbed them dry on his handkerchief, and drew two hundred naira from his breast pocket. Then he sat waiting for the shouting to subside. From the sound of things, it wouldn't be long before the man realised he had the lost the fight.

'Nah because of oyibo you dey talk to me anyhow!' growled the labourer in a final burst, and before the woman could retort he leapt over the benches, slapped aside the lace curtains with his food-smeared hand, and stalked out.

'Where you dey go – pay me my money!' the food seller screamed. She made to rush after the man, but Furo, horrified at the thought of a scuffle breaking out at the entrance of the buka while he was still inside, threw out his arm, grabbed the woman's wrist, and spoke without thinking. 'Please, madam, I beg you, let him go. I will pay for his food.'

'Why you go pay?' the woman demanded, straining against Furo's grip. 'That agbero chop my food finish, curse me on top, and e no get money to pay! Hah, no way o. I go show am today sey I be Okpanam woman. Abeg leave my hand!' With a heave she yanked her arm free, then spun around and bounded through the curtains.

Furo felt a twinge of relief as he returned the two hundred naira to his pocket. After glancing around the buka in search of an exit plan that didn't involve wasting good money, he reached for the bottle of Pepsi the labourer had left behind. He wiped the bottle mouth clean and drank down the chilled cola as he sat waiting. When he heard sounds of the fight – shouts of many voices and the stampeding of feet – he set down the emptied bottle, picked up his folder, stood up from the bench, then strode to the side curtain and slipped out of the buka.

Late afternoon, the red-faced sun slinking off west: offices shut and the shops shutting, the traffic hawkers multiplied in the frenzy of the day's dying, the motorways choked with cars and the sidewalks with crowds, the zombie drag of feet drumming the earth. As Furo wondered where to go, he wandered around Ikeja, caught in this surge, the headlong rush of Lagos at the end of day. Inside and outside, from the pull of his thoughts to the push of his surroundings, nowhere was there respite from the muddle of images, sounds, smells.

Inside, he thought:

The streets of Lagos at night were dangerous for anybody, more so for him; and sleeping on the streets was an option only for the insane, the gang-affiliated, or the suicidal.

Outside, he saw:

Surly faces, ferocious stares, armies of swinging legs – a burst pipe in a roadside gutter. It spouted water in a fine spray, the ground for metres around churned into mud by feet.

He thought:

He couldn't afford a hotel, and police stations were to be avoided. He would most likely be arrested as a foreigner with no papers.

He saw:

Splotches of faeces lining the ground beside a flyover whose concrete sides were plastered with posters of pastors and politicians; and, under the bridge, littered around, their edges fluttered by the draughts from passing cars, were torn newspaper pages, crumpled notebook sheets, discarded lottery tickets, streamers of tissue paper, all stained with shit.

Inside:

He was sure he could find a church, they were scattered around all corners of Lagos, but finding one that left its doors open at night was another matter. Even churches had learned the hard way that robbers in Lagos had no fear of the Lord.

Outside:

Hills of festering garbage at street corners, and mounds of blackish sludge along the edges of gutters from which they were shovelled out, and everywhere rubbish – punctured plastic, shattered glass, mangled metal, rain-pulped paper – covered the ground.

Furo thought: There is nowhere to go.

Near the end of a deserted street Furo had turned into to get reprieve from the stares and the noise, he saw a three-storey apartment block with a collapsed roof. The building was uncompleted, abandoned-looking – it seemed defeated by the ambition of a middling architect – and there was a clandestine gap in its fence of bamboo posts. Furo cast a quick look around to make sure no one was watching, and then he approached the fence, dropped to his hands and knees, and squeezed through the opening. The ground on the other side was thick with elephant grass; through the waving blades he saw islands of stacked concrete blocks, their sides and tops washed by the sun's rays and dotted with sunbathing lizards. He rose to full height and listened, then picked up a rusted tin that lay at his feet and flung it through the open doorway of the house, and listened again. The house echoed with silence. The lizards raised their bright red heads to gleam at the intruder from motionless eyes, and stiffening their blue-speckled tails in readiness to flee, they communicated their displeasure at the disturbance by doing push ups on the baking blocks.

Wading through the tall grass, which nicked his hands as he slapped the blades aside, Furo approached the building and entered. Desiccated mould, dust-heavy cobwebs, crumbling exoskeletons, flaking rust – the smell of neglect filled the large room he stood in. The floor was covered with cement dust in which insects burrowed; a shovel with a broken haft lay half-buried in the dust; a wheelbarrow missing its wheel was upturned in one corner; an opened cement bag lay under a window, its contents hardened into jagged rock. The holes punched in the walls for scaffolding rods and electrical wires gaped open, and the concrete slab that ceilinged the room was studded with wood chips, tangled wires, glass shards, the wishbone of a bird.

The rest of the ground-floor apartment was in a similar state of incompletion, and Furo, after investigating for signs of recent visitors, mounted the staircase. His footsteps rang eerie in silence, and the creep of his shadow sent smaller shadows scuttling into darkened cracks. As he crossed the first-floor landing, he caught sight of a decayed carcass sprawled in the apartment doorway. Discoloured fur still clung to the bones, and traces of its mouldy odour hung in the air. For as long as the dog had lain there, and likely longer, the house had seen no human visitors, Furo was sure. He decided that the second floor with its fallen roof was too dangerous to explore. After giving the first-floor apartment a cursory once-over, he settled on the master bedroom, which was far enough from the dog's remains to ignore its lingering presence. With his feet he cleared the ground of debris under the window that opened on to the frontage, and then he set down his folder, sank on to it, and drew up his knees, rested his head on them. He was trying to read the time from the sun's position when he fell asleep.

It was dark when Furo opened his eyes. He stared at his surroundings, confused about where he was, until he saw his hands, pale in the gloom, and he remembered. Something he hadn't thought of – mosquitoes. Those Brit-massacring heroes of West Africa's anti-colonial resistance: the un-acknowledged national insect of Nigeria. The air was thick with the malarial bloodsuckers. Bomber squadrons of them circled over his head, whined past his ears, tickled his cheeks with their wings, and needled his imagination. His skin itched from their strikes, and when he grew tired of slapping himself he stood up, leaned out the window, and stuck his face into the coolness of the night. The grass below swayed and whispered in the breeze; the muted buzzing at the back of his mind rose to the shrill of crickets. The street beyond the bamboo fence had faded into blackness. There was nowhere to go, he thought, the blackness was closing in. By now his parents would be wondering about his absence. His mother must have discovered he had left his phone behind, and first she would whinge to his father about how dangerous Lagos was and how could Furo be so stupid as to go out without his phone, and by ten o'clock, when she had abused his father's tolerance to her own limits, she would start phoning her bosom friends with the same complaints before contacting his own friends to ask if they knew where he was. Eleven o'clock would surely find her keeping a lookout outside the front gate, and by twelve, while his sister searched through his bedroom for clues of his whereabouts, she would be fixed in front of the TV as she watched the midnight news for announcements of hit-and-run collisions and petrol tanker explosions and motor park insurrections. After that he had no idea what she would do. He had never stayed out this late without informing his family.

Furo could imagine, though, the terror his mother would feel. He could see the look of long-suffering that slackened his father's jaw and reddened his eyes. He could hear his baby sister's anguished sobbing as clearly as the swishing of the grass below him.

It was too much.

It was too painful to think about the pain he was causing others.

He turned away from the window and sank down to his haunches. Closing his eyes to the darkness, he made an effort to return to sleep.

But he couldn't.

He couldn't replace the lid on the emotions bubbling within him.

He wished he had someone with whom to share his burden. If only he could go to his mother and say, 'Mummy, something is wrong, look at what happened to me!' And his mother would take control just like she did when he was seven and caught chickenpox from school. She would pacify his fears with promises of ice-cream binges. She would strip off his clothes and bathe him in warm, Dettol-smelling water, then rub him down with calamine lotion and set him loose to run shrieking around the house, her little war-painted savage. But he was thirty-three, too old now for blind belief in a mother's healing powers. And, also, the chickenpox only lasted a few days; the calamine lotion soothed him, and the white coating it left on his skin could be washed off. This was the right thing to do, going away, the unselfish path to take, best for all concerned, of that he was sure. For his was not a condition like cancer, where his mother would spend her life savings seeking a cure; or a condition that allowed for denial, say schizophrenia, where she would spend the rest of her life as his carer. At least for cancer his family would know that their misfortune was shared by others across the world, and for schizophrenia there was still the hope that once in while the son they recognised would emerge from behind the phantasmal fog of his mind. What he had was neither physical nor mental, not in a sense that made any sense, and so it was as inexplicable to him as it would be to everyone else.

If Furo were only able to sit across from his family, he would ask forgiveness for not opening the door to his mother. He would tell his parents to not worry too much about him, that things were looking up, that he'd finally found a job, and he would even share any particulars his curious sister might want to know about his adventures; but the one thing he couldn't tell any of them was how he felt about going back. That was another truth he now admitted to himself, that from the instant he opened his eyes this morning he had felt a momentum building inside him, a feeling of freefalling that had grown stronger with each decision that pointed him away from his family. Alone in the darkness of this abandoned building, and despite the stinging mosquitoes, in spite of everything he had suffered through, the mere thought of a reversion to his former stasis was anathema to him. To make this admission even harder was his awareness of how much his family, and his mother especially, would mourn his absence. He was her son, flesh of her flesh and blood of her womb, and grieve was what mothers did when they lost a child; but beyond that, he knew she also counted him as her second chance to succeed in everything his father had failed at. She had said as much all his life, in roundabout adages and through her straightforward actions. His was the fortune and fulfilment his father had never attained. That was a son's duty to a mother who had sacrificed her freedom on the labour bed.

It had always been Furo's duty to achieve for his mother's sake. He kept his part of this umbilical pact by always giving his best, if not at his studies, then at examinations, and, as the dice rolls in the crapshoot of academic success, his best, for a time, was enough to satisfy her. All through primary school he never took any less than sixth-best position in class, and in the second term of his second year of secondary school, when he came top in class for the first time in his life, he remembered how his mother took him straight from school to her office in Onikan and announced to her colleagues, 'My small husband has killed me with happiness!' From that pinnacle there was nowhere left to go but down the hill. He still gave his best, he always did, as he tried to hold the bar of achievement that the small husband had set for him, but for reasons only tangentially related to a flowering interest in girls and their breasts, Furo found that the higher he went in school, the less acceptable his best was for his mother. By the time he got into the third-rate university at Ekpoma (and this after two failures at JAMB) even his mother knew that his employment prospects were too far downhill to ever kill her with happiness again.

It was his mother he feared the most. She lurked in his earliest memories, memories so full of her that they had to be her memories too. Even now he remembered how, as a child in nursery school, she would arrive to pick him up at the clang of the closing bell, and the sound of her voice mingling with the other parents' in the anteroom always awakened a stiffness in his shorts. Back at home, while she boiled ripe plantains for his lunch – this memory predated his sister's crying existence – and then asked him, as she

41

scrambled the eggs, to tell her all about his day at school, his chest would swell to tightness from his eagerness to obey. She listened, really listened, because he would later listen to her describe, almost lisp-for-lisp, his playpen escapades to his father when he returned from work at night. Did his father listen? He watched TV. Not the Betamax cartoons that Furo wanted, but the local news. Every day, schooldays and weekends, he would oust Furo from his TV throne and switch to News at 5, News at 7, News at 9. He drank his beer as he watched the droid-voiced newscasters, his face getting sadder and angrier, his haggard eyes stuck to the screen even when he threw back his head to suck from the bottleneck; and now, thirty years later, Furo recalled how he used to wonder why his father watched so much TV when all it did was make him ugly.

Furo couldn't remember when he began to see his father as a failure. His awareness might have sprouted earlier than 1991, but in that year he knew that something was wrong when his mother, in addition to running the house out of her purse, as she'd done ever since she gave up housewiving and took up a banking job that paid four times more than her husband earned, also took over the paying of her children's school fees, because, as she explained, his father's entire salary was being saved up for a major business venture he was on the verge of starting. Several years and many pay cheques later – by which time Furo, in his final year of secondary school, had learned from experience to stop speaking to his father on any matter concerning money – his father resigned from his eighteen-year service at the Federal Ministry of Agriculture, handed in his official Peugeot 504 and vacated his government residence in Victoria Island, and after moving with his family into the house his wife had finished building all the way over in Egbeda, he finally embarked on the long-vaunted adventure: his chicken farm.

The farm was an obvious failure from its third month of operation and Furo, who in the meantime had finished secondary school and taken up unpaid employment with his father while awaiting the results of his JAMB examination, was there to see the unravelling of the dream. His father's troubles started with the ten-thousand-egg incubator he had imported from China. This backbone apparatus, his proudest and most expensive investment in the farm, floated into Apapa port seven weeks later than promised, and after another five weeks of begging for receipts for the paid-up custom duties and arguing over demurrage charges incurred as a result of the withheld receipts and bargaining down the amounts demanded as bribes by custom officials for the release of the receipts, the incubator at last arrived at the farmland in Iyana Ipaja, only to be unpacked from its crates and discovered as an empty shell that would never hatch a chick. On that unlucky day Furo saw his father weep for the second and third times in his life, the second being in the afternoon as he realised he had been duped, and then again at night as he reported the calamity to his wife. While soothing her husband, Furo's mother had suggested what everyone else was afraid to say to a sinking man seeking straws, that maybe it was just a packing error, but she was wrong, it was not, as every effort his father made to contact the company in Qingdao only proved he was the victim of fraudsters, and in the end he had to give up all hope of ever recovering his money, because, as his wife explained to his children, the NITEL payphone costs were gobbling up his left-over capital and, besides, the woman who always answered his desperate midnight phone calls only responded in Mandarin to his threats of litigation.

The chicken farm never recovered from that blow. Neither did Furo's father, who kept the business open mainly as an excuse to escape the house every day. By the time Furo gained admission to university and departed for Ekpoma, his father's business was nothing more than an in-house joke and his mother had accepted her everlasting role as the sole financier of everything Wariboko. She covered Furo's fees as well as his sister's; she kept the house in food and settled the utility bills; she bought his father a second-hand Peugeot 405 so he could do the household shopping while she was at work; and every December, when the wild rush for Christmas chicken quickened the hearts of failed farmers across the nation, she granted the loan for the few hundred broiler chicks his father bought and fatted for pocket change. Furo couldn't remember when it began to dawn on him that his father had settled for defeat in a war he still pretended to fight. He likely knew earlier than 2009, but it was that year, after he returned to his mother's house upon completion of his youth service, that he realised it was his father he pitied the most.

It was his sister he envied the most. Her confidence in herself had always exasperated her older brother, whose self-esteem was further bruised by his awareness that her self-belief was in no way misplaced. She seemed able to accomplish anything she set her mind to. Even as children she would win her own battles in the playground and then rush forwards to help out with his; she learned to whistle before him, despite being five years younger; from when she was three years old, whenever she and he left the house together, she insisted on crossing motorways without his assistance; even into their teens, whenever they were both caned for some wrongdoing, her tears always dried first. Then again, she had never faced the parental pressure he did – a woman can find a husband to take care of her, but a man must take care of his wife, Furo's father was fond of saying – and yet she excelled at her studies to the point that even their mother accepted that her daughter was the best chance the family had of producing a success story. Aside from academics, his sister had a ravening appetite for leisure reading, and she was the only one in the family who spent money on magazines and novels. Sometimes it seemed there was nothing she didn't know. It was from her that Furo learned how to start up and navigate through a computer (this process occurring over the holidays she had spent transcribing his handwritten final-year thesis into digital format), and after he graduated and returned to Lagos to seek a job, it was she who urged him to join Twitter – which she wasn't on but knew enough about to assist him with opening his account – as it was perfect for self-advertising. She had even appeared on national TV. She did this through her own efforts, and in the face of her brother's scoffing dismissal of her ambition, by trying for and making the hot seat of 'Who Wants to Be a Millionaire?' – which, by the way, she might have been if her boyfriend Korede, who was her 'phone-a-friend' lifeline, hadn't failed her at the eleventh question. She departed the show with winnings of two hundred and fifty thousand naira and arrived home to a hero's welcome from her parents, and, from her brother, as ever, adoring envy.

Furo was certain that by leaving he'd escaped the almighty struggle to convince his family that he was still the same person, son and brother. Even if he succeeded in suspending their disbelief, there were then the frantic efforts they would undertake to regain what was lost: the medical investigations, the money it would cost them, the media circus that must follow; and, probably, for his mother, whom he knew would be desperate enough when all else had failed, the recourse to consultations with spiritual healers. Now, with his disappearance, they would expend effort and spend money in attempting to solve the mystery, but at least they would be left with an image of him that they could hold on to.

Yes, he was doing the right thing, he was even surer.

Better his family retain their image of him and he his of them.

Furo awoke to the caress of the early sunlight streaming in through the window above his head. After a quick glance to check that nothing had changed – his colour was the same, as white as night becomes day – he sat unmoving for a long time, his ears tuned to the city. Hunger came, and the harder he resisted the stronger the pangs became. His neck resumed its ache. His palms, when he dropped them from rubbing his nape, were oily with grime. Beneath the dirt, the skin was paler than any hand he'd ever studied, and the lifelines were etched fainter, the palm edges and pads reddened with coursing blood. Not bad-looking as hands go, he said to himself . . . but owning these, calling them his, that was too much to handle.

Dropping his hands to the ground, Furo pushed up into a crouch, then picked up his folder and slipped it under his arm as he straightened to full height. He stood motionless for some moments inhaling the grass-dew smell of a new day, but when he started brushing off his clothes, the cement dust of abandonment flooded his nostrils, choking him with sadness.

It was time to move forwards.

Again the stares. The hawker from whom he bought a seventy-naira loaf of Agege bread stole glances at him as she knelt beside her wooden tray, sawed open the loaf, and spread ten naira worth of mayonnaise on it. The woman who sold him three sachets of pure water stared with open amusement as he squatted by her icebox and washed his face and his mouth and his hands and drank what was left. And the pedestrians, the sleepy-eyed taxi drivers, the minibus passengers with their work-ready faces, the road sweepers and roadside beggars and policemen standing useless at clogged intersections – all followed him with their eyes as he strode by.

Under the sun's glare, almost as hard to bear as the stares from which there was no hiding place, Furo trekked from Ikeja to Maryland. He didn't plan his direction: it was set out for him when he found himself beside the police college's long-running fence on which was painted at intervals RESTRICTED AREA: KEEP MOVING. He obeyed this instruction until the fence was passed. He kept on moving, past the landscaped grounds of Sheraton Hotel & Towers and the red-and-white facade of the Virgin Atlantic building. He slowed his steps to skirt a cluster of commuters at Onigbongbo Bus Stop and quickened his pace as he approached the thumping roar of a helicopter rising from the bowl of OAS Heliport. Onwards he went, throwing step after step along the sun-cracked sidewalk until he reached the watering-hole bustle of Maryland Junction.

Foremost consequence of Furo's journey was the burning sensation on the bridge of his nose, which made his eyes water when he mopped his sweating face with his handkerchief. But the gruelling trek, and the unrelenting lash of the sun, the total pointlessness of his fatigue, also bleached his mind of clinging delusions and helped him decide where to go. To Lekki, stamping ground of the Lagos rich. He would go to The Palms, the largest mall in Lagos.

There, at least, the air conditioning was free.

And it was far from Egbeda, as far from his family as he could go in Lagos.

And then again, there would be others who looked like him.

Getting to Lekki from Maryland would involve hopping buses. There was a BRT bus terminus at Maryland Junction, and Furo, opting for the cheaper ride over the faster mini-buses, approached one of the ticketing agents. After surprising the woman with his accent, he bought a one-way ticket to Marina. He boarded the bus, chose a window seat near the back, and rested his tired head against the sweat-smudged glass. While the bus was filling up with passengers, Furo avoided looking at his face in the glass, a wasted effort, because by the time the bus set off, he had noticed that his hands were shaking from hunger, and that the spray of hair on his forearms seemed to change colour from red to orange in the slant of sunlight, and that some of the glances he drew from the other passengers were sympathetic, concerned, almost pitying of the plight that was evident in his skin. During the bumpy, unhurried, many-stop ride, he also noticed, always in front of him, the persistent presence of a nose that smarted from sunburn.

He had lunch at Marina. Again eba and egusi soup, and again in a buka, but this time with no incident more remark-able than cheering cries from a gaggle of area boys, motor park hooligans, who gathered outside the buka to watch him eat. After he settled the bill, he strode blank-faced through a swarm of child beggars till he reached the BRT bus stand,

48

and when the last of the beggars, the most determined, a pretty Chadian girl who tugged at her pigtails as she recited her tired script, finally gave up and shuffled off, he settled on to the bench to await the arrival of the bus to Lekki. The skyline ahead of him was the postcard image of Lagos, the agglomeration of high-rises that landmarked the financial district of Broad Street, and averting his eyes from this view in boredom, Furo gazed over the murky waters lapping against the marina behind his bench. On the far shore floated a metropolis of cargo ships and derrick rigs. Canoes and old tugboats crawled across the waterway, their paddles digging and outboard motors chugging. Scavenging egrets soared and squabbled over the sluggish waves of Five Cowrie Creek: that dumpsite for market refuse and road-kill carcasses; that open sewer into which the homeless and the shameless emptied their bowels in public view. Furo could see them now, men mostly, squatted along the marina wall with trousers rucked around their ankles and faces straining from the pleasure of bursting haemorrhoids. The familiar smell of Lagos motor parks, marijuana and tobacco smoke mingled with the stench of petrochemicals and moonshine alcohol and human effluence, blew on a breeze from the water's edge: a dizzying mix that Furo was happy to turn his back on as his bus pulled up.

He arrived at The Palms with ninety naira in his pocket.

Who did Furo see but a white person striding towards him as he passed through the glass doors of The Palms. A long-haired woman with a large mole on her chin, she wore a lavender summer dress and green oversized Crocs. In both hands she grasped the big yellow bags that boasted of lowest prices. Faced with this test, this face-to-face with a white person, Furo realised he was unprepared for the encounter. He was worried how they would see him. Could they tell by sight that there was something wrong with him? If they could, then why, how, what was it they saw that black people couldn't? Thinking these thoughts, Furo halted in front of the glass doors, his attention fixed on the woman. She drew close, her gaze flicked over his face, and then she was past, her Crocs clopping and ShopRite bags rustling.

The woman's lack of reaction to his presence proved nothing, Furo told himself, but he feared that before long he would find out the truth, because in the crowded passage ahead of him were several oyibo people, some Indian- and Lebanese-looking, some Chinese, walking alone or in small groups, laughing, chatting, gesturing at the bright lights in storefront windows: all of them as indifferent to their difference as he wasn't to his. Then he thought he had stood too long in the same spot, that people must be staring at him and wondering, and he looked around but caught no eyes, they seemed to ignore him in the midst of plenty. Buoyed by this glimmer of a chance at a normal life — one where he wouldn't always be the cobra in this charmless show of reality, the centre of attention — he started forwards into the chill of the mall.

Furo's fear came to nothing, as none of the oyibo who looked at him gave the impression that he was something he shouldn't be. The few glances he attracted came from his own people, and even they seemed more interested in his dusty shoes, his wrinkled trousers, his sweat-grimed shirt, his cheap plastic folder, all the signs showing he wasn't kosher in the money department. That was a look he was used to from before, and so it didn't worry him. Better the scorn he knew than the admiration he didn't. But above all, better the people who ignored him than the ones who didn't. Moving through the crowd, he began to feel more at ease with the approach of non-blacks. There was no uncertainty about their reaction to sighting him. They would see him and maintain stride, see him and keep on talking, see him and show no surprise, every single time. With the others, the majority, it was hit-and-miss. And after some near misses, a woman hit on him.

He was almost at the entrance of the lavatory when he heard a hiss behind him. He spun around to find her standing there. Though he had never seen her before, he recognised her at once. She was one of those youngish women who dressed not so much to kill but rather to mimic teenagers – which sometimes they claimed they were, rarely truthfully – and spent their days stalking the mall in a hunt for lone white men. In two words, she was a runs girl. In one, a prostitute. She had the worn-out sensuality, the overbearing perfume, and the arsenal of glances. While her mouth said, 'Hello there,' her eyes were busy telling Furo, *I'll be good to you, baby.* Or something to that effect. Perhaps, on some other day, he might have responded to the promise in her eyes, but today he didn't even reply to her greeting before whipping back around and striding away from the lavatory.

He arrived at the food court to find it brimming with voices. After-work hours on weekdays were busy periods for The Palms, as commuters killed time there – eating dinner, watching movies, browsing the shops – in a bid to wait out the worst of the traffic. Looking around for somewhere to sit, he saw that most of the tables were occupied by whispering couples or chattering groups of office colleagues, but near the centre of the dining area stood a table with three empty chairs, the fourth taken by a man reading a book. Weaving a path through the jumble of conversations, Furo approached the silent table, and the man raised his head. His dreadlocked hair was neck-length, and his beard stubble was sprinkled with grey, as was the hair on his chest, which showed through the V-neck of his T-shirt. Despite the greying, he was about Furo's age.

'Hello,' Furo said. 'Can I share this table with you?'

'Please,' the man replied, and waited until Furo sat before returning to his book.

After placing his folder on the table, Furo raised both hands to massage his neck, at the same time throwing a look of resentment at all the happy people seated about him. He envied them. Unlike him, they all had homes to return to. He knew that the food court and all the shops in the mall would be closed by ten, and the mall would be emptied of people and locked up after the cinema upstairs finished its last showing around midnight. And then where would he go? He couldn't risk illness, not when he had no money, and spending another night in an abandoned building full of mosquitoes seemed to beg for malaria. But what choice did he have today, tomorrow, the day after, until he began work at Haba! in a couple of weeks? In an effort to get away from these insoluble worries, Furo returned his gaze to the table, and narrowed his eyes at the book across from him. *Fela: This Bitch of a Life* – the words on the front cover. The man's short-nailed hands gripped the book cover, pinning it open. Head cocked to one side, eyelids lowered, face expressionless, his lips moved silently as he read.

This bitch of a life indeed, Furo thought. There he was, living his life, and then this shit happened to him. He had always thought that white people had it easier, in this country anyway, where it seemed that everyone treated them as special, but after everything that he had gone through since yesterday, he wasn't so sure any more. Everything conspired to make him stand out. This whiteness that separated him from everyone he knew. His nose smarting from the sun. His hands covered with reddened spots, as if mosquito bites were something serious. People pointing at him, staring all the time, shouting "oyibo" at every corner.

And yet his whiteness had landed him a job.

Furo blew out his cheeks in a sigh. Dropping his hands to grasp the table, he pulled in his chair. The metal legs screaked on the floor tiles. At this sound his tablemate looked up, and Furo, seizing the chance, said to him, 'Sorry to bother you, but can you please tell me the time?' The man nodded yes, put down the book, reached into his trouser pocket, and pulled out a phone. He said, 'It's almost five thirty,' to which Furo responded, 'Thanks.' As the man returned the phone to his pocket, Furo said, 'Funny how time drags.'

'When you're bored,' the man said. He smiled and added: 'And when you're waiting.'

Furo forced a laugh. 'Also when you're in trouble.'

'That too,' the man agreed. He waited a beat. 'Do you mind saying what the trouble is?'

'Ah . . . no,' Furo said. 'It's not something I can talk about. But thanks for asking.'

The man leaned forwards in his chair and crossed his hands over his book. 'But we can talk if you want. To pass the time.' He tapped the book. 'That's one good thing about books. You can always pick up from where you left off.'

'I have to confess I'm not a big fan of books myself,' Furo said. He thought a moment, and then chuckled. 'I shouldn't say that in public. I just got a job selling books.'

'What sort of books?'

With a glance at the man's shock of hair, Furo said: 'Probably not your type. Business books, that's what the company sells.'

'What's the company's name?' As Furo hesitated, the man said, 'I ask because I used to work for a publishing house. I might know your company.'

Furo nodded. 'Haba!'

'Excuse me?' The man's puzzled expression deepened as Furo raised his hand, but when he drew a line in the air with his forefinger and jabbed a hole under it, saying at the same time, 'Haba with an exclamation mark, that's the company's name,' the man's face brightened with comprehension. Furo finished drily: 'I can see I'll have trouble telling that name to people.'

The man snorted in laughter. 'Yah, they'll be surprised hearing haba from your mouth. Which is a good thing for a bookseller, I suppose. It will leave an impression.' After a pause, he said, 'I haven't heard of that company.'

They relapsed into silence. The air in the food court was thick with aromas from the quick service restaurants, and Furo felt his stomach stirring in response. He'd eaten a large meal barely two hours ago, and his belly was still tight with undigested starch, yet the smell of food, the sound and sight of others eating, tensed him with craving. He was grateful for the distraction when his companion said, 'I haven't introduced myself,' and held out his hand. 'I'm Igoni.'

Furo's brow puckered as they shook hands, and he repeated: 'Igoni?'

Igoni nodded yes.

'*Tobra?*' Furo said.

Igoni's eyes widened with surprise. '*Ibim.* You speak Kalabari?'

'Not really. I can understand a few words. My father's from Abonnema, Briggs compound. I'm Furo Wariboko.'

'Imagine that,' Igoni said. His eyes sparkled at Furo. When he smiled, his parted lips revealed a flash of thumb-sucker's teeth. 'You must have one hell of a story.'

Furo wanted to ask what Igoni meant, but he thought better of the impulse. He had a sneaking feeling he'd already revealed too much. And so he remained silent as Igoni closed his book, then took up his laptop bag, stuffed the book into it and, rising from his chair, said, 'I'm going to the cafe round the corner for a smoke. Can I buy you coffee or something?' Surprised by Igoni's offer, Furo responded, 'I'd like that.' He stood up quickly, picked up his folder, and followed Igoni into the stream of shoppers in the mall's passageway.

As the first Nigerian mall of indubitably international standard, the unveiling of The Palms was a milestone event not only for the Lagos rich, but also for yuppie teenagers, music video directors, and politicians eager to showcase the investment paradise that was newly democratic Nigeria. At the time of the ribbon-cutting in 2006, Furo was at university in faraway Ekpoma, and so he had to make do with his sister's recounting of the mall's abundant pleasures over the telephone. Two warehouse-sized supermarkets, one fancy bookstore, many fast food restaurants, bric-a-brac shops, branded boutiques and jewellery outlets, a sports bar, a bowling-alley-cum-nightclub, a multiplex cinema, and scores of ATMs: any means by which to part the dazzled from their money, The Palms provided. And yet in all these years since he returned to Lagos, despite countless visits to the mall to watch the latest from Hollywood and spend his weekends with girlfriends he wanted to impress, Furo had never entered the mall's sole cafe.

Approaching the glass facade of the cafe, Furo saw that

a majority of the tables were occupied by oyibos. That was the reason he'd never set foot in the place: he assumed that any hangout that drew so many expats was too exclusive for someone unemployed. Which Igoni, going by appearances, was not. They had reached the entrance, and a private guard in visored cap and paramilitary uniform jumped up from his folding chair and eased the door open, then stamped his boot in greeting. Heads turned to watch them enter, and then turned back to pick up their conversations. The interior was lighted by shaded lamps pouring down soft yellow beams, and the floor tiles shone, the metal tables gleamed. From the walls hung flatscreen TVs showing news channels with the sound turned down. One half of the cafe was announced as non-smoking by wedge-shaped signs on the tables, and the other section was overhung by a haze, this fed by trails of smoke from all the hands clutching glowing cigarettes, smouldering cigarillos, sputtering cigars, and, here and there, hookah pipes. Igoni headed for the smoking section, Furo followed, and they settled into a red loveseat backed against the far wall.

The prices were as Furo imagined. Too high for him, now especially, when every naira he spent felt like spurting blood. He read the menu with mounting indignation until a waitress arrived for their orders. 'Cappuccino, please,' Igoni said, and when Furo felt his hairs bristle at her attention, he chose, 'Chocolate milkshake,' then closed the menu, set it down on the table, and stole a glance at his host. The embarrassment he felt at the price tag of his order, the cost of six full meals in a roadside buka, was nowhere apparent in Igoni's face. In that instant Furo felt the bump of an idea falling into place, and the tingle that announced it a good one.

The waitress collected the menus and left before Furo

spoke. 'If you don't mind my asking,' he said to Igoni, 'what do you do for a living?'

'I don't mind,' Igoni said. 'I'm a writer.'

'Of books?'

Igoni nodded yes, and reaching into his pocket, he drew out a Benson & Hedges packet. Furo waited till the cigarette was lit. 'What kind of books do you write?'

'Not business books,' Igoni said with a quick sly grin, and then leaned back in the loveseat, crossed his legs, and blew out smoke. 'Fiction, short stories, that sort of thing.'

'I see,' Furo muttered in distraction, as his attention was diverted by a passing angel, the sudden dip in the hum of conversation. The cafe door had opened to let in a woman alone. Long seconds ticked while she stood in front of the entrance, her head turning with imperial slowness as she searched through faces. Then she struck for the smoking section. She wore yellow high heels, carried a bright yellow handbag, and the balloon-skirt of her black gown, which bounced at each stride she took, showed off her long legs. To Furo it seemed every eye in the cafe was fixed on her, but she relished the attention, her eyes twinkled with awareness of it, and on her lips played a smile that grew bolder the closer she came. After she slipped into the loveseat beside Furo's table, the chatter in the cafe picked up again.

The waitress arrived bearing a tray, and after setting down Furo and Igoni's drinks, she crossed over to the newcomer. Furo glanced around at the first sound of the woman's voice, but it was her prettiness that kept him looking. He noticed the waitress closing her notebook, his cue to look away before he was caught staring, but he waited till the last moment, the tensing of the woman's temple as she realised she was being watched, to swing his eyes away from her face to the TV above her head, which showed a crowd of Arabs chanting and waving placards written in English. His neck soon tired of straining upwards to no purpose, and abandoning this ruse, he turned forwards in his seat and reached for his drink.

The first sip of the chocolate milkshake heightened Furo's hunger. The second cloyed his tongue with sweetness. The third gave him gooseflesh. Each time he sucked on the straw he took care to hold the liquid in his cheeks, to swill it round his mouth, and only when his cheeks were stretched tight and his gullet throbbed from the effort of remaining closed, did he gulp down the drink. It left its sweetness in his mouth and spread its coolness through his skin, and this, added to the cosiness of the cafe, lulled him into a state approaching contentment. Until he glanced to the side, caught the stare of the woman, and felt a flush melting away the pleasure from his face. He dipped his head and sucked furiously on the straw.

Igoni finished his cigarette in silence and picked up his cappuccino. As he drank, Furo watched him openly. Igoni seemed friendly enough, he also appeared to have some money, and he was Kalabari, almost family without the drawbacks. Furo decided it was now time to ask the favour of Igoni that he'd intended since he realised that fate was finally dealing him a good hand. And so he said Igoni's name, and when Igoni looked at him, he spoke in a halting voice:

'I know it's a bit odd, but I want to ask you a favour.'

'Go ahead,' Igoni said.

'I need a place to stay in Lagos. Only for a short time, about two weeks. I'm hoping, if it's possible, if it's not too much trouble, that I can stay with you.'

'Oh,' Igoni said in a surprised tone. 'That's a big one.'

Furo jumped into the opening. 'I know,' he said, 'but I don't have anyone else to ask.'

Igoni leaned forwards, rested his elbows on his knees, and cracked his knuckles. He stared at the ground between his feet until he raised his head. 'I'll be honest,' he said, his eyes seeking out Furo's, and then swinging away as he continued in a voice shaded with regret. 'Any other time I would be happy to have you over, but I'm in the middle of some writing, so I really can't, not now.'

Furo's voice was hoarse as he said, 'I understand.'

Igoni was about to speak again when his phone rang. After mumbling a few words, he hung up the call, and then reached for his wallet. 'I have to rush off,' he said as he flipped it open. 'The person I was waiting for has arrived.' He pulled out four crisp five hundreds and placed the notes by his saucer. 'That will cover the bill.' Rising to his feet, he slung his laptop bag over his shoulder. 'It was nice meeting you, Furo. Bye now.'

Furo watched Igoni until he disappeared into the milling throng outside the cafe's glass front. Returning his gaze to the table, he noted that Igoni hadn't finished his drink. He picked up the cup, and after swirling around the leftover cappuccino, he drank it down. As he clacked the cup on the saucer, the money caught his eye. Maybe he should have asked Igoni for money instead, he thought, and then heaved a coffee-scented sigh.

'May I join you?'

Furo whipped his head around. The woman in yellow heels had turned in her seat till her bared knees pointed at him. Her smile did not reach her eyes.

'Is it OK to join you?' she asked again.

At his nod, she took up her handbag, rose to her feet

and, with a waft of perfume, slid in beside him. Her knee bumped his under the table. 'Oops,' she said, and threw him a smile only just warmer than her last. 'I'm Syreeta.'

'Furo,' he said.

'That's a Nigerian name.'

'I'm Nigerian,' Furo said. Some resentment escaped into his tone, and he met her gaze. Her brown irises were steady pools from which his face stared back. 'You sound Nigerian for sure,' she said at last. 'But you're the first Nigerian I've met who has green eyes.'

Furo blinked in surprise, and to cover his confusion he raised his hand to his nape, where his fingers began to rub. When Syreeta asked, 'Is your neck paining you?' he nodded and rubbed harder. 'Stop rubbing it like that, it won't help, it will make it worse.' After he dropped his hand, she said, her tone conversational: 'What you need is a massage. I can give you one if you want.' She held up her hands, showed her palms to him. 'I'm good with my hands. And my house is not far from here.' She took his silence for agreement. 'We'll go after my food comes.'

Head reeling from the speed of things, Furo bent forwards and grabbed hold of his straw. As he slurped the last of his milkshake, his eyes watched Syreeta's hands, her scarlet fingernails drumming the tabletop. Her offer had caught him unawares, as he hadn't expected it of someone as well-heeled as her. He understood what she wanted, the same as that other one, the runs girl who had accosted him by the mall's toilet, had wanted. The white man's money, that's what. Appearances had deceived him and her, because he had misjudged her morals as completely as she his pocket. She was loose, he was broke, and the rules of this game were fixed. He had to set her straight. Despite the tinder of hope that her offer had sparked, he had to douse it before the flames overcame his common sense.

Furo straightened up and found his voice. 'Look, I don't—'

'Shush,' Syreeta said, and Furo followed the direction of her look. The waitress was headed their way with a tray from which steam rose, and as she drew up to them, Syreeta said, 'Sorry dear, I've changed my mind, I'm leaving now. Pack the food for me. And bring our bills.'

Alone again, she said to Furo, 'You wanted to say something?'

'I don't have any money,' he blurted out.

Her face hardened. 'Did I ask you for money?'

'But you want me to go home with you!'

'And so what?' she said in a flat voice.

Furo stared wordless, aghast at her shamelessness.

'Do you want to or not?'

He closed his mouth and nodded yes.

'Then stop talking plenty and come,' Syreeta said with a toss of her braids.

In the car park of The Palms, Syreeta beeped open a silver-coloured Honda CR-V. 'Your belt,' she said to Furo after he climbed into the passenger seat, and when he was buckled in: 'I'll make a quick stop before we go to my place.' She switched on the ignition. The flash of dashboard lights, a blast of stereo music, streams of air from the vents, and the machine purr of an engine eager to go. The car cruised out of The Palms, and when Syreeta accelerated (even though he couldn't drive, Furo could tell that she handled the wheel with panache, to which the Honda responded like a dance partner) towards the Lekki highway, the easy motion of the car pulled Furo into a sinkhole of comfort. Every breath he drew, every rub of his tired shoulders on the soft leather seat, every sensation contributed to his need to pee.

Her quick stop was the five-star-looking Oriental Hotel. Furo realised this when the Honda swept through the gateway into a parking lot overflowing with millionaires' toys, and by the time Syreeta found a spot and reversed into it, he'd convinced himself of the quickie reason for her stopover, the abysmal state of her morality, and the dangerous nature of her daring. She demolished his assumptions by asking him to follow her in. Together, side by side, they walked into the hotel's lobby. To the right of the entrance was the reception counter, and Syreeta turned left. She clicked past a knot of men dressed in bankers' suits, and pausing in their conversation, they stared after her, their eyes burning with the fever of acquisition. Furo skidded across the smooth stone floor in his efforts to keep pace with her, and when she halted in front of the elevator, he felt a vicious stab in his bladder. He couldn't hold it in any more.

'I need to ease myself,' he whispered to Syreeta.

'Let's get upstairs first,' she responded, but a quick look at his face changed her mind. 'Go on, the loo is that way,' and she pointed. 'I'll wait here.'

Furo trotted towards the lavatory, and once he was through the door he hopped from foot to foot and fumbled with his fly before bounding to the nearest urinal. He panted at the first spurt, pungent and steaming, the colour of factory waste, a whole day's worth topped with a cup of milkshake, which splashed into the glistening ceramic and rattled the coloured mothballs and foamed in the drain. His nerves calmed with his stream, and soon he glanced around to confirm he was alone, and then down at his trousers to ensure he had no reason to be self-conscious. He finished and gave a yawn, closed his zipper, and then, as his eyes caught the brand stamped on to the urinal, he barked with laughter. He hadn't noticed he was peeing into a Toto – a vagina. *Yes, a dirty joke*, he thought as he strolled chuckling to the washbasin, but when he saw his face in the mirror, his mirth caught in his throat. *A monstrous joke, a monster's joke: that's what this is.*

Syreeta was standing where Furo had left her but she was no longer alone. A portly Chinese man wearing rumpled cargo shorts and a crocodile-patterned shirt was speaking to her (her face was averted from his fixed, unctuous smile) and indicating with his hands that she follow him. When Furo arrived at the elevator, the man dropped his arms to his sides and fell silent. 'Done?' Syreeta asked, and when Furo answered yes, the man veered his face towards him, his smile wiped off. Syreeta poked the elevator button, the doors slid open, and the man backed away.

They rode up in silence, all the while looking down at the spread of the city through the elevator's glass wall. Reaching the second floor, they emerged into a corridor, and Syreeta led the way across its deep carpet. In the last few feet to the corridor's end, as Furo saw that the door ahead was inscribed 'African Bar', he hastened around her and held the door open. With a quick look at his face, she brushed past him into a dimly lit hall. Spinning disco lights, their gaudy pinpoints ricocheting off swaying silhouettes, showed a path across the dance floor. The moody melody of Bobby Benson's 'Taxi Driver' boomed from speakers in the ceiling. Arranged along the walls were widely spaced tables, many occupied and shimmering with drinks. Near the entrance, a man and woman danced with their arms around each other's waists, their heads on each other's shoulders, and their feet scraping the floor in a sleepy harmony that paid no heed to the music.

Syreeta headed straight for the bar, whose long wooden counter was decorated with a pair of imitation elephant tusks stuck upright in pedestals, one at each end. Behind the counter stood a drinks cabinet stacked full of liquor bottles, their cognac browns and campari reds and curaçao blues highlighted by narrow beams of halogen light. As Syreeta climbed on to a bar stool, the barman came forwards with a happy-to-see-you smile and greeted her by name.

'Evening o, Clement,' she responded. 'How work today?'

'Work dey, my sister. I no fit complain.' To Furo he said, 'Good evening, sir,' and after Furo returned the greeting, he reverted to Syreeta. 'Make I bring the usual?'

'No, I'm not staying,' Syreeta said. 'I just want you to do something quick-quick for me.' She opened her handbag, drew out her BlackBerry, and fiddled with the keypad. 'Abeg take a picture of me and my friend. Come to this side – I want the bar to show behind us.'

'No problem,' said the barman as he accepted the phone from Syreeta's outstretched hand. He walked to the end of the counter, lifted the flap door and passed through, then stopped a yard away from their stools and, holding up the phone, said, 'Tell me when you ready.' Syreeta turned to Furo. 'Put your arm around my shoulder.' He hesitated, mystified about where she was going with all of this, but spurred on by her stare, he obeyed. She leaned into his embrace before saying: 'Don't face the camera, look at me.' He locked his gaze on the clear skin of her forehead and pulled a tense smile, and when she called out, 'Ready,' the camera flashed.

Back in the car, after switching on the engine and

adjusting the blow of the vents, Syreeta held her phone two-handed against the steering wheel and tapped the keypad for several minutes. 'Rubbish!' she muttered at last. With a hiss of annoyance, she tossed the phone along with her handbag on to the back seat. Then she said to Furo in a composed tone: 'Time to go home.'

Home was just around the corner from The Palms. The car turned off the highway and sped through a succession of side streets that threw off Furo's bearings, and then cruised down a stretch of blacktop which ran from end to end of a housing estate. On the left side of the road stood a high fence, beyond which was the rest of the world. On the right, arranged in a barrack sprawl of identical roofs, was Oniru Estate. Syreeta parked by the side of the road, metres away from the second gate and, after climbing down barefooted from the car, she opened the back door and took out her red-blinking phone, her handbag, the plastic bag containing her packed meal, and a pair of rubber slippers, which she slipped her feet into before beeping the car locked. Furo followed her across the road to a plank footbridge balanced over the roadside gully, and then through a pedestrian gate into the residential area. White sand, a deep layer of it, covered the pathways between houses. They trudged through this seabed, her slippers flinging grains back at him, his feet sinking with every step. Sand slipped into his shoes and chafed his ankles, and by the time they arrived at her apartment, there was sand gritting between his teeth.

Like most houses in Oniru Estate, Syreeta's was as down-to-earth as a concrete bunker. The slapdash architecture only allowed for one design flourish, which was the whitewash on the walls. The front door opened on to the kitchen. Syreeta had switched on the kitchen light when her phone, which had kept ringing during the drive from the hotel, started up again. She didn't take the call until she led Furo to the parlour and sank down beside him on the settee.

'What do you want?' The phone pressed to her ear with her right hand, she inspected the fingernails of her left. Almost a minute passed before she spoke again. 'I'm not your property. Tell that to your wife.' As she listened, she dropped her hand in her lap, tugged up her skirt, and scratched the inside of her thigh. Catching Furo's eye, she stuck out her tongue at him. 'I met him at The Palms. I was bored and he asked me out. Did you think I would sit there and wait for you all night?' A pause, and then she yelled, '*Don't shout at me!*'

Furo sat as still as a photograph: Syreeta looked like an explosion waiting to happen. Whatever was going on between her and her boyfriend wasn't his business. Especially as Syreeta seemed intent on involving him. He hoped she knew where she was taking this game of hers.

There was a loaded silence as the other man did all the talking, and he seemed to be saying the right words, because Syreeta's face began shedding its tension – her mouth, at some point, parted in a reluctant smile – and when she spoke her tone was calm. 'I'm not at home.' She listened and then retorted: 'You should have thought of that before you stood me up. I have to go back to my friend. Call me tomorrow if you want.' Ending the call on that dagger thrust, she tossed the phone on to the settee, but after a moment's thought she snatched it up, pressed down the power button until the screen went blank, and then slipped it into her handbag. She yawned and stretched, throwing her arms wide and her legs forwards. Her yawn morphed into a grin. 'Let's get ready for your massage,' she said to Furo. And in a serious tone: 'But you have to bathe first. You smell of Lagos.' Gathering up her handbag and the plastic bag of food, she rose to her feet and strode to a door, nudged it open, flicked a switch, and then spoke from the lighted doorway. 'Give me a few minutes to dress the bedroom. You can start removing your clothes.'

With Syreeta out of sight, Furo cast a look around him, hoping to get a sense of this creature from her den. Her house seemed clean enough, there were no cobwebs in the ceiling corners and the paint job was unsmirched under the light switches. He also noticed that the parlour was furnished with mismatched items, none of which seemed handed down. The settee on which he sat was upholstered in blue corduroy, and the rest of the sitting arrangements, two armchairs, were vermilion chintz. The chairs were cardinal points to the magnetic centre of a round black table, with the settee taken as south and the armchairs as east and west; and due north, up against the facing wall, stood a pinewood cabinet stacked with electronics: glossy black widescreen TV, ceramic-white DVD player, green-and-silver stereo, and a DSTV decoder in metallic plastic. Everything spoke of new money and no eye for colour planning.

Reconnaissance finished, Furo bent down, undid his laces, and removed his shoes. Wrinkling his nose at their fungal stink, he dropped the shoes out of sight behind the settee. Then he gathered all the banknotes in his pockets (two thousand and ninety naira, as Syreeta had paid his bill at the cafe and let him keep Igoni's money) and folded the lot into his wallet. He stood up to undress, and then piled his shirt and trousers on the rug along with his soiled handkerchief. After placing his wallet and folder on the centre table, he sat down again in his boxer shorts and singlet and resumed inspection of the apartment. The floor from wall to wall was covered in a thick fawn rug. The ceiling was white plaster, the walls were painted blue, and he counted four doors leading out of the parlour. One opened to the kitchen, another to Syreeta's bedroom, and the third bore a sticker that announced: *In this house the toilet seat stays down!* The fourth door he assumed led to another bedroom, which meant that Syreeta either had a flatmate or the space for one. He was sucking his teeth over this discovery when a movement caught his eye from the lighted doorway, and he turned his head to see Syreeta standing there, unclothed except for sheer black panties. Her breasts were smaller than he'd imagined. Her areolas were the darkest part of her. Her navel was a deep hole from which no light escaped. Her voice broke his concentration.

'Don't tell me you plan to bathe in your underwear.' She stepped forwards and tossed a towel at him. 'Wrap that if you're feeling shy.' Walking towards the bathroom, she said over her shoulder, 'I hope you don't mind cold water,' and after the bathroom light came on, Furo heard the splash of running water, followed by her voice: 'Come in when you're ready.' She was brushing her teeth over the washbasin, her braids swinging to the fierce motion of her hand. Furo watched her with sidelong glances from the doorway, until he saw she didn't mind, and then he looked openly, his eyes stopping at the twin dimples above the swell of her buttocks, like a creator's finger marks. From slender ankles to straight calves to the deep curve of her back she had the carriage of an athlete, but in her hips she was as soft as a mother.

'Stop staring at my ass,' she said as she finished gargling. She picked out a cellophane-wrapped airline toothbrush from a tumbler on the washbasin ledge and handed it to Furo. While he squeezed out toothpaste, she climbed into the shower stall and ran water from the tap into a bucket. Then she watched him in turn until the bucket ran over. She closed the tap, stepped out of the stall, and on reaching the bathroom door, she gave a final instruction:

'Hurry up. I don't like waiting.'

There was no light in the parlour when Furo emerged from his wash. Treading the darkness, he arrived at the bedroom door and knocked before opening. The bedroom was also unlit and the hum of an air conditioner tickled the silence. Furo stood in front of the door, unsure of where to turn, and he shivered in that spot until Syreeta said, 'You don't talk much, do you?'

Turning in the direction of her disembodied voice, he moved forwards till his leg struck wood. He bent down and felt around in pit-bottom darkness: his hand found a mattress before touching skin. 'Lie down,' Syreeta said, the bed swaying as she moved aside. He climbed in and lay on his back, and her hand brushed his scalp, bumped his nose, and clasped his chin. When she said, 'Turn over,' he rolled on to his belly. He felt her fingers searching around his waistline. With a sure-handed pull she removed his boxers, and throwing her thigh across him, straddled his back. Through the shock of her weight on him he heard the rasp of a bottle cap before his senses were sent scattering by a perfume so strong, so sweet that a mournful sigh eased from his lips at the same instant he felt the splash of liquid on his back. And then Syreeta's hands – rubbing, spreading the oil into his skin. He groaned when her fingers gripped his neck.

'Feels good, doesn't it?' she said as her hands worked. 'Just relax.' She began to hum.

Furo lost count of all the times he gasped and grunted as she squeezed and thumped his neck and shoulders. The dig of her fingers, the scratch of her pubis, the grip of her knees on his ribcage, every sensation pinpricked his nerves.

69

When she lay down on him – her tender-skinned breasts squashed against his back, her oil-slicked legs entangled with his, her breath brushing his nape – the pleasure grew so intense that it squeezed from his eye corners. He pressed his face into the pillow and caught his breath, but still the sobs burst out, each one racking his shoulders.

Syreeta halted all movement when she realised Furo was crying. She remained quiet awhile, as if uncertain for the first time how to respond to his foreignness; and then, bringing her lips close to his ear, she whispered, 'Let it out.' She pushed her arms under him, linked her hands around his chest, and in that position they were both soon rocked to sleep.

It was still dark when Furo awoke. The bedroom curtains were parted, the air conditioner no longer sounded, and the world was swathed in that bottomless silence particular to wildernesses and power cuts. Furo realised what had roused him when Syreeta shook him again.

'I'm awake.' He pushed aside the bedcover and sat up. 'Is something wrong?'

'You sleep like a dead man.' Her voice was sleep-husky. 'It's almost six. Don't you have to get ready for work?'

It took him a moment to realise she didn't mean sex. 'No.'

'You don't have a job?'

'I do. But I start in two weeks.'

'Oops, sorry,' and her yawn drifted into his face. After she lay down, he asked, 'Do you want to go back to sleep?'

'Not really. Why?'

'Can we talk?'

'Uh-huh.' She rolled around to face him in the darkness. 'I'm listening.'

'How many bedrooms are in this house?'

'Two.'

'Do you live alone?'

She hesitated before saying, 'Yes.'

'What of your boyfriend? Doesn't he—'

She cut him short. 'That's none of your business.'

'I'm sorry, I just meant . . .' His voice trailed off. He took a deep breath and tried again. 'What I meant to ask was: does anyone use the second bedroom?'

'No. It's my guest room.'

Through the window, the sky's edges were turning mauve. The darkness was lifting.

'Why are you asking? Do you want to live with me?'

Furo jumped on the chance. 'Well, yes,' he said. Syreeta said nothing; he wished he could see what she was thinking. 'Please,' he continued. 'I don't have anyone else to ask for help. I just need somewhere to stay for a few days, till I start work.' And still she remained silent. In the distance Furo could hear the highway, the honks that marked its trail. He began to count time, his lips moving in silent prayer. Ten seconds, twenty – time was going too fast, so he slowed his keeping – eighty-four seconds by his tally before she spoke.

'I don't know anything about you. Except that you're white. And that you say you're Nigerian.' In a gentler tone: 'And that you're a softie. Lagos will kill you.' She raised her hand, ran her fingers through her braids, and the scent of sleep-tousled hair drifted to Furo. 'I went and sent your picture to my man last night,' she said with a sigh. 'What will I say when he finds out you're staying with me?' She sighed again. 'I knew you would ask. I heard you asking that guy in the cafe last night.' The bed shifted as she adjusted. 'OK, you can stay.'

'Thank you,' Furo said, his voice breaking from the weight of his gratitude. 'Thank you,' he repeated, 'thank you, Syreeta.'

Furo couldn't help admitting that some part of his gratefulness was due to his new appearance. Syreeta was helpful to him because he looked like he did. He was almost sure of that, because why else would she do all she had for him? She had paid his bill at the cafe, allowed him into her bed, massaged him to sleep last night, and now, at some risk to her relationship (odd affair though that was, one where she made her man jealous by sending him a staged photo of herself in the arms of another man), she had solved his problem of a place to stay. He was grateful to her, and yet he was also mindful of who she thought he was and why women like her usually moved with men like him. Her big new jeep, her well-furnished apartment in Lekki, her living alone in style and among gadgets, her ease with money and trendy places, her apparent lack of an office job or a home-run business, all of these pointed to her status as woman who knew what was what. A woman who knew how to handle men. Who knew how to live off them. Who knew the going value of a white man in Lagos. And Furo, for all the street savvy and survivor skills he prided himself on, had no idea where Syreeta was leading him.

The sky had faded into a seashell blue. Birdsong assailed the air. Voices shouting in greeting filled the streets. A nearby car vroomed into life. A new day rising.

Syreeta rose with the day, strolled across to her cluttered vanity table, and stooped beside it to open a cabinet fridge. She straightened up and turned around to face the bed with a Five Alive carton clutched in her hand. Left arm akimbo, she threw back her head and gulped from the carton. Red juice spilled down her chin, flowed between her breasts and into the trimmed V below her belly. With an 'Ah' of pleasure she pulled the carton from her lips, and looking at Furo, she raised it to him in question. When he nodded yes, she said: 'Come and get it.'

She watched with a knowing smile as Furo searched through the rumpled bedclothes for his boxer shorts. Giving up, he swung his legs to the rug and stood up, his hands hanging down by his sides. Her smile widened to reveal teeth as he walked towards her. He reached for the juice carton, but at the last moment she whipped it behind her back. 'I have some rules in this house,' she said. 'You'll wash your own plates. You won't drop rubbish on my floor or leave your clothes scattered about. You'll do your own share of the housework. You must inform me whenever you plan to stay out late. And if you ever bring a woman into this house—' She left the threat hanging and stared him in the eye. 'I hope we're clear?'

'Very clear,' he said.

'It's just better for you to know my rules from the start,' she said, holding his gaze, 'so we don't have trouble later.' She glanced down at his crotch and gave a soft laugh. 'As for that one, I don't know o. It's now complicated. We'll see how it goes. Here, have some juice, maybe it will cool you down.' Still laughing, she brushed past him as he raised the carton to his lips.

Furo's eyes avoided the vanity table in front of him, the tall mirror affixed to it. Through the window above the fridge he saw the morning face of the sun suspended in the cold-coloured sky, and behind him he heard Syreeta tumble into bed. Then a muffled scream punched the air, and Furo, coughing up juice, whirled around to find Syreeta staring.

She raised her hand, pointed a stiffened finger at his groin, her movements slow, her eyes rounded as she said:

'What happened?'

He glanced down in fear. 'What?'

'Your ass, your ass! I mean your ass!'

Furo spun around, saw his reflection; then turned again and looked over his shoulder.

'Your ass is black!' Syreeta cried, and as Furo stared in the mirror, frozen in shock, she flung up her arms, flopped on her back, and wailed with laughter.

@_IGONI

The ice cream you see in TV commercials
is actually mashed potatoes.

—@UberFacts

Furo Wariboko persisted in my thoughts after I left him at the mall, and so I did what everyone does these days: I Googled him. The search results pointed me to either Facebook or Twitter, and since I was no longer on Facebook (I deleted my account after I started receiving homophobic messages over my personal essay on wanting to be a girl), I followed the Twitter links. Now is the time to admit this: from the first moment I saw Furo I suspected I'd found a story, but it was when I heard him speak that I finally knew. A white man with a strong Nigerian accent, stranded in Lagos without a place to stay, without any friends to turn to, and with a job as a bookseller for a company so small I hadn't heard of it? Even if I hadn't met the hero myself, hadn't gleaned the details directly from the source, and even if I had plucked the whole fiction out of the air, there was no way in hell the writer in me was going to miss the rat smell of the story. What I didn't know though was the scale of the story. For that discovery I have Twitter to thank. It was there that I found out about the Furo who had gone missing in Lagos one day before I met my Furo. And it was from the tweeted photos of that lost Furo that I realised my own Furo used to be black.

Furo's story didn't emerge abracadabra-quick. It took me some time to weave the fragments I gathered from Twitter into any sort of narrative. (The thing with Twitter is: to get what you want from it, you first have to give it what it wants. As with most social networking platforms, the currency on Twitter is the users who sign up and the content they generate. Every currency holds value for someone somewhere, whether that value is based on gold or the stock market or, in the case of Twitter, popularity; that blanket word, which, for the pinpoint purpose of metaphor, I will now proceed to formularise as $P = U \times C \times T$. Extrapolating this to Twitter, popularity equals '500 million users' multiplied by 'content generated by users' multiplied by 'time spent on Twitter by users'. Yes, time – the terminus of all rigmaroles.) And so I, @_igoni, spent bundles of time on Twitter. Hours spent lurking on the timelines of virtual strangers. Hours spent snooping through megabytes of diarrhoeic data. But my investment paid off, I got what I wanted, I found @pweetychic_tk, whom I realised was Furo's sister as I read this tweet of hers:

> *Pls help RT. This is my missing bro Furo Wariboko in the pic. He left home Monday morn & no news of him since. pic.twitter.com/0J9xt5WaW*

I followed her on Twitter, of course, and going through her timeline hour after hour and day by day, reading her tweets for hidden meanings in her abbreviations and punctuation choices, and searching for mood flaggers like what news stories she retweeted and favorited, and monitoring her movements from the geotagging of her shared photos and videos, I began to get some insight into a part of Furo's story that cannot be told better than by the family he left behind.

@pweetychic_tk: Wednesday, 20 June

09:08 | Hello Twitter! #myfirstTweet

09:10 | Pls help RT. This is my missing bro Furo Wariboko in the pic. He left home Monday morn & no news of him since. pic.twitter.com/0J9xt5WaW

09:26 | RT '@RubyOsa: My cousin @pweetychic_tk has just joined Twitter. #Follow her. Her big bro got lost in Eko 2 days ago!' Thanks Ruby.

10:14 | @RubyOsa Furo is also on Twitter. His handle is @efyouaruoh

10:31 | Thanks! RT '@lazyeyedben: Hello @pweetychic_tk. I dig your pic. I'm now #ffing.'

11:01 | I'm fed up with this ASUU strike. 2 whole months without school!

14:37 | I'm hungry.

14:59 | Without @efyouaruoh the house is lonely. Mum & Dad are looking for him. I'm getting afraid. Maybe something has really happened.

16:35 | I'm starting a hashtag for my missing bro. See the attached picture for details. #Furo needs us! (RT if you have a heart.) twitpic.com/bz7htc

17:52 | RT '@RICHnaijakids: Lord in heaven, you've been good to me. Finally found the Air Retro 7s Bordeaux http://tmblr.co/ZX-9nta1U9bm'

17:55 | @RICHnaijakids Enjoy your riches oh. But we KNOW your fathers. #corruptleaders

18:58 | Today is K's birthday. I should call him. I should be the bigger person. But I won't.

19:41 | Mum & Dad just got back from the police. They've still not heard anything about Furo.

19:59 | I ask Mummy a simple YES or NO question & she gives me a 20-minute speech!

20:02 | How can the police at Akowonjo Station tell Dad to pay them to go and find Furo???

20:05 | I'm just tired of everything.

22:47 | Going to bed. Goodnight everyone.

From early on I distrusted the persona of @pweetychic_tk. I didn't know why at first, as she seemed sincere enough in her tweets about herself, and so I put my scepticism down to my own suspicious nature. (Just to press home that point about my suspicious nature, here's my first tweet upon opening my account: *To make money off selling us to ourselves for free, that's the business model of social media.* Given the tone of this tweet, I'll understand if netizens find it hard to believe when in future I declare that actually I don't disapprove of social media. But I don't and can't and won't. For one thing, I'm too much aware that my disapproval wouldn't matter a Facebook poke to the billions who have adopted Facebook and Twitter as if they were new-age versions of Christianity and Islam. And then again, as @_igoni, how can I, in honesty, oppose the very medium responsible for my existence? My efforts would be better served in renouncing Jehovah from the pulpit of a Kingdom Hall. Jesus wept and the hashtag exists, that's gospel, so I'll move on to the real crux: my distrust of digital personas.) I was wrong to think that my scepticism was unfounded, as the more I learnt about Furo's story, the more certain I became that his sister's persona had to be either contrived or schizophrenic. For here was a young lady whose full-blood brother had just gone missing, and there she was on Twitter collecting followers and trading jokes? If her digital persona was not misleading, then her real one had to be full of shit.

@pweetychic_tk: Thursday, 21 June

03:36 | I think I'm starting to understand this Twitter thing oh . . .

09:11 | Morning Twitterfam! See the sunny weather we're enjoying in Eko!

09:30 | Phone app lets women rate men like restaurants http://hfpv.to/629Nv via @HuffPoVidz

09:31 | If that app had come out b4 it might have saved me from my rubbish ex! (See last tweet.)

09:37 | Did anyone watch yesterday's episode of Who Wants to Be a Millionaire?

10:16 | Not a single retweet or mention since morning! #bored

10:20 | The biggest #COCK I've ever seen belongs to the aboki who has a kiosk near my hostel!

10:21 | FOOL => RT '@RUDEbwoyDeji: This #Unilag okpeke @pweetychic_tk has just fessed up that she likes aboki cock ha ha ha!'

10:23 | @RUDEbwoyDeji Silence is the best answer for a FOOL.

12:36 | WOOHOO! 104 new followers! #COCK tweets rule!

12:47 | Some people are sending me angry DMs oh. #COCK

12:50 | Confession time! #COCK

12:51 | For all you tweeps who RTed my #COCK tweet, I meant CHICKEN! The aboki keeps a big fat chicken as a pet. #gotcha #LWKMD

13:47 | Hmm. Follows have stopped since #COCK became CHICKEN. #justsaying

13:50 | O se! :-) RT '@lazyeyedben: #ff @pweetychic_tk, one of the realest chics on Twitter.'

15:27 | LOL RT '@drbigox: NEPA promo = Pay your bills regularly and win a generator.'

16:01 | I miss @efyouaruoh. Where are you? Mum & Dad went to the newspapers today. This is not funny any more oh. #Furo

16:06 | I'm sad :'(@efyouaruoh won't reply to his mentions & FB messages. Or is he lost 4 real?

21:54 | See me see wahala! This ugly FOOL @RudebwoyDeji is still looking 4 my trouble!

22:19 | Some people on Twitter are stupid sha. They think they can just say anything. But that's easy to fix. @RudebwoyDeji, you're BLOCKED.

22:43 | Too much animosity on Twirrer tonight mehn . . . get a life you haters. #goodbye

While searching for Furo's story, I, too, underwent a transformation. I was more relieved than surprised by this happenstance. The seeds had always been there, embedded in the parched earth of my subconscious. I had heard their muted rattling in the remembered moments of my sleeping life; I had seen their shadowy branches overhanging the narrow road that wound into my future. As is usual with Damascus journeys, I only understood the portents after my conversion. (One such portent – or, rather, evidence of my subliminal preoccupation – can be recognised in this quote from an interview I granted a magazine a few months earlier: *No human being has ever directly seen their own face. It's impossible within nature – the most you can do is glimpse your nose and, for those with full lips, the curve of your upper lip. And so we only see ourselves through external sources, whether as images in mirrors, pixels on the screen, or words on the page, words of love from a mother, words of hate from an ex-lover.*) Long before Furo's story became my own, I was already trying to say what I see now, that we are all constructed narratives.

09:45 | This thing is getting real. It's now 4 whole days since my big bro #Furo got lost. See his missing ad in today's (cont) http://tl.gd/ktdfkbt

09:53 | I'm still disgusted at how the Christian Taliban twisted my #COCK tweet yesterday. It was just a joke – GET IT? #hypocrites

09:54 | 4 all the #hypocrites who attacked me, I now have 1856 followers! Eat your hearts out!

10:32 | WHAT have I done to this one AGAIN??? => @Nu9jaYoots

10:41 | @Nu9jaYoots Who dash you #YOOT Leader? You can't even bloody spell! #mschew

10:52 | By their tweets we shall know them, Twitter #YOOT Leaders. With achieve-nothings like YOU no wonder PDP has a 68 y/o grandpa as Youth Leader!

10:55 | Why am I even wasting my time? For my new followers, abeg see my next hashtag.

10:57 | #Furo #Furo #Furo #Furo #Furo #Furo #Furo #Furo #Furo #Furo #Furo #Furo

10:59 | RT '@lazyeyedben: @pweetychic_tk Who is Furo?' YOU don't know? And to think you were my Twitter crush! You're dumped! *stomps away*

11:06 | :-) RT '@lazyeyedben: @pweetychic_tk *singing* Please don't go, don't gooo . . .'

11:42 | I love Twirrer.

11:42 | Facebook is sooo yesterday.

11:43 | RT '@Lurv_Facts: Women are biologically attracted to a-holes because their traits resemble those needed for survival in the wild.'

11:44 | Retweets are NOT endorsements!

11:49 | I just lost 3 followers. WTF. Why can't I get to 2000???

14:49 | For those who haven't seen this yet, here's my big brother's missing advert in today's newspaper: twitpic.com/yjs75Np #Furo

17:30 | God I LOVE this picture! twitpic.com/bzR76on via @JimmyChooLtd

17:31 | I'll gladly endure the pain of wearing a tight pair of shoes . . . if it looks good LOL.

20:03 | I'm not pregnant. That's a relief.

20:40 | _|_ (-.-) _|_ to @emem_1987 & @anpasticru

20:42 | Twitter is beginning to piss me off sha!

20:44 | Some RATS don't know when to choke on their evil thoughts @emem_1987 @anpasticru

20:45 | I came here to look for my missing bro. Every other thing is dirt off my shoulder.

20:49 | This! RT '@lazyeyedben: I'm digging your style @pweetychic_tk. Don't mind the olofofos.'

20:49 | THANKS @lazyeyedben! You're such a cool dude!

21:04 | Co-sign => RT '@Rihanna: The one person you can't run from is YOU!!!'

21:05 | I ♥ @Rihanna! #justsaying

21:15 | Mum & Dad have returned. Mum is crying again. My life is so not fun right now.

21:41 | OMG!!! Mummy wants to go to the mortuary 2moro to look for Furo!!!

22:17 | 2moro is officially the worst day of my life. #goodnight

My handle is @_igoni and I was born into the Twitter stream in January 2009. Apart from tweeting links to my online publications as well as other articles I'd enjoyed reading, I didn't have much to do in my short existence. Until, that is, I found @pweetychic_tk and, through her, @efyouaruoh. Furo's Twitter page displayed as its profile photo an image of sunglasses-wearing Neo from *The Matrix*, and the profile name was 'FW', while the bio read, 'Lagos-based job hunter,' and so, if not for his sister's tweets, @efyouaruoh would have remained a cipher for ever vanished into the dead-end alleys of the Web, just another one of hundreds of millions of unverified Twitter handles with a meagre following and a preference for the pseudonymous; and, to boot, a digital persona whose final breath was drawn at 00:13 on 18 June. 'Nepa bring light abeg,' he tweeted, and then nothing ever again. Silence, on Twitter, is as good as death, and if life hadn't intervened to bring us together on the day after his final tweet, I might never have found myself scrolling through the timelines of the dead, searching for the POVs of the real person in the ghosts of their digital personas.

@pweetychic_tk: Saturday, 23 June

11:15 | This is NOT a good morning. Dad is driving us to the #mortuary in Ikeja. We're going to search for #Furo there!

12:21 | I just knew the place would be UGLY twitpic.com/bzT67oM #mortuary

12:27 | It STINKS inside!!!! twitpic.com/c4KnnIP #mortuary

12:33 | RT '@Nneka_Or: omg can this be Lagos?? RT @pweetychic_tk: It STINKS inside!!!! twitpic.com/c4KnnIP #mortuary'

12:33 | RT '@PrinceofmoJo: RT @infoeNGine: Lagos govt shuts down smelly #mortuary http://dlvr.it/2NLieR @pweetychic_tk'

13:03 | THOSE ARE DEAD PEOPLE!!! twitpic.com/bzs24bP #mortuary

13:05 | RT '@asiwajuayo: WTF! Naija should suffer a natural disaster! RT @pweetychic_tk: THOSE ARE DEAD PEOPLE!!! twitpic.com/bzs24bP #mortuary'

13:05 | RT 'enugu2coventry: This is unspeakably shameful. RT @pweetychic_tk: THOSE ARE DEAD PEOPLE!!! twitpic.com/bzs24bP #mortuary'

13:06 | RT '@PrinceofmoJo: RT @punchonthenet: Rear Admiral's missing daughter found in Lagos #mortuary http://dlvr.it/2NLtuM @pweetychic_tk'

13:33 | When I die I want to be cremated! On the same day! twitpic.com/ZvY80pQ #mortuary

13:48 | O_o RT '@gambianfaust: @pweetychic_tk My granny died & I wanted 2 keep a part of her with me. So after her cremation, I snorted the ashes.'

13:48 | RT '@MarkyMona: @pweetychic_tk Thx 4 raising awareness abt this prob. See the #mortuary they kept my father in! pic.twitter.com/rU1ogDtS'

14:07 | I just threw up a little in my mouth. Even dead people don't deserve this. #mortuary

14:22 | RT '@PrinceofmoJo: RT @HMNews: Nigeria | Floods: #Mortuary Attendants Stack Corpses on Rooftops http://dlvr.it/2NLdG @pweetychic_tk'

14:26 | @PrinceofmoJo Stop tweeting those links at me you PERVERT!!!

14:27 | Apologies 2 my followers 4 the error, but please don't RT or click on @PrinceofmoJo #mortuary links. They're porn.

14:44 | RT '@asiwajuayo: Yay! @pweetychic_tk is the reason! RT @TrendsLagos: 'mortuary' is now trending in #Lagos: http://trendsmap.com/ng/lagos'

15:12 | Thanks ALL!!! My phone battery's about to die, I have to go now. #mortuary

23:17 | OMG!!!!!! @DONJAZZY retweeted me!!!

When I'd learned enough about Furo's story to be sure I was committed to following it to the end, I tweeted @pweetychic_tk. In remarkable time she had become a Twitter celeb, gathering seven times as many followers in a week as I had in four years, so I wasn't certain she would respond to a Twitter lightweight like me. (Question: How did she get so many followers so fast? Answer: Check out the first page of the Google search for 'get Twitter followers fast'. In other words, she did the work.) With this in mind – 'this' being my dread of getting rebuffed in public – I pondered on the approach most likely to succeed, at the same time studying her timeline for any clues that might help with my decision, which I indeed reached upon seeing a serendipitous tweet of hers. From meeting her brother I knew about our shared ethnicity, and so, to indicate to her that we had a connection deeper than Twitter *esprit de corps*, I greeted her in Kalabari before offering to buy her ice cream. Calculation always trumps sincerity on social media. Yet I must admit that when she not only replied my tweet but also accepted my offer, I was buffaloed.

@pweetychic_tk: Sunday, 24 June

07:33 | Good morning folks! Thanks for all the RTs & mentions yesterday!! #mortuary

07:33 | And happy Sunday to ALL my new followers! Have you seen my hashtag #Furo yet?

07:35 | So @DONJAZZY RTed me yesterday & my phone hasn't stopped buzzing. #Thank you

08:45 | I'm off to church. Yes oh, I believe in all that bible stuff ;o)

09:41 | I'm seriously craving ice cream. It's all this hellfire talk I'm sure!

09:57 | Pastor finish soon oh so my Daddy can buy me ice cream LOL!

09:59 | TWITTER FIGHT ALERT!!!

09:59 | RT '@kweenofsheebah: I'm Ethiopian and I'm SO offended by @afrikais1country'

10:01 | O_o RT '@kweenofsheebah: @afrikais1country Ethiopians are a proud people. We're not like the rest of you African booty scratchers. #HornPride'

10:04 | RT '@kweenofsheebah: @VJ_Singhing If @afrikais1country wants to mock that way of thinking it should be called AFRICA-IS-A-CONTINENT.'

10:06 | RT '@kweenofsheebah: @VJ_Singhing YOU shouldn't even be on this topic of Africans! You look like you eat curry in Mumbai.'

10:08 | TWEEPS!!! See #HornPride for the latest. I'll only retweet the best insults ha ha!

10:10 | #HornPride RT '@kweenofsheebah: @naijapalaver Nigeria was colonised just like the rest of Africa. Ethiopia was NOT.'

10:13 | #HornPride RT '@_igoni: @kweenofsheebah Seems you need reminding that tiny Eritrea kicked your butt. @pweetychic_tk'

10:15 | #HornPride RT '@kweenofsheebah: @_igoni Don't tell me about butt-kicking when your people were dragged to the US to pick cotton & get whipped!'

10:15 | See my last retweet! @kweenofsheebah is subbing NIGERIANS!!! #HornPride

10:35 | NOooo! RT '@kweenofsheebah: @pweetychic_tk Stop hashing my tweets you repulsive Nigerian troll!' #HornPride

11:01 | Church is finally over!!!

11:05 | Have you seen @kweenofsheebah bio? @afrikais 1country #HornPride

11:06 | @kweenofsheebah YOU live in CANADA & yet you talk shit about AFRICA???

11:31 | #HornPride RT '@kweenofsheebah: Shut up all you poor Africans. Go fix your starving 3rd world countries. That should keep y'all busy.'

11:50 | My fingers hurt from all the RTing, but this has got to be the best fight ever! And a BIG hello to all my new followers!!! #HornPride

11:51 | :-) #HornPride RT '@kweenofsheebah: All you Nigerian scammers tweeting threats at me, I've nothing to say to you.'

12:11 | YAY! RT '@lazyeyedben: #HornPride is trending! 2 days in a row @pweetychic_tk has put Lagos on the map! I love that gal!!'

12:43 | No more tweets from @kweenofsheebah in the last 20 minutes. She's run off to lick her wounds. Good riddance to bad rubbish!

13:00 | Time for ice cream!!!

13:11 | Aargh! Mum is still waiting to see Pastor! I'm stuck here with Dad until she's done. No ice cream! *sheds angry tears*

13:13 | Ooh yes please! RT '@_igoni: Tobra, @pweetychic_tk. I'll buy you ice cream. Least I can do after you provided my Sunday entertainment.'

13:14 | @_igoni I'm at the Winners Chapel on Akowojo Road in Egbeda.

13:49 | Just got off the phone with my new Twitterpal @_igoni . . . #crazyexcited

13:57 | @_igoni arrives! twitpic.com/bzBvv3h

15:43 | Eating ice cream with @_igoni at The Palms in Lekki! twitpic.com/bzFu2dl

20:03 | Today's stupid rain couldn't spoil all the fun I had with @_igoni! Now heading home in one of those new metro cabs! #enjoyment

20:14 | 4,743 RTs & 86 favs of my first-ever tweet about #Furo (You guys ROCK!!!)

21:37 | Mum needs to chillax! I can't go out again because Furo got lost???

22:31 | I'm thinking about the long talk @_igoni and I had about #Furo today.

22:35 | @_igoni And imiete for the @ColdStone ice cream!!!

23:22 | :o))) RT '@_igoni: @pweetychic_tk The pleasure was mine. See you again soon.'

23:45 | Ooooh just 2 followers short of 7,000!!!

23:46 | *staggers across bedroom* *flops on bed* *hugs teddy bear* #happy #goodnight

Five days after I found her on Twitter, I got a chance to meet @pweetychic_tk. I was conflicted about that move – should the artist probe too deeply into the mundane lives of their characters – but grabbed the chance anyway. We met by arrangement at the gate of her church in Egbeda on an over-cast Sunday afternoon after the close of service and, at her suggestion, I took her to The Palms in Lekki for ice cream. Her name was Tekena. (When she asked what she should call me, @_igoni or just plain Igoni, I joked, 'Call me Morpheus.')

BLACKASS

'I scarcely dared to look
to see what it was I was.'

—Elizabeth Bishop, *In the Waiting Room*

On Thursday, 21 June, Syreeta gave Furo an old phone that she no longer used, and after she loaded it with airtime, she made a call to someone she knew at the passport office in Ikoyi. A new passport would cost nine thousand naira and take three months to process, but through her contact it would take three days and cost seventeen thousand. Furo didn't have the money, and he said so in a voice shocked into loudness after hearing Syreeta say into the phone, 'We'll come tomorrow,' but she shushed him with a finger pressed to her lips, then muffled the phone against her chest and whispered to him, 'At least see the man first, get the application form.' Furo shut up in agreement, and on Friday morning she drove him to the passport office, parked the car by the gate, and handed him an unsealed envelope. 'That's twenty thousand,' she said, and when his outpourings of gratitude had dragged on too long, she interrupted, 'Go on. The man is waiting.'

The arrangement was for Furo to wait by the flagpole at the passport office entrance until Syreeta's contact came to fetch him. Easy instructions to follow: so easy that Furo dreaded the difficulties that must arise. It seemed to him imprudent, provoking – a clear-cut case of trouble dey sleep, yanga go wake am – to walk into the lair of immigration officials and stand under the Nigerian flag. But the previous day, after the set-up phone call, when he disclosed his misgivings to Syreeta, she had laughed them off. Her confidence only served to bolster his doubts, which grew even bigger after he got down from the car and watched her drive off to her appointment at the beauty salon. But he had no time to dwell on his superstitions, as his appearance had caused a tidal wave of excitement in the horde of informal agents, the hustlers, young men and the odd woman who rushed about offering help to everyone who approached. When this crowd fell on him with their frenzied cawing, their begging stares and smarmy smirks, he hurried forwards with his hands guarding his pockets and his lowered head shaking no until he entered the gate of the passport office, through which none of the hustlers ventured. After he halted beside the flagpole, he placed the call. 'It's Syreeta's friend. I'm here, under the flag,' he said into the phone, and the man grunted in acknowledgement, then ended the call. Furo glanced around, searching for a face that matched that voice. The man's number was stored in the phone as Passport Man. Furo had asked Syreeta for his real name, but she didn't know it and neither did her friend who had recommended his services to her. For safety from sting operations and disgruntled customers, Furo supposed. Another reason to worry.

The passport office comprised two long rows of office blocks whose patios were sealed off by wrought-iron bars. Immigration officials in khaki uniforms marched down the patios and into the open doorways of the front office block, through which Furo could see desks and queues of people. A man, a uniformed officer, emerged from one of the doorways. After staring in Furo's direction for meaningful seconds, he lifted his nametag from around his neck, stowed it in his trouser pocket, and started forwards. Though he looked younger than Furo had imagined from the voice on the telephone, he had to be Passport Man. This was confirmed when he called out from several paces away, 'Wariboko?' At Furo's nod he showed no emotion, and on reaching his side, he said, 'Come with me.' He led Furo out through the front gate, and after calling over a sly-faced man from the throng of informal agents, he told Furo, 'Go with him.'

Furo trailed the agent to a plywood shack by the fence of the passport office. On the shack's doorstep a pass-my-neighbour generator coughed out fumes, which, over time, had blackened the front wall. The cramped, smoke-darkened interior held a laminating machine, an inkjet printer, a bulky photocopier, an electronic binder, and a desktop computer atop an old rickety table. The agent stopped at the table, selected a sheet from the papers strewn across it, then pulled a biro from his pocket and bent down in preparedness to write. With a frown of concentration on his upturned face, he asked Furo his surname.

'Wariboko,' Furo answered.

'Abeg spell it for me.'

Furo extended his hand for the biro. 'Let me write it.'

'No,' said the agent. 'Just spell.'

Furo spelled out his surname, and after the next question, his first name, too.

'What is your place of birth?'

'Port Harcourt.'

'Spell Harcourt. I have forget how many Rs.'

With a groan that didn't pass his lips, Furo did as asked.

'What is your date of birth?'

'Six, May, 1979.'

'You're a male,' the agent stated, and ticked that section. Glancing up, he asked, 'Do you know your state of origin?'

'Rivers,' Furo said.

'What of your local government area?'

Furo had had enough. 'I can read,' he said curtly. 'Let me fill the form myself.'

The agent straightened up as if his back was cramped, then met Furo's gaze and said: 'Don't worry, oga, relax yourself. This nah my work, I know what I am doing. The smallest mistake can spoil your passport finish. Let me handle everything so your money will not waste.' He bent again over the table. 'Oya, talk now, what is your local government?'

'Akuku Toru,' Furo replied in a resigned voice. He understood now that the agent knew his job indeed. For Furo, it was too much effort to resist the haggling etiquette of jobbery.

'I know that one spelling,' the agent responded, and wrote it out before asking, 'What is the name of your guarantor?'

Furo stared in puzzlement. 'What do you mean by guarantor?'

In a voice of gloating, the agent said, 'See what I was saying! That's why I'm doing the form for you. Nah small things like this wey fit scatter your application.' He waited for Furo to stew in his ignorance a few more seconds before he explained: 'A guarantor is somebody who will guarantee you're Nigerian. No be just anybody o, it must be an adult who has a good job. But no worry yourself, leave am to me, I go take care of that.'

After the agent finished filling in the form, he inserted the single sheet into a cardboard folder and handed it to Furo with the words, 'Give this to your man.' Drawing closer to Furo, he said in a tone of instruction: 'During your interview, if perchance they ask you for the name of your guarantor, tell them it is Joseph. And if they ask you for his workplace, you can tell them anything. Better you say he's a civil servant.'

'What about his surname?'

'Don't worry about that one.'

'Are you sure?'

The agent laughed. 'You're still doubting me? But I done tell you sey this nah my work.'

'If you say so,' Furo muttered, and made as if to leave. The agent cleared his throat, and when Furo glanced back at him, he hardened his face into a grin and spoke in a coaxing tone, 'Ah, oga, you want go just like that? You no get anything for your boy?' Furo pulled out his wallet, and as he flipped it open, the agent added, 'I'm not charging you o, but you're a big oga, oyibo man like you.' He plucked the two hundred banknote from Furo's fingers. 'God bless you, sir! In case of next time, if you want to do new passport, or even yellow card or international driving licence, just come straight to me. I will handle everything for you for a better price. Why not take my number? You can save it as Passport Deji. The spelling is D-E-J-I.'

Passport Man was finishing a cigarette under the flag. As Furo arrived, he flicked away the butt, took the folder from Furo with his left hand and thrust out his right, then raised his eyebrows with a meaning that was unmistakable. Furo counted out three thousand naira from the envelope and handed over the rest. Passport Man thumbed through the thousand-naira banknotes, pulled out two, slipped them into Furo's folder, and shoved the envelope into the same pocket he had put his nametag in. Then he said in a sharp tone, 'Walk behind me. When I stop, you stop.'

He led Furo through a doorway in the first office block. By the front wall of the room a cluster of people were seated on wooden benches, and across from them was a desk at which presided a female immigration officer. A man wearing a rumpled French suit sat before her in a straight-backed chair with his hands stuck together between his knees and his shoulders hunched forwards, and whenever she addressed him he nodded his halo of hair before uttering a response. The occasional Yoruba phrase floated to Furo where he stood just inside the doorway. Finally the woman closed the man's folder and slid it across to him, and as the chair creaked under his rising, Passport Man raised a hand and hurried forwards, Furo following. The woman's eyes caught Furo's face and stuck to it. But she looked down when his folder landed on her desk. 'Special,' Passport Man said in his rusted voice, and then backed away, leaving Furo feeling exposed. He hadn't foreseen that he would be left alone to face an official armed with a system.

The woman raised both hands to adjust her beret, after which she drew Furo's folder closer with one hand and dropped the other under the desk, as if to scratch an itch. She indicated the empty chair with her chin, and after Furo sat down, she pinched open the folder, bent forwards to eye the contents, then pulled open a drawer and tipped the folder into it. When she replaced the folder on the desk and flipped it open, the money was gone.

'Kedu aha gi?'

'Excuse me?' Furo said. He smiled in apology. 'I don't speak Igbo.'

'I don't speak Kalabari,' the woman retorted, 'but I doubt you do either.' Picking up a red pen, she asked in a churlish tone, 'What are your names?' Her following questions all came from the form in the sequence Furo remembered, but she stopped before arriving at the question he feared the most, about his guarantor. While she wrote on the form Furo watched her hand – corded with veins, hard nails covered with chipped brown polish – as it guided the pecks and scratches of the pen. She finished writing, closed the folder, spun it across to Furo, and '*Dalu.*' Goodbye.

He rose from the chair and turned around to see Passport Man beckoning from the doorway. By this time it was clear to Furo that the process was moving along much more smoothly than he'd expected. The bribe-sharing, the queue-jumping, the fact non-checking, and the customer-handling were as efficient as any system whose design was alimentary: in through the mouth and straight out the anus. He was no more than a bite of food for a subverted system, which chewed him up for money and, to avoid the cramp of constipation, shat him out fast. It was bad business for Passport Man to fart where he ate, and so, for his own sake, he put real effort into guiding Furo around the hiccups in the bureaucracy. Step by step Furo grew surer of the ground he walked on, and with new confidence he followed Passport Man into the next office, where his photo was taken and his fingerprint biometrics collected by another paid-off official, and then on to the third office, where yet another official fulfilled his stomach duty by stamping a slip and instructing Furo to return with it on Monday for passport pick-up. Emerging with Furo from this office, Passport Man said, 'We have finished. Call me when you get here on Monday.' He permitted himself a smile for the first time since Furo set eyes on his commando face. 'You're now a Nigerian, officially.'

Vultures, hyenas, Lagos taxi drivers, in rising order of cunning, greed, hard-heartedness, Furo was convinced after forty minutes of standing by the roadside opposite the passport office. And when his legs grew tired, he walked some distance away to a new spot along the road, but that didn't help, every taxi that pulled up – ordinary yellow, special red, metro black, or unpainted kabu-kabu – sped away empty, the drivers unwilling to reduce their inflated prices. Furo knew why, as did everyone who witnessed his heated haggling. A white man in Lagos has no voice louder than the dollar sign branded on to his forehead.

Furo's frustration turned to anger. Anger directed everywhere. Everywhere he turned he made discoveries about this new place he had lived in all his life. Life in Lagos was locked in a constant struggle against empathy. Empathy was too much to ask for, too much to give: it was good only for beggars to exploit in their sob stories aimed at your pocket through your heart. Heart, in Lagos idiom, meant guts, mettle, even recklessness, but rarely compassion. Compassion was a fatal fracturing in hearts bunkered against the city's hardness. Hardness so evident in the hiking of taxi fares and the drivers' refusal to look beyond a white face and hear a weary voice bargaining for understanding . . . that was the Lagos he was discovering afresh.

A smiling lady came to his aid. She was passing on the sidewalk when the last taxi driver called out his last price, four thousand naira, and then drove off after Furo held up his fingers in a peace sign that meant two thousand. As Furo stepped back from the road with a muttered curse, the lady approached him and said hello. At his grudging response, she threw him a cordial smile that raised his hackles and made his voice crackle with resentment. 'Can I help you?'

'I see you're having trouble getting a cab,' she said airily.

'Yes,' Furo replied in a rude tone, but his decision to cut short the conversation was overcome by the yearning to spread around his bitterness. 'Can you imagine these bloody drivers? See the prices they're calling! For what – where am I going?'

And when the lady indulged him by asking where he was going, he cried out: 'Just Lekki, near The Palms!'

'Ah-ah, but that's not far at all.' Her tone was soft with sympathy.

'It doesn't make any sense,' Furo said. 'I've been standing here for nearly an hour and I've stopped how many taxis, more than ten, and yet none of them has agreed to go below four thousand. I've even offered two!'

The lady smiled at him again, a mouth-and-eyes smile whose genuineness was almost telepathic, and then she raised her hand and patted the air before her chest in a soothing motion. 'Take it easy,' she said with assurance. 'I'll help you stop a cab.' Feeling his anger ebb at the flow of her voice, Furo aimed a long look at her, took in her youth, the cheerful spirit reflected in her face, and he returned her smile at last and said, 'That's sweet of you. Thanks.' He was about to ask her name when she spoke. 'Don't mention. You'll have to move away though. We can't let these drivers know we're together. Go now, quickly, a cab is coming.'

Furo hurried over to a Toyota Tundra parked about three yards away. He leaned against the driver's door, folded his arms across his chest, and tried to look bored. From where he stood he heard the lady speaking to the taxi driver in Yoruba. When she gave a low whistle, he glanced in her direction to confirm it was OK to abandon his owner's stance, then pushed away from the Tundra and walked towards the yellow taxi, an ancient Datsun saloon. The lady straightened up from the passenger window at his approach, rolled her eyes at him and gave a playful shake of her head, then opened the door. He slipped into the car, and as she pushed the door closed, he looked at the driver, a long-necked man with wrinkles almost as deep as the tribal marks in his cheeks.

He wore pink cutwork trousers, a fishnet singlet, a white skullcap, and he met Furo's gaze with the most astonished look his sun-leathered face could manage. Furo swung his eyes to the window when he felt the lady's hand on his shoulder. 'You'll give him one thousand naira,' she said. Then to the driver, 'Baba, this is my friend, please treat him well. *E se, e le lo.*' She stepped back from the window, returned Furo's wave, and resumed her stroll to sainthood.

As the taxi sheered away from the curb, Furo strapped on his seatbelt and prepared his mind for a rough ride ahead. The driver was transmitting his unhappiness to the car through his rough jabbing of the gearstick. He was aware he had been tricked into asking an honest fare, and if he could find a way that left his self-respect some wriggle room, he would renegotiate. Furo had already made up his mind to resist the move that, sure enough, barely a minute after they set off, the driver made. 'The go-slow today is bad, very bad.' This said in a sociable tone and followed by a sidelong glance at Furo, who remained silent. As weather was for Londoners, traffic for Lagosians was the conversation starter. The taxi driver tried again. 'You speak English?' The question was asked this time with a fixed stare. Furo, not wanting to be rude to the older man, nodded yes. 'That's good,' said the driver. 'You like Lagos?' At Furo's indifferent shrug, the driver grew voluble. 'Lagos is a good place, enjoyment plenty. Nowhere in Africa is good like Lagos. Money plenty, fine women dey, and me I know all the places where white people are enjoying. Like Bar Beach. And Fela shrine – you know Fela?' When Furo made no reply, the driver began searching through the cassette tapes scattered on the dashboard. 'Let me play Fela music for you.'

'No, please,' Furo said. 'I know Fela.'

'Maybe next time,' the driver said as he braked the car.

Catching Furo's eye, he jerked his head at the stalled cars ahead. 'See what I was telling you. And we never even reach where the main go-slow go dey.'

Furo snorted with amusement, but when he spoke his voice showed irritation. 'Baba, this is not go-slow. The traffic light is showing red. See, the cars are moving already.'

The driver grabbed the gearstick, the chassis grumbled, the car jerked forwards, and the ensuing silence lasted for several minutes of rally racing. Finally he raised one hand from the steering wheel and scratched his nose, then wiped his fingers on his trousers, and said, 'Abeg, excuse me o, I'm very sorry for asking, but how come your voice is sounding like a Nigerian?'

'I've lived in Lagos a long time,' Furo said. 'Watch that okada!'

The taxi swerved to the driver's startled yell and the front bumper only just missed the motorcyclist's knee. The taxi swerved again as the driver leaned out the window to shout back angry insults. After retracting his head, he turned to Furo, his eyes glinting with excitement.

'*Okaaay*,' he drawled, nodding his head. 'So you are a Lagos person. That is how come you and your girlfriend played me wayo.'

It took Furo a second to catch the man's meaning, and then he said with a laugh, 'She's not my girlfriend.'

'But you played me trick, talk true?'

Furo's tone was mock aggrieved. 'How can you say I tricked you, ehn, Baba? My friend asked you how much to Lekki and you told her your price. Where is the trick in that?'

'Lagos oyibo!' the driver said with a hacking laugh. 'You funny sha. I like you.'

This old baba was a wily one, Furo thought, and turned

his face aside to hide his smile. But the man was wise enough to know when to ease up, as it turned out. Silence followed their arrival in Victoria Island and the journey down Ozumba Mbadiwe Way, but as the car drew up to heavy traffic by the fence of the Lagos Law School, the driver spoke again.

'So you are living in Lekki?'

'Yes,' Furo answered.

'Ehen!' the driver said, and then waited for Furo's curiosity to show itself. When Furo looked his way, he said, his tone imploring, 'You that are living in Lekki, if you are taking taxi every time, you know this is the truth. That price I charged your friend is not the correct one. I called little money because she is my Yoruba sister. I am not complaining o, nothing like that. I just leave it for you to add something for me.'

'I hear you, Baba.'

'That's OK. We are nearing Shoprite. Where is the exact place I will drop you?'

'Oniru Estate.'

'Oba Oniru. I know there well. Which side are you going? Is it first or second gate?'

When the taxi pulled to a stop at the second gate of the estate, Furo handed the baba two thousand naira. Effusive blessings, an offer of marriage to one of his daughters named Bilikisu, and finally Furo was out of the car. *All in all not a bad day*, he thought as he ambled towards the gate, and turned around at the driver's shout to wave back at the departing taxi.

The apartment was empty when Furo entered. After a few quiet minutes of lying on the guest-room bed, he shook off his torpor and sent Syreeta an SMS. She responded at once with a phone call to say she was spending the weekend at a friend's and that she would return early on Monday. 'There's fried chicken in the fridge, cook something,' she said, 'but please don't burn down the house,' and because her pause seemed to call for it, Furo laughed before saying, 'I've heard you,' then ended the call. Realising he had to be careful not to wear out his clothes before he acquired new ones, he rose from the bed and began to undress. He stripped down to his boxer shorts, hung his shirt and trousers in the wardrobe, then padded barefooted across the guest room, his bedroom now – after two nights it didn't yet feel like his, but he loved the thick Vitafoam mattress, the ingenuity of mankind's small comforts that it represented – and threw open the door. He made a beeline for Syreeta's bedroom and halted in the doorway. The unmade bed, the electronic hum of the fridge, the gauzy curtains stirring in the breeze, the imposing vanity table – its surface piled with cosmetic jars, gaudy bottles, squeezed tubes: all in doubles, twinned in the mirror – and in the corner the raffia basket of used underwear, like an outsized potpourri. He pulled the door closed and crossed the parlour, the TV following his movements with a dull grey stare. On the centre table rested two remote controls. He picked, pointed, pressed, the TV screen blinked blue, and as the DSTV decoder scanned for signals, he sank on to the settee.

He had the house to himself for the weekend.

A bed, two even.

And food, TV, anything he wanted.

Furo locked his mind on the TV, which showed a Nollywood movie, and in the scene a weeping woman sat in jail with a bloodied, shirtless man. The woman's crying sounded strained, the movie jail was a real garage – motor oil spots on the floor, filigreed grille for a door – and the make-up blood looked like make-up blood. Furo changed the channel, and kept on changing, his thumb tapping the keys, the remote wedged against his belly, his knees spread apart and his shoulders slouched, his eyes blinking as the TV flickered and switched voices in mid-sentence: here's some peri peri, a much stronger bite, dominate the headlines, nothing but Allah's favour, love potting around, *Jerry! Jerry! Jerry!*, cocoa boom era, hungry man size, avoid Gaddafi's fate, last scrap of hope, her majesty the queen, we make our own beef, terrible for tennis, *stadium crowd chanting*, still capable in spurts, battle to reach each level, *xylophone tinkling*, accused of phone hacking, can withstand his might, right to be proved wrong, *hit you like ooh baby*, off the starboard bow, what happened elsewhere, love can save the universe, *loud audience laughter—*

His phone rang: he could hear its plaintive jangling below the TV's barrage. He jumped up from the settee and ran into the bedroom and grabbed the phone from the bed. It was Syreeta calling. 'Phone was in the bedroom,' was the first thing he said. And then, 'I was watching TV.'

'Enjoy,' Syreeta said. 'I just remembered I hadn't asked you how it went. Your passport.'

'Oh yes, it went very well. I'm supposed to collect it on Monday.'

'We should celebrate. Do you plan to go out tonight?'

'No.'

'What of tomorrow?'

'No plans for tomorrow.'

A teasing note entered her voice. 'Don't you do clubs? Come on, it's the weekend!'

'No clubbing for me,' Furo said with a forced laugh. 'I can't afford it.'

'OK then,' Syreeta said. Her voice had reached a decision. 'I'll return on Sunday, in the evening. I'll take you out, my treat. We must wash your passport.'

'I'd like that,' Furo said, to which Syreeta responded with

a quick 'Cheers,' and then, as he began to express his thanks, the line went dead. Lowering the phone from his ear, he stared at it without seeing, thinking about Syreeta and her puzzling kindnesses. He knew she felt sorry for him, and he suspected she even liked him in her own hard-boiled way, but now it also seemed she trusted him, at least enough to leave her bedroom unlocked. But all of that didn't explain why a Lagos big girl was so free with her favours, especially as she knew he had no money. He had nothing she could want, nothing at all. After all, she had seen everything, even his buttocks.

That morning, when she and he discovered his buttocks together, was branded on to the underside of his consciousness. He had awoken several times in a fright on Wednesday night, her laughter ringing in his mind. But the bigger terror was that the blackness on his buttocks would spread into sight, would creep outwards to engulf everything, to show him up as an impostor. That it hadn't yet happened didn't mean it wouldn't still. That he didn't have a hand in what he was didn't mean he wasn't culpable. No one asks to be born, to be black or white or any colour in between, and yet the identity a person is born into becomes the hardest to explain to the world. Furo's dilemma was this: he was born black, and had lived in that skin for thirty-odd years, only to be born again on Monday morning as white, and while he was still toddling the curves of his new existence, he realised he had been mistaken in assuming his new identity had overthrown the old. His idea of what he was, of who the world saw him as, was shaken by the blemish on his backside. He knew that so long as the vestiges of his old self remained with him, his new self would never be safe from ridicule and incomprehension. Syreeta, clearly, had shown him that.

Thinking these troubling thoughts, Furo spent the rest of Friday with his eyes stuck to the TV screen until he tumbled off the cliff edge of his mental fatigue. He awoke what felt like mere minutes later to the human noises of Saturday morning, and after he freshened up with a quick bath and a light breakfast, after the power went and the wild clatter of generators swelled in all corners of his mind and the housing estate, after he stared at the dead TV for so long that his eyes stung from the rub of the thick-as-mud air, and then, after he fiddled with his phone until he figured out how to turn off the Caller ID, he called his old phone. It rang on the first try, and before he could recover from the shock of the expected, that voice he recognised even better than his own jolted him awake to the horror of his mistake, a mistake he only salvaged by biting down on his tongue to control the urge to reply to his mother's hopeful hello. He cut the call, switched off the phone, removed the battery, and then bowed his head to the pounding of the generators, the machine rumble of the world.

Later, when he'd calmed himself enough to breathe easy, he made every effort to close back the portal from which the past was leaking into his head.

Saturday passed slowly, but it passed.

He rose with the sun on Sunday and washed his clothes, then wrapped his towel like a sarong and stepped out of the apartment for the first time since Friday. The yard was empty, as were the estate streets, because sunny Sundays were bumper days for churches. After hanging his washing on the clothesline, he went back inside and swept the floor, dusted the furniture, beat the hollows out of the settee, and washed his piled-up dishes. The sun's face was sunk in a mass of thunderclouds by the time he was done with housework. He gathered in the sun-scented laundry, ironed his shirt and trousers, and took a bath. By four o'clock he was ready for Syreeta's return.

The rainstorm struck at five. From afar the rain approached like a crashing airliner. At this sound, a rising whine that left the curtains curiously still, Furo hurried into his bedroom and stared from the window above the bed, which gave the clearest view of the sky. He smelled the raindrops before he saw them. A lash of thunder roused the wind, which rose from the dust and began to swing wildly at treetops and roof edges and flocks of plastic bags ballooning out to sea. Raindrops swirled like dancing schools of silver fish and scattered in all directions, splattering the earth and the shaded walls of houses. Furo sprinted around the apartment shutting windows.

Syreeta arrived in the rain. As was usual during a storm, the power had gone, and Furo was stretched out on the settee, not asleep but drifting there, lulled by the drumming on the roof and the wind whistling outside the windows. He started upright when he heard the key in the lock. The door banged open, Syreeta rushed in, turned around in the doorway to close her umbrella and shake water from it, then kicked the door closed and bent down to rest the umbrella against it. She was barefooted. The bottoms of her jeans were rolled up to her knees. Her braids were gathered in a shower cap, and when she came closer Furo saw she was shivering. Her face was angled with annoyance.

'You came in the rain!' Furo exclaimed in welcome, but Syreeta made no response as she strode into her bedroom and slammed the door.

Furo stood up from the settee and skulked off into his bedroom. He took off his clothes and hung them in the wardrobe to preserve their freshness, and then slipped into bed and pulled the blanket over his head. Syreeta's mood had dampened his, and the excitement he'd nursed all day at the thought of their going out was now a fluff of fear in his belly. He felt like a chided child, driftwood in angry currents, at the mercy of whims as changeable as Mother Nature's.

'Furo?'

When he lifted his head from under the blanket, Syreeta was standing in the bedroom doorway. In the splash of rainwater he hadn't heard her open the door. Beyond the doorway the shadows thickened, night was falling, but Syreeta was as clear as a spectral warning in the white towel that wrapped her from chest to thigh. She spoke in a voice adjusted for crashing thunder.

'Thanks for closing the windows. The house would have flooded if you weren't here. And thanks too for cleaning up. How was your weekend?'

Furo sat up in the bed. 'It was quiet. I got some rest. And yours?'

Waving aside his question with her left hand, with the right she grabbed the fold of the towel just as it loosened, and tightened it again over her breasts as she said, 'This nonsense rain has spoiled my plans for today. We can't go out any more. The traffic out there is crazy.'

'That's OK,' Furo said. As the silence that followed seemed awkward for him alone, he dropped his eyes from her face. But when she said with a sigh, 'I'm going to lie down,' quicker than thought he responded with, 'Can I join you?' His glance caught the flash of her smile. She waited long enough for him to suffer for ever, and then she turned around without replying and walked away without closing his door. Furo caught his breath at the creak of her bedroom door, and by the time he was convinced the door wasn't closing, he was almost gasping for air.

No refusal and two open doors.

Furo stood up and went through, shutting both doors behind him.

'How is your neck?' They were lying on their sides under the bedcover, Furo with his back to Syreeta. Her breath warmed his shoulders. The hairs on his neck prickled from her stare.

'There's still some stiffness,' Furo said, and turned around to face her. His arm brushed her breast as he settled. He added quickly, 'The massage helped a lot though.'

Her eyes were half-closed, her face slack with drowsiness, but she reached out her hand and tapped his nose with a fingertip. 'Your nose is peeling, it's sunburn. I'll give you some lotion later.' She curled her tongue in a yawn before saying, 'How long has it been paining you? Your neck,' and as Furo replied, 'About five years,' her drooping eyelids flew open in surprise. 'Five years! That's a long time. What happened?'

Furo found her stare distracting, so he moved his gaze to the heave and fall of the bedcover over her chest. 'I strained it in university. Too much study.'

She yawned again, her tongue trembling pinkly against the roof of her mouth, and then rubbed her wrist across her eyes. 'Which university did you attend?'

'Ambrose Alli.'

Again surprise lighted her features. With a breathy laugh, she said, 'You? In Ekpoma? How the hell did that happen?'

'It's a long story,' Furo said.

'I'm sure it is,' she said in a lowered tone, as if speaking to herself, and then her voice turned back to Furo. 'And I'm sure it's a strange one too. You're very strange, you know that?'

At this question she pushed her hand along the pillow till her fingers touched Furo's cheek, and then her hand slid upwards to his scalp and began stroking. 'I've been meaning to ask: why do you cut your hair so short?'

'No reason. I just like it.'

'You're not going bald, are you?' Her fingers tightened on his scalp, her long nails digging in. Forcing his head down, she raised herself on her elbow to stare at his crown. 'You're not,' she confirmed, and released her hold before sinking back on to the bed. 'Your hair looks red and gold, sort of orange. Let it grow. I want to see it full.'

Confusion flooded Furo. 'I don't want to grow my hair,' he said at last.

'But why not? Or you want me to say please? OK, *please*, do it for me.'

At the seductive lilt in her voice, a notion entered Furo's head, and in a split second it metastasized into a tumescent stirring in his groin. He pursed his lips, creased his brow, held his pensive look for several moments before saying, 'OK, I'll grow it,' a pause, 'if you kiss me.'

Syreeta coughed with laughter, her legs kicking under the bedcover. 'Only because of hair?' she finally said. 'Keep gorimakpa if you like, see who cares!' Her giggles seemed to hold an invitation, and surrendering to the propulsive bubbling of his instincts, Furo pushed his head forwards and pressed his lips to hers. He felt her laughter splutter against his teeth, but when he drew back his head, he was reassured by the look on her face. 'You're in trouble now,' she said in a mock-serious voice. 'You can't cut your hair unless I give you permission.' Then she raised her arms, hooked them around his neck, and pulled his face into hers.

Time slowed to the splash of raindrops, breaths quickened,

the air warmed, and someone kicked away the bedcover. When Syreeta pulled back to catch her breath, her crinkled nipples caught Furo's eyes. He felt cramped by his boxer shorts, and, rocking forwards on his knees, he tugged them off, all the while pinning Syreeta with his eyes until his mouth closed on her breast, the left one, then the right, her hand guiding his head. The bed dipped under the shifting of hips, the push of a knee, the spreading of thighs. Raising his head from her chest, Furo asked, 'Can I kiss you there?' and she widened her eyes at him before nodding once. He slid downwards and stuck his head between her thighs, and as his tongue flicked and tasted, his mind noted facts: too sensitive, more tongue less teeth. Her whimpers washed over him. And then: 'I'm ready,' she said. He, too, was ready, but she stopped him with her thighs. 'No. Condom.'

Furo stared at her as if from a long distance. 'I don't have any.'

'On my dressing table,' she said and unlocked her legs.

Furo felt trapped. Despite his dislike for the rub of rubber, he would wear two if Syreeta wanted. He would stand on his head if she told him to. But nothing would convince him to turn his back to her, not after what happened the last time she saw his buttocks.

Syreeta raised her hands to cup her breasts. 'What is it?' she asked. Drawing hope from the quaver in her voice, he placed his hand on her belly and trailed a finger along the hairline leading down. 'Can I?' he said softly. 'I want to feel you.'

She searched his face. 'You want to fuck me without a condom?' Then she sighed, shook her head. 'Ah Furo, I'm not sure.'

'Please,' Furo said, and touched her where she was softest.

She stiffened and sucked in air. 'Please,' he repeated and rubbed her again. Her knees slowly parted. Her hands fell away from her breasts. And moans later, she agreed.

Furo awoke to what felt like an old day in a new century. Sunlight bounced off the zinc roof of the house opposite, voices trilled in the street outside the window, and a car with a tired engine rumbled past, its tyres splashing through puddles. A footstep sounded in the doorway, and then Syreeta entered the bedroom with a swing in her hips. She held a juice carton in one hand, her toothbrush in the other. She wore a G-string, flesh-coloured. Her left breast shone wet.

'You're awake,' she said brightly as she padded up to the bed. Climbing on and straddling Furo's belly, she tipped the juice carton to his mouth. 'Drink, sleepyhead. Get your energy back.' Her braids tumbled over his face as chilled apple juice poured down his throat. After he'd drunk enough, he nudged aside the carton, then reached up and tweaked her nipple. For soundless seconds she glowered into his face with longing eyes; then she slapped away his hand. 'Not now, when we come back.' She jumped off the bed. 'I'm taking you out. We're going to visit my BFF.' Halting in the doorway, she cast a mischievous look back at him. 'Oya, come,' she said and waved her toothbrush in his direction. 'Let's bathe together.'

He had swung his legs off the bed before he remembered. He remained seated at the bed's edge, and said to Syreeta, 'I just remembered I have to pick up my passport today. Let me get my clothes ready. You go ahead and bathe first.'

'If that's what you want,' Syreeta said and blew him a kiss. He faked a dive to catch it, groaned under its weight, and flopped back on the bed. She strode off laughing.

His buttocks felt like a weight dragging him back to a

place he wanted badly to forget. Syreeta had avoided the topic ever since she apologised for laughing at him, but he knew it had left an impression, he suspected she would bring it up in coming days, and he hoped to impede that conversation for as long as he could. He had answered her questions that day by telling her that he was born with it, the blackness an outsized birthmark, and yet what he told her was one thing and what he knew was another. He knew he had to efface the blackness from his buttocks, from all memory. Feeling dejected by the enormity of this conundrum, he stared across at Syreeta's vanity table with its science lab-like collection of cosmetic bottles. In that moment, the sound of running water from the bathroom splashed into his mind and washed up the hull of an idea.

As Furo saw it, his black behind was a problem to be solved. The step he was about to take was better than doing nothing. Better than sitting around hoping. His failure or success would come through his own hands, and if he failed, at least he would know he tried. He had no choice in the decision that had got him where he was, but now that he was here, he would steer his own course. On this thought, he stood up from the bed, strode to the vanity table, sat on the stool before it, and picking up cosmetic bottles one at a time, he read their labels. He wasn't sure what he was searching for, but he knew when he found it.

The cheapest-looking of the skin-whitening creams was a pink-and-green tube called Lovate Cream. Hydroquinone and octyl methoxycinnamate, and other exotic chemicals only meant that it burned when Furo squeezed out a smidgen and rubbed it on to his wrist. The other whitening creams he found, which were branded more overtly (in one plastic tube, Pale & Lovely Winter Fairness, and in the other ampoule-type bottle, Daudalie Radiance Serum Skin Correction), both left his skin with no sensation more unpleasant than a cool slickness. The descriptions on all three labels promised what he wanted, and he decided against using the facial scrubs and alcohol cleansers he had piled to one side during his search. These strong-smelling potions made no claims to bleaching skin, and the risk of discovery he ran using them seemed much greater than any rewards. He couldn't imagine what explanation he would give Syreeta as to why his buttocks smelled like her face.

Pale & Lovely was the largest of the creams, the one that Syreeta was least likely to notice being depleted, and Furo decided he would apply that every morning after his bath, followed by Lovate in the afternoons, and then the smallest bottle, Daudalie, at night. He would be careful with everything, from the amounts of cream he applied to the replacement of the bottles on the vanity table, because he couldn't let Syreeta find out he was using her whitening creams, as that would only end in the conversation he was avoiding. At the thought of her catching him with his finger in her jars, Furo quickly arranged the table as he had found it, then he took up the Pale & Lovely and squeezed the pinkish cream on to his palm. After he returned the tube, he stood up from the stool and hurried out of the bedroom. In the bathroom he could hear Syreeta singing.

At Ikoyi passport office, Syreeta waited in the Honda as Furo went in. When he returned with his new passport grasped in his hand, she reached out for it, and after reading the identification page, she handed it back and asked how come his surname was Nigerian. Furo's answer:

'I've already told you I'm Nigerian.'

'But you're white!' exclaimed Syreeta.

'So you mean I can't be white *and* Nigerian?'

'That's not what I'm saying. I'm asking how it happened.'

This question had been expected by Furo for some time, and over the long weekend he had thought through his answer. He'd considered saying he was mixed race with a Nigerian father and a white American mother, but while that explained his name and his black buttocks, it raised other questions, the most irksome being a white extended family and his lack of ties to the US embassy in Nigeria. The second story he'd considered was that his white family had settled a long time ago in Nigeria and along the line had changed their name, but on further thought that idea seemed absurd and so he discarded it. Nigerians readily adopted European and Arab and Hebrew names. It never happened the other way around.

The story he settled on appeared to him the most plausible, the least open to rebuttal – it answered every question except that of his buttocks. But then, he told himself, nothing in life is perfect. To Syreeta he said:

'I don't like talking about it so I'll just say this quickly. My parents are Nigerians. They lived in America for many years, my father was born there, and while they were over there they adopted me. My mother couldn't have children. They returned to Lagos while I was still a baby, and they quarrelled when my father married a second wife. My mother took me away, we moved to Port Harcourt, and I haven't heard from my father in nearly twenty years. My mother passed away last year. I came to Lagos and got stranded. Then I met you. That's why I have this name. That's why I have nobody. Now I'm hungry. Can we stop somewhere to eat?'

'Of course,' Syreeta said, and after she faced forwards

and guided the Honda on to the road, she added in a voice hoarsened with awe:

'I didn't know it was possible for black people to adopt white people.'

And so it happened that Syreeta stopped over at The Palms to buy lunch at the cafe where she and Furo had met six days ago, and by three o'clock they were back on the Lekki–Ajah highway, in after-work traffic, headed towards her friend's house in Victoria Garden City.

Seated beside Syreeta as she steered the Honda through traffic, Furo realised why radio DJs were superstars in Lagos. The car radio was tuned to Cool FM, and many times on the drive from Lekki to Ikoyi to pick up Furo's passport and back to Lekki for lunch and on to Ajah to visit her friend, Syreeta had danced in her seat and squealed with laughter at the music selections and the banter of a host of DJs who seemed never to run out of something to say. With the Honda now stuck in a monster traffic jam on the outskirts of Ajah, Furo began to think that for the millions of commuters who spent hour after hour and day after day in Lagos traffic with only their car radios for company, these feigned accents and invented personalities became as dear as confidantes. The more he thought about it, the more he was struck by blinding flashes of the obvious, a whole rash of ideas marching into his head to the beats from the car radio. Persistent power cuts in Lagos, in the whole of Nigeria, meant that battery-operated radios were the entertainment appliance of necessity for both rich and poor, young and old, the city-based and the village-trapped, everyone. Radios were cheap to buy and free to use, no data bundles or subscription packages or credit plans, and they were also long-lasting, easy to carry around, available in private cars and commercial buses, and most important, they were independent of the undependable power grid. Mobile phones even came with radios, as did MP3 players; and computers had applications that live-streamed radio; and thinking of it, the rechargeable lamps that everyone owned also had radios built into them. Then again there were those new Chinese toys for the tech-starved: radio headphones, radio sunglasses, radio caps, radio wristwatches. It was endless. Radio was deathless. Radio DJs were superstars.

Furo lost interest in this line of thinking when the DJ cut the music to announce that it was time to pay the bills so don't touch that dial. After several minutes of jolly-sounding jingles, most of which seemed aimed at schoolchildren and petty traders, a spanking-new Tuface single was introduced by the DJ, and as the song sprang from the speakers Syreeta threw up her arms and hooted with joy, and then glanced over at Furo with a lopsided grin.

Syreeta showed a clear fondness for local music. Pidgin hip-hop, Afrobeat electronica, Ajegunle reggae, highlife-flavoured R & B, even oldies disco crooned to a lover named Ifeoma. Nigerian music dominated the Lagos airwaves, and Syreeta seemed to know the lyrics to every song. Rihanna's anthems might be enjoyed, and Drake's rap acknowledged with sporadic nods of approval, but when P-Square warbled, Syreeta hollered back. Furo also listened to Nigerian pop – he had two P-Square albums on his old phone – though he couldn't say he had a particular taste for it. But now, hearing Syreeta sing along to lyrics that preached money and marriage and little else, he found himself hating P-Square a little.

The song ended, the DJ resumed his adenoidal chatter, and Syreeta said, pointing with a finger straight ahead, 'See where those buses are turning – and that LASTMA man is just sitting there looking! OK now, I'm going to follow them.'

Furo stared through the windscreen at the congested road: in the confusion that met his eyes he couldn't find what Syreeta was pointing at. The road should have resembled a Mumbai train station at rush hour – lines and lines of stilled cars stretching into the distance, armies of hawkers darting about in rag uniforms, the air sluggish with exhaust fumes and exhausted breaths – but it didn't, it had a chaos all of its own. It looked exactly like after-work traffic in Lagos was supposed to look. A sprawling coastal city that had no ferry system, no commuter trains, no underground tunnels or over-head tramlines, where hordes of people leaving work poured on to the roads at the same time as the freight trucks carting petroleum products and food produce and all manner of manufacture from all corners of Nigeria. The roads were overburdened and under-policed, and even in select areas where road-expansion projects were under way, the contracted engineers worked at a pace that betrayed their lack of confidence in the usefulness of their labour. They knew as well as the politicians that Lagos was exploding at a rate its road network could never keep up with.

The cars ahead revved and spat out smoke, the Honda rolled forwards a few inches, and finally Furo saw the reason this section of the road was gridlocked. Metres ahead, in the middle of the highway, an excavator was breaking blacktop and scooping earth, and at the spot where it heaved and clanged, a new roundabout had been partitioned out with concrete barriers that narrowed the road into a bottleneck. A small band of touts, led by a cap-wearing man, whose white goatee caught the sunlight, had pushed aside one of the barriers, opened a path to the other side of the road – which was free of traffic – and they collected money from any car that squeezed through the breach. It was mostly minibuses that turned off to disgorge passengers and rush back into town, but a few private cars also took the opening. A state traffic warden sat on the tailgate of a patrol wagon adjacent to the breach and calmly watched proceedings. His crisp uniform shirt, the yellow of spoiled milk, was tucked into his beef-red trousers, and his black boots gleamed as he swung his feet back and forth. Heavy-shouldered and round-bellied, he appeared too comfortable in his position, too dapper for roadside work.

Furo turned to Syreeta. 'I've seen the opening. Do you want to turn around? Aren't we going to see your friend any more?'

'We are,' Syreeta replied. 'See where the petrol station is? VGC gate is right beside it. I'll cross over and drive by the side of the road till we reach the gate. If I stay here I'll have to go too far ahead, I'll have to follow this traffic till after Ajah Junction, then turn around and start coming back. With this go-slow, that will take us at least another thirty minutes.'

Furo was tired of sitting, his buttocks ached, and yet he wasn't eager for Syreeta to take the shortcut. He felt too conspicuous to break laws openly.

He spoke. 'I don't trust that LASTMA guy.'

'He won't try anything,' Syreeta responded, and turning to smile at Furo, she added in a teasing tone: 'You white people fear too much.'

Furo didn't return her smile. 'I think it's safer to stay on the road.'

Of course Syreeta ignored his warning, and after she forked out two hundred naira for the illegal toll – special fee for special people, white goatee said with a brooding glance at Furo – and drove through the breach, of course the traffic warden jumped down from his perch and bolted

125

forwards to accost the car. Syreeta tried to drive around him, but the man was nimble despite his paunch and he also seemed to have no regard for his life. When he leapt on to the bonnet and bumped his forehead against the windscreen, smearing the glass with sweat, Syreeta braked the car to a stop, pressed the control button for her side window, and yelled out through the opening, 'Are you crazy? Do you want to break my windshield?'

The traffic warden made no response as he slid off the bonnet on his belly, this action soiling his shirtfront and dishevelling his tucked-in hemline. Then he dashed to Syreeta's side and tugged at the door handle, but finding it locked, he squeezed his arm through the window crack and grasped the top rim of the steering wheel with some difficulty. 'Your key,' he puffed, and his eyes darted towards the ignition. He blinked as he realised it was out of his reach. Unless Syreeta lowered the glass for him to lean in and grab the key, she was out of his power. The only option open to him was to coerce her into ceding control. These machinations were exposed by the whole range of expressions that played across the man's features in the instant before he raised his gaze, and as he glowered at Syreeta with his sun-darkened face only inches from hers, his chest rose and sank with each baleful breath that clouded the glass barrier between them. His knuckles bunched on the steering wheel; the edge of the glass dug into the flesh of his upper arm. In a voice whose threatening tone had jumped several notches, he repeated his demand:

'Give me your key, madam.'

Syreeta gave a mirthless laugh. 'Are you joking? I'm not giving you anything,' she said and shook her head in emphasis, then leaned back in her seat, calmly returning his stare.

'You this woman, I'm warning you o, give me the key!'

'Why?' Syreeta shouted back. 'Oya, tell me first, what did I do?'

'You don't know what you did, ehn? OK, I will tell you after you give me the key. Just do as I order. Obey before complaint.'

'No fucking way,' Syreeta said.

'You're looking for trouble.' This said quietly, his tensed forearm trembling through the window. Vapours of cold air wafted out of the car into his shiny face.

'You're the one looking for trouble,' Syreeta said. 'Didn't you see other cars passing? How come it's me you want to stop? You think you've seen awoof? You better get out of my way if you know what's good for you!'

'If you move I will show you!' the traffic warden growled in warning, at the same time shoving his second hand through the window to grasp the steering wheel. His flexing muscles seemed prepared to wrest out the steering wheel, and his expression showed he would try, but Syreeta, to Furo's growing wonder, didn't appear in the slightest bothered by the suppressed violence of those arms in front of her breasts. With a mocking laugh she averted her face from the traffic warden and stared straight through the windscreen. It was a deadlock.

Furo knew there was nothing he could say to defuse the situation, and nothing he could do in his broke state, but still he felt compelled to act. He leaned across Syreeta, met the traffic warden's hostile eyes, and said in a beseeching tone, 'Excuse me, oga,' but Syreeta whirled around and shushed him with a curt 'No.' He settled back in his seat. Syreeta was handling this all wrong. She should be ingratiating herself to the traffic warden, not provoking the man to arrest her. With her car impounded she would pay a fine many times larger than the bribe that had prompted the traffic warden to pick on her, while he, for all his scheming and exertions, would get nothing except paperwork to fill.

The traffic warden broke the silence. 'Abeg answer me, madam,' he said in a voice so rude it could pass for a vulgarity, and Syreeta did, she veered her face around and told the man in haughty tones that she would have his job for the embarrassment he was causing her. Furo rolled his eyes in exasperation at her words. *But surely she must know what to do*, he thought. Nobody who had been in Lagos more than a few hours could remain ignorant of the survival codes, and yet Syreeta flouted rule after rule. The traffic warden had begun shouting the familiar threat that showed he had reached the end of his routine: he demanded to board the car and lead Syreeta to the nearest LASTMA office. Bureaucratic hellholes, LASTMA offices, and if the traffic warden made good his threat then Syreeta would be lucky to retrieve her car before the month's end. And only after paying a heavy fine as well as settling the bill for mandatory driving lessons and a psychiatric evaluation, this last a precondition for allowing her back into the madness of Lagos roads. Furo felt he had to warn her, and he opened his mouth to do so, but Syreeta spoke first.

'Furo, I'm sorry, please get down from the car.'

He tried to catch her eyes. 'This is not the best way—'

'I know what I'm doing,' she cut him off, her right hand cleaving the air in time to her words. 'I'll deal with this idiot my own way. Just get down.'

Sighing in resignation, Furo reached for the door handle, and as he flicked it unlocked, the traffic warden released his grip on the steering wheel and sprinted around the car's front.

When the man grabbed the open door and yanked it wider, Furo looked at Syreeta. 'Should I sit in the back?' he asked. 'I don't mind following you to the LASTMA office.'

'No need,' Syreeta said. Then she noticed the anxiety on Furo's face, and her expression softened, she curved her lips in a smile intended to reassure. 'Don't worry, I have this under control.' She cast a look at the surrounding area, which was crowded with roadside stalls and noisy from all the people milling about, spilling their feelings into the air. 'But there's no place for you to wait around here,' she muttered, as if chiding herself. 'Oh, I know. Why don't you walk to VGC? Go inside and wait for me near the gate. I won't be long.'

Behind Furo the traffic warden snorted with derision, and Syreeta threw him a vicious look. Furo spoke quickly to forestall the attack gathering in her face. 'If that's what you want,' he said, and climbed down from the car, then stood watching as the traffic warden jumped in and slammed the door. He heard the harmonised clicks of the car's central lock, followed by the whirr of Syreeta's side window closing. When Syreeta and the traffic warden turned on each other with furious faces, Furo spun around and strode away from their muffled yapping.

Avoiding the curious stares of the pedestrians he passed, Furo walked quickly to the filling station, then cut across its concrete expanse and approached the double gates of Victoria Garden City. Two lines of cars flowed through the estate gates, entering and leaving. In front of the entry gate, right beside the sleeping policeman, stood a private guard. Hands clasped behind his back and feet spread apart, he eyeballed each car that clambered over the bump. He raised his head as Furo approached, and his shoulders stiffened, his features hardened into a scowl. Furo realised there was someone walking behind him. A man wearing black jeans and a white T-shirt, his hair cornrowed, a rhinestone stud glinting in one ear. Furo turned back around, and slowed his steps to a shuffle, unsure if he should walk past the guard or state his business. Deciding on the action least likely to cause offence, he halted by the guard and said, 'Hello.'

'Good afternoon, sir,' the guard replied, smiling in welcome. 'Are you here to visit?'

'Yes,' Furo said.

'I see, I see,' said the guard, and ran his hands down the front of his epauletted shirt, smoothing it out. He ignored the cars entering the estate; he stared hard at Furo's nose. 'Who is the person you want to see?'

'I don't know her name . . . she's the friend of my friend,' Furo said. 'Well, actually—'

'I see, not a problem,' the guard interrupted. He threw a suspicious look at the cornrowed man waiting behind Furo. 'What is her house number?'

'I don't know,' Furo said. 'The thing is, I'm supposed to—'

'Not a problem,' the guard said and wrinkled his brow in contemplation. At that moment the cornrowed man made an impatient noise in his throat, and then he moved forwards, muttered 'Sorry' to Furo, and said to the guard, 'I'm going to Mr Oyegun's house.'

The guard aimed a furious stare at him. 'Can't you see I'm attending to somebody?'

'I'm in a hurry,' the cornrowed man said, his voice urgent. 'Mr Oyegun is expecting me. I know his house, I've come here before.'

'Respect yourself, mister man!' the guard barked at him. 'Or you think anyone can just walk in here anyhow? Who are you anyway? Move back, move back – can't you hear me,

I said move back!' He flapped his hands in the chest of the cornrowed man, drove him back behind Furo. 'That's how we Nigerians behave, no respect at all,' the guard said to Furo with a grimace of apology. Lowering his voice, he asked: 'Do you have your, erm, friend's phone number?'

'I was trying to explain,' Furo said. 'I'm supposed to wait for someone to pick me up here. If you don't mind I'll just stand in that corner.' He pointed to a spot inside the gate.

'I see, I see,' the guard said, nodding his head as he waved Furo in. 'Not a problem at all, you can go inside. Should I bring a chair for you?'

'I'm OK,' Furo said. He passed through the gate, strode a few paces to the grass shoulder, and turned around to face the gate. The cornrowed man had moved forwards, he was speaking with the guard, who shook his head with vehemence and remained standing in the way. The cornrowed man flung up his hands and uttered a complaint, then reached into his pocket, pulled out his mobile phone, dialled a number. After repeated attempts at reaching someone on the phone, all seemingly unsuccessful, the cornrowed man again spoke to the guard. The guard ignored him, he stood with his chest puffed out and his fists clenched and his boots planted apart, glaring at passing cars. The cornrowed man gave up with a gesture of dismissal. Pocketing his phone, he whirled around and stalked off, and the guard glanced over at Furo. 'Are you sure you're OK, sir?' he shouted across. 'You're sure you don't want a chair?'

Syreeta drove through the gate barely five minutes later. Furo started to raise his hand, but let it fall when he realised she'd already seen him. She pulled up alongside, and he climbed into the Honda's chill, which was spiced with a whiff of the traffic warden's sweat. The skin over Syreeta's cheekbones was stretched tight, a vein beat in her temple, and the car radio was off. Furo knew better than to ask about the traffic warden, how she had got rid of him so quickly. He held his gaze away from her face and stared through the windscreen. Road signs whizzed past. *No honking. No hawkers. No litter. No parking. No okadas and danfos.* The quiet through which the car sailed was deeper-rooted than the fact of the silent radio. No crowds, no roadside garbage, no traffic jam, no noise. The Lagos he knew was far from this place.

The Honda cruised down avenues bordered by mansion after mansion. Furo looked out the window till his eyesight blurred from the monotony of affluence, and then he craned his neck around to stare back at a black stallion (wild-eyed, it reared its head and chomped at the bit, yet trotted smoothly on) ridden by a man wearing jodhpurs, a jockey hat, and a sleeveless dashiki. He faced forwards as the car swept past a chain-fenced tree park with children's swings, slides, and sand-pits; and turning into a side street, it slowed to a stop in front of a townhouse with an immaculate white fence and Doric gateposts. Through the grilled gate Furo spied a fleet of sleek vehicles, their bodywork glinting and windows sparkling. He finished counting the high-priced playthings – seven in all, the least exotic a Jaguar coupé – before blurting out in astonishment: 'Is this where your friend lives?' Syreeta nodded yes while tapping her horn, and after the gate slid open of its own accord, she drove in and parked to the side of the broad driveway, which bordered a lawned garden flashing with wild colours in a backdrop of tamed greenery. From the tree boughs dangled wind chimes and birdhouses. Furo swung the car door open to the smell of wetted earth, which mingled in the breeze with the frail scents of flowers. The monastic quiet was deepened by the gurgle of water from a stone cupid endlessly pissing into a fishpond. He climbed down the car and gazed around him, up at the security cameras hanging in the eaves and down at the clam shells covering the driveway. At the crunch of feet, he spun away from this vision of fortified Eden and followed Syreeta towards the front door.

The housemaid who answered the door was dressed in a starched white gown. Her smile of welcome announced she knew Syreeta and was pleased to see her, but in greeting Furo the smile faltered and she dropped her eyes, then dipped her head and pressed her hands against her belly in a mannered gesture of respect, after which she said in response to Syreeta's enquiry about her madam, 'She dey for visitor's parlour.' Following a trail of children's laughter, Syreeta and Furo passed through two doorways and a museum-piece hallway before reaching an air-conditioned, brightly lit lounge that whiffed of cedar polish. The window curtains were drawn, the outsized TV was on – it showed Johnny Bravo in swimming trunks on a HD-coloured beach – and from the high ceiling a silver chandelier shone golden light. The sitting area was a dais with three steps leading up. Two sides of it were closed off by an L-shaped couch, burgundy red like the curtains, and under the chandelier stood a malachite table with nude cherubs for legs. A bottle of Remy Martin VSOP was on the table, and on the couch five ladies lolled, all clutching cut-glass goblets in which cognac swirled. Near the TV several beanbags were scattered on the parquet floor. On these were sprawled six children – all of them woolly-headed, fair-skinned, half-white.

'*Syreeta darling!*' a lady sang as she bounced to her feet and skipped round the couch. She was younger than Syreeta; she seemed barely out of adolescence. Her hair was cut low and sprayed silver, her fingernails curved blackly around the bowl of her glass, and the thin fabric of her white miniskirt was stretched so tight that Furo saw the flower patterns on her underwear. Tearing away his eyes, he glanced at the other ladies staring at him over the low backrest, and then he looked back at the one who breezed past him in a cloud of perfume and woody liquor. She hooked her free arm round Syreeta's neck, and they pressed cheeks, exchanged babbles of affection, then the lady whirled around to face Furo. Her smile looked dazed. 'So this is you!' she said huskily, and after handing her drink to Syreeta to hold, she spread her arms wide and leaned into Furo so abruptly he had to hug her to keep his balance. She snuggled into his arms, rested her head on his chest, and brushed her hips against him. 'Yum-yum,' she said in a whisper meant to be heard by all, and then, with a ribald laugh, she disentangled from him. 'I'm Baby,' she said. 'Syreeta has told me every-thing about you.' Her appraising gaze swept down his body and rose again to his face. 'Almost everything,' she added with a chuckle.

Furo and Syreeta took their seats with the rest of the company, all of whom knew Syreeta, Furo realised from their greetings. As Baby bent over the table to pour drinks for the newcomers, one of the ladies, Syreeta had called her Ivy, asked Syreeta, 'Where is he from?'

'He's American,' Syreeta said in a tone whose casualness did not hide her satisfaction. 'But he's lived in Nigeria for so long that he's now one of us.' Like a presiding queen, she raised her hand in the direction of Baby, who arrived at that moment and handed one drink to her and the other to Furo before flopping on to the couch.

'I just got back from Atlanta,' said a lady whose large feet were emphasised by her zebra-striped tights. She uncrossed one leg and immediately crossed the other. Balancing her glass on her knee, she shot a questioning look at Furo. 'Lovely city. I attended a business conference with Gianni, my husband. He's Italian.'

Furo raised his glass and drank. The alcohol landed a sucker punch to his throat, and struggling to keep his discomfort from showing, he raised his swimming eyes to find the ladies' faces waiting. 'Ever been?' the Italian's wife asked with a hint of impatience, and into the silence Furo gasped, 'No,' and then began to cough from the burn of the cognac. Syreeta placed a hand on his back and patted gently. 'Breathe slowly,' she whispered to him. In a tone of wry amusement she said to the ladies, 'He likes milkshakes,' and the wave of coos that rose at her words lightened the grip on Furo's chest.

The ladies reminded Furo of his university days. They were a type he recognised but hadn't gotten a chance to mingle with at close quarters, to sit beside and be addressed by. They were the very ones who had partied at the trendy nightclubs that ordinary students could only dream about, who had travelled three hundred miles every Friday from Ekpoma to Benin City in the chauffeured rides of their aristos and returned in flocks on Sunday with excess cash and branded clothes and stories of their carouses that were the grist of campus gossip and front-page news of local celebrity rags. In a school system where money, sexual favours, and sugar daddy's influence had black-market value in the acquiring of grades, these campus queens were only a few points down from straight-A students. They graduated from university with little trouble, with few carried-over courses, and without any employable skills, and after serving their country during youth service by playing truant at those high-paying jobs they always landed in either Lagos or Abuja or Port Harcourt, they set aside their degrees and put their talent to work in turning the same tricks that had served them thus far. Within toddler years after graduation the most successful of them ended up as Baby and her friends: sipping cognac in the mansions of their moneyed husbands. These women were hustlers, plain and simple, and Furo, back in those days of neck-cramping study and eating beans five times a week because his allowance had to be managed, had despised them almost as much as he wanted to befriend them. But now, with Syreeta in his life, he admitted to himself that his view of them had softened.

In the time that followed his arrival in their midst, Furo learned that Baby was married to a Dutchman, Ivy to a Canadian, Chika to an Englishman, Ego to a German, and Joy to the Italian. Chika was a buxom lady with heavily ringed hands, which she waved around for emphasis while she spoke, and her accent was the least Nigerian in the room, the most accomplished in its transatlantic melding of Peckham twang and Harlem slang. Between Chika and Baby sat Ivy, and when she rose to pour herself a refill from the cognac bottle, Furo saw how much taller than him she was. She wore pink high heels, black pencil jeans and a white tube top. On her lower back the lanky, long-tailed figure of the Pink Panther was tattooed in black ink. Ego sat furthest from Furo, and yet his eyes kept returning to her bleached blonde hairpiece, which cascaded down her right shoulder and curled around in her lap. Her eyelashes were so long they threw shadows on her rouged cheeks.

From the topic of their husbands the ladies moved on to their children. They all had one each, except for Ego, whose boy and girl were three and five years old. The youngest child, a plump two-year-old named Romeo, was Joy's. His attachment to mamma was almost umbilical, as he toddled up to her again and again to blub at a slight by the other tots or to point squealing at the cartoon antics showing on screen. Joy spoiled him with attention, the other mothers warned, she fed him too much pasta and not enough of the yams needed to build his muscles, and they spent laughing minutes offering her advice on how to man him up in time for kindergarten. 'In Naija a man must be strong o, even if he's oyibo,' Baby declared, and turning to face Furo, she asked with an elfin smile if he didn't agree.

Baby's girl Saskia was nearly four. When her mother called to her to come and greet uncle, the child pranced over and climbed into Furo's lap without a word. 'What a cute girl,' Furo said to the preening mother, though to call her cute was an injustice to her prettiness. Her soft curls smelled of baby shampoo, her ripe banana complexion glowed from rich feeding, and her full lips trembled with pinkness. Her large grey eyes shone with boredom at adult worship. Furo found her insufferable. Syreeta, however, couldn't hide her fascination. 'Oh yes she is!' she exclaimed in response to Furo's words, and leaning across him, she kissed the girl's cheeks and dimpled chin, then set down her drink and lifted Saskia from Furo's lap into hers. In a Teletubby tone of voice she asked the child simpering questions about school, her bedroom, her toys, about how she got that naughty-naughty scratch on her knee, all the while nodding encouragement as Saskia lisped her replies. Questions exhausted, with a magic flourish Syreeta pulled a shiny box of milk chocolates out of her handbag and pressed it into Saskia's hands. The child's delighted yelp drew smiles from all the mothers, and it was with reluctance that Syreeta released her to return with her prize to her waiting playmates.

The conversation among the ladies turned to past boyfriends. In the zeal to one-up each other, their affected accents skidded and crashed, and from this wreck of grammar the mangled sense was rescued by a reversion to pidgin – the shortest distance between two thoughts. The straight-talking bluntness of the vernacular caused their mingled voices to beat the air like wings of released doves. Higher the voices rose and quicker the glasses tipped liquor down throats. The nature of the conversation also influenced the language, as the ladies' speech slipped further and further into the maze of slang, seeking those shaded places where meaning hid in plain sight.

'That my agaba Nikos nah proper olingo man sha.'

'Nothing do you kpakam!'

'Yemi still dey chop adro for inside Dublin?'

'Your oko jus' dey love up like person wey chop kognomi!'

'Make una hear original gist o! This one fresh pass fresh fish—'

Their chatter was wide-ranging: from an ex-head of state who fixated on the feet of soldiers' widows to overheard gossip of Abuja politicians who had a thing for orgies with boys. Then it was on to exotic cars and swanky restaurants and the latest kerfuffle in *Keeping Up with the Kardashians*. The lifestyles of the Lagos glitterati: who was cheating with whose daughter in Victoria Garden City, whose husband had just acquired a beach house in Tarkwa Bay, and which police commissioner's son was spotted in a sex tape on xHamster. Now and again one of them would glance at Furo and, stopping herself on the cusp of a revelation, she would rise from the couch to pour a refill of cognac, only to resume from the juncture her empty glass interrupted.

The conversation petered out when the housemaid arrived pushing a serving trolley. Plates of coconut rice and boneless barbecue chicken were placed before the children and Furo, while the mothers and Syreeta were served steaming bowls of either catfish or cow-tail or goat-head pepper soup. After the housemaid withdrew, Ivy said a quick prayer to bless the food, and then everyone settled down to the business of eating. The sound of chewing was a poor substitute for table-talk, and so Baby, crunching on the biscuit bone of a goat's ear, turned to Syreeta and asked about the drive down. Syreeta described the heavy traffic she'd gone through, to which the ladies responded with sympathetic noises. Except for Joy and Syreeta, they all resided in VGC, and their poor husbands had to endure the Ajah traffic on those days they couldn't evade it by flying home in a chartered helicopter. The horror stories of Lagos traffic that the women shared soon led to Syreeta telling of her fresh experience with the LASTMA traffic warden, and after the oohs and ahhs that egged her on, after the multi-lingual curses directed at the traffic warden and his generations yet unborn, it was Ego who finally asked the question that was irking Furo.

'How did you get rid of the pest?'

Baby laughed. 'Ah-ah Ego, don't you know who Syreeta's man is? He's a big oga—'

A sharp movement from Syreeta made Baby choke on her soup. Recovering from her coughing fit, she shot a guilty look at Furo, and then changed the topic to the havoc wreaked in Lagos by the rainstorm of the previous day. Her friends all piled in with tales of flooding.

Baby's blunder had cast a pall over the party, and as Furo finished his meal, Syreeta stood up and announced their departure. 'Aw!' Baby exclaimed, staring up at Syreeta. 'I was hoping you could wait until Erik returns. It would have been so nice for Furo to meet him.' Then she rose with Furo, and after he and Syreeta said their goodbyes to the ladies, she walked them to the front door. Night had fallen; the house front was lit by halogen searchlights, under which Baby's silver hair glowed. Baby hugged Furo by the door of the Honda, then held him at arm's length with her fingers hooked in his trouser pockets and thanked him for visiting, asked him to come again. He guessed from her distracted air that she wanted a moment alone with Syreeta, so he said goodnight, climbed into the car, and shut the door. But before Baby arrived at Syreeta's side, the house door flew open, Joy rushed out with her sleeping child in her arms, and halting in front of Syreeta, she said, 'Can I ask a favour please? You're going to Oniru, abi? Can you drop me at Chevron? By the junction, you don't have to drive in.' She adjusted her son's head on her shoulder and turned to Baby. 'Sorry to rush off like this, I have to take Romeo home to sleep, and to be honest I feel too tipsy to drive. I'll send the driver to pick up my car in the morning. By the way, that catfish was delish! Ring you later to get your caterer's details. Ciao-ciao.'

On Tuesday morning, while Syreeta was in the bathroom washing away the slick of lovemaking, Furo rolled off the bed, crossed to the vanity table, and applied his morning dose of whitening cream. Syreeta returned and, snuggling up to him under the bedcover, she said, 'I'm going out later.' Too drowsy to speak, Furo nodded acknowledgement. Moments later he was sunk in a post-coital slumber.

He awoke to the sound of a door opening and the aroma of food entering, followed by that voice that was now as familiar as the scent of her skin: 'Sweetie?' Furo opened his eyes to find Syreeta's face above. She pulled aside the bedcover with one hand; in the other she grasped a plate. Half-moon slices of boiled yam, three sunny-side ups, and a splattering of tomato gravy. Furo's stomach sat up with joy, and after he followed suit, he gave a yawn that became a moan of pleasure. With a trill of laughter, Syreeta placed the food on the bedside table, and then said, 'I'm ready to go.' She was bathed, dressed. Her car keys dangled from a crooked finger.

'Don't go, not yet,' Furo said. He didn't want to be left alone. 'Are you in a hurry?'

'Kind of,' she said. 'But I can wait a few minutes.' She sat at the bed's edge, tossed her keys to the floor, and placed a gentle hand on Furo's chest. 'Eat.'

He ate quickly. The last mouthful gone, he rose from the bed and walked to the fridge, took out a bottle of water, and stared out the window as he drank. He had overslept: his muscles felt waterlogged and the ache in his neck was more insistent than usual. He'd intended on washing his clothes today, but now he felt too lazy. Glancing down at his boxer shorts, he tugged at the waistband and checked it for grime. When Syreeta said, 'You've been wearing those for days,' he released the waistband with a snap, and raising his hand to rub his neck, he said to her: 'It's the only pair I have.' He started towards the bed. 'I need to get some new clothes.' He sat beside her, then lifted her hand from her thigh, turned up her palm and covered it with his. His fingers were longer, blunter, fish-belly pale. A muscle flexed in her wrist.

'Milk and chocolate,' Syreeta said. Her eyes rose to his face. 'Is something wrong?'

Letting go of her hand, Furo bent forwards and clasped his temples in his palms. 'I miss my mother,' he said.

'Oh!' Syreeta exclaimed softly, and reaching out with both

141

arms, she drew his head against her bosom. Her heart raced beneath his cheek. 'How did she die?'

Furo raised his head and stared aghast at her.

'Your mother – what happened?'

He had forgotten. His mother was dead, his father had abandoned him, and his sister was someone he had never met. He lived with a woman who fed and fucked him. He was white.

'Cancer,' he said. He pulled away from Syreeta, flopped back on the bed, and the jolt of the mattress reminded him of his neck. 'Can you give me a massage?'

'I really should get going.'

'Then go.'

He felt the force of her stare before she stood up from the bed. He heard the clink of a bottle on the vanity table, and then her footsteps returning. When she said, 'Turn on your belly,' he opened his eyes to see her unscrewing the bottle cap, the fragrance of eucalyptus oil escaping as she lifted it off. He adjusted himself on the bed and arranged a pillow under his head. As she bent forwards with the bottle poised, he asked, 'Won't you remove your clothes?'

'Fuck it, Furo! I have to go out.' Her voice had lost its patience.

He threw her a wide-eyed look from an awkward angle. 'But that's why you shouldn't get oil on your clothes,' he said with innocence. And then he grinned.

Syreeta gave a grudging laugh and glanced over her shoulder at the wall clock. 'OK,' she said as she unhooked her dress. 'But I'm out of here in ten minutes.'

'If you say so,' Furo said, his voice muffled by the pillow.

Sometime during the night, Furo felt Syreeta stir beside him and then stand up to switch off her singing phone. When she slipped back into bed, he rolled closer and spooned her, nestled his face in her fragrant braids, and then drifted off in the sudden quiet.

Wednesday morning. Furo was curled on the settee watching *Mr Bean* on TV when a loud rapping on the front door killed his chuckles. Syreeta was in the kitchen peeling plantains for breakfast, and as Furo looked in her direction at the second round of knocking, he saw her peering through the window netting. Then she leapt back and whirled around and ran on tiptoe out of the kitchen with the knife grasped in her fist. Furo was on his feet by the time she reached the settee. He started to speak but she raised the knife to her lips and, grabbing his arm, she pulled him into the guest room. 'Please stay here, lock the door,' she begged in a whisper, her fingers digging into his forearm. Furo nodded in assent, after which she loosened her grip and began absent-mindedly stroking his reddened skin with a nervous look on her face. The knocking had grown louder, the in-between pauses shorter. Syreeta's eyes refocused on Furo's face as she said to him, 'Don't come out until I tell you,' and striding out of the guest-room door, she eased it closed behind her. Furo reached the door in a bound. He turned the key and removed it from the lock, but still he felt exposed, so he rushed to the windows and drew the curtains, then returned to the door and dropped to a squat beside it. Still the pounding sounded; the blows were furious. But they stopped when a door slammed in the house, Syreeta's bedroom door, and she called out, 'I'm coming, don't break my door!' The sounds of the front door opening, Syreeta's cry of surprise, and then a deep male voice, which followed Syreeta's into the parlour. The settee huffed as the man, still talking, sank into it. Furo could hear him clearly through the thin wall that concealed

143

their nearness. His voice was a rich baritone, brandy- and tobacco-roughened, and it seemed to emerge from a thick body. His words, as he asked Syreeta if she was punishing him, were accented with the mellifluous timbre of Yoruba.

'I'm telling you, Bola, I'm not angry any more,' Syreeta responded, to which the man fired back in tones of annoyance: 'So why didn't you show up yesterday? And why are you not picking up your phone? I was calling all night!'

'I went to bed early. I wasn't feeling well,' Syreeta said. Furo had never heard her so submissive. From the man's tone when he spoke again, he wasn't surprised by this side of her. 'Riri, Riri, Riri,' he repeated with rising reproach. 'How many times did I call you, you this troublesome pikin? You couldn't even call back? I waited at our place for over an hour!'

'I'm sorry.' After a pause she added: 'But now you know how it feels.'

'Shut up there,' Bola said lightly. 'How is your body?'

'I'm feeling better.'

'That's good. So you're strong enough to give me some sugar? You know I've missed you. I had to cancel an important meeting today. Just so I could see your face.'

Syreeta's voice now came from a different place, somewhere further away, nearer the bathroom. 'Give me a moment to get ready. Are we going to Oriental?'

'I'm here already,' Bola said. She made no reply, and he continued, 'We haven't spent time in this flat since you moved in. I don't even know what your bedroom looks like.' Furo barely had time to interpret the creaking sounds from the settee when, as Syreeta called out with urgency, 'No Bola, that's the guest room!' the door handle turned. Furo stared at the door with evangelical awe, the sweat dripping from his face like the last grains of sand in a fatal hourglass. 'Is it locked?' Bola asked, rattling the handle, each swing tugs the string that was snagged in Furo's guts. And then, 'Why is it locked?' His voice, to Furo's ears, was sibilant with suspicion.

'No reason,' Syreeta said. 'I hardly ever use the guest room and so I locked it. I misplaced the key somewhere. I've been meaning to get a carpenter, but I keep forgetting.'

Again the handle turned under Furo's terrified gaze. 'Do you want me to force it open?'

'Hell no, you'll spoil the door! Leave it alone. I'll take care of it later.' Her words were followed by rapid footfalls, and after her door opened, she said, 'This is my bedroom. Come and sit here and wait for me, I'm going to bathe. I'll finish now-now.'

While he listened to Bola's voice rising and falling in telephone conversation, Furo began to recover from his overdose of adrenaline. His outpaced heartbeats still left him short of breath, and his skin was cold with sweat, the wetness squelching in his armpits and between his thighs, yet he was calm enough to steer his thoughts to the trough of common sense. This much was clear: Bola was Syreeta's sugar daddy, her lover and benefactor, her man. Furo had always suspected how Syreeta afforded her lifestyle, but now he knew it was to Bola as much as her that he owed his gratitude for the comfort he was provided. The roof over his head, the bed he slept in, the twenty thousand for his passport, the food he ate and the fruit juices he drank, he knew from whose pocket everything came. If Syreeta was the breast at which he sucked for favour, then Bola, though unknowing, was the father figure. As this notion flashed through his head – that he was fucking the woman of the man who sheltered him, a man whose voice this moment was bubbling from behind the wall that

– Furo felt a twinge of remorse. He
.vay. Going by what he'd gathered, the man was
.adulterer. Syreeta was free, unmarried, her own
.nd from the sound of things, probably half Bola's
.nyone deserved pity, it wasn't Bola.

The slam of the front door signalled the departure of Syreeta and her man. Through a chink in the curtains Furo tried to catch a look at them, but they had turned in a direction that was beyond the window's angle of sight. He knew they were off to lunch, because after Syreeta emerged from the bathroom, he had overheard her and Bola discussing where to eat, and while she was dressing, they reached a decision to do the English pub on Sinari Daranijo. From Bola's arrival in Furo's life to his exit from the house no more than two hours had elapsed, but that was time enough for him to mark Furo's hideout with his dominant smell. New bank-notes in old leather, laundered fabric sprinkled with eau de cologne, and the pewter whiff of heavy jewellery: the smell of a man used to having his way. Before emerging from Syreeta's bedroom Bola had handed over her pocket money for two weeks, two hundred thousand naira Furo had heard him say. Syreeta's thank you, to Furo's shocked ears, was unimpressed-sounding.

Furo's phone rang. The sound came from Syreeta's bedroom, and so he let it ring on. Seven missed calls later, by which time it was apparent that whoever was calling wasn't giving up, Furo unlocked the guest room door and crept into Syreeta's bedroom to find the phone under the bed. As he'd suspected, his caller was Syreeta, who said when he picked up the call, 'Why didn't you answer?'

When Furo made no response, she continued in a calmer

tone, 'I just wanted to tell you, I put the plantain in the fridge. Can you fry dodo?'

'Yes.'

'Is there still light?'

'Yes.'

'You should warm the stew in the microwave before light goes.'

'OK.'

Her next words were weighted with casualness. 'I've gone out with my friend. I'm not coming back tonight. I'll return in the morning.'

Furo said nothing.

'Are you all right?' Her tone was touched with defiance.

'I'm fine.'

A pause, then a slow sigh, and she said: 'Till tomorrow then.'

'Tomorrow,' Furo said and hung up.

After plugging his depleted phone into the wall socket beside the vanity table, Furo headed to the kitchen. He took the peeled plantain and the covered dish of tomato sauce out of the fridge, placed the plantain in a pan of groundnut oil on the gas burner, and while the slices sizzled and caramel-ised, he heated up the sauce in the microwave. Afterwards he trotted over to the bathroom to pee, and on the stroll back to the kitchen, he caught sight of a folded newspaper on the centre table. Bola's no doubt; even the toilet smelled of him. His meal ready, he set it on a tray and bore that to the settee, then drew the parlour curtains, turned on the TV, and returned to the kitchen to fetch a can of Maltina from the fridge. The big new fridge, the glitzy microwave, the IKEA tableware, his appetising meal, he knew whose money paid for all of this. The fridge door closed with a *whump*.

As Furo sank down on to the settee to eat, he winced from the pain in his rump. His buttocks felt bruised. He had first noticed the sting in the morning as he rubbed on the whitening cream, but he made nothing of it, too much sitting around he supposed. The smarting had gotten worse this afternoon, it was becoming painful to sit, and it now seemed his right cheek had a sore. And so, after he finished his feast and put away the dishes, he entered the bedroom to look in the mirror.

The whitening creams were working: the skin of his buttocks had brightened. No doubt about it, a layer of shade had sloughed off, and the reddened skin underneath shone like a good egg held up to the light. And yet, seen beside the whiteness of his back and legs, his rump looked black and angry. The bleaching action had opened a sore on his right buttock, the size of a large coin, raw-red in the centre and ringed by encrusted ooze. It looked even worse than it stung.

There it was.

It was easier to be than to become.

Furo was certain he had made the right decision. He was determined not to give up until his ass was as white as the rest of him. But for now, faced with the mirror, he admitted the painful truth: until the sore healed, he had to stop bleaching his buttocks.

Around midday on Thursday, Furo was inspecting his laundered clothes in the parlour when he heard the scratching of a key in the front door lock, and the door swung open to reveal Syreeta awash in the avenging light of the bright sun. Her chipper tone, as she spoke from the kitchen, seemed forced to his ears. 'I have a surprise for you.' She moved forwards and left the door open, then stared at the blaring TV, avoiding Furo's eyes. 'Dress up. We're going out.'

On the drive down Syreeta refused to tell him anything about the surprise. She fended off Furo's questions, only revealing that they were headed to a place near Alpha Beach. Their destination turned out to be a shopping complex at the mouth of a wide sand road that ran straight as a chalk line towards the crashing ocean. Syreeta spent some time finding a spot in the jam-packed car park, and after they got down from the Honda, she led Furo past several blocks of shops. The row they turned into was lined on both sides with shops whose fronts teemed with party-dressed, white-looking mannequins. Furo guessed the nature of the surprise even before they halted in front of Success Is the Lord's Clothings, 'stockists of Italian suits and ties, British shirts and shoes, American wristwatches and belts, French perfumes & etc.,' as the signboard announced. Chuks Yelloman Emmanuel was the MD/CEO. When Syreeta rapped on the sliding glass door and called out his nickname, he approached and wrestled the door open, then pressed his shoulders against the wall so they could squeeze past, and once they were through, he shoved the door closed as if anxious to keep in the clouds of frost blowing from the air conditioner.

'Madam the madam!' he said in stentorian tones as he engulfed Syreeta's hand in both his massive paws. Pulling her deeper into his blue-lighted shop, he barked at his young assistant to move his yansh from the only seat in sight. Syreeta settled into the deckchair, and placing her handbag in her lap, she crossed her legs. While she responded to Yelloman's animated greetings, Furo admired the painted toenails of her dangling foot, his eyes following her baby-oiled shin all the way up to her pampered knee, which peeped out from under the frilly hem of her skirt. Then he turned his gaze to the shoes spread across the floor like a horde missing its bodies. Every bit of space in the shop was taken up by all manner of fashion items. Folded on ledges and swinging from hangers were authentic designer clothes as well as their Aba imitations – but the real and fake were segregated, displayed with varying degrees of esteem. It was obvious to Furo why Syreeta had brought him here. The shop owner practised business with conspicuous candour.

It struck Furo that Yelloman hadn't yet greeted him.

Syreeta addressed Furo. 'This is it, the surprise. We need to get you some clothes for work. I can spend . . .' She shot a glance at Yelloman's averted face, and then held up her hands, one with fingers spread and the other curved in a fist. Furo's eyes widened as she mouthed, *Fifty thousand*. He had never spent that much on clothes, not at one time. And never had he needed clothes as much as now. He felt a boiling need to express his joy, his relief at a problem solved. He wanted to fling his arms around Syreeta and squeeze her till she understood.

'Thank you,' he said in a quiet, even voice.

It was time to choose. He needed shirts, trousers, ties for the office, a set of underwear. But where to start? The shop was stuffed so full it seemed futile to search. No matter what he found, no matter how right for him it might seem in the blue light of the buying moment, the dim lighting of the shop, there would always be something better he had missed. He glanced at the corner where the assistant had scurried to, but the youngster was no longer there, he had slipped out the back door. And so Furo turned to Yelloman. 'I want some shirts that look like what I'm wearing, but a bit cheaper than this. Can you advise me?'

Yelloman was standing perhaps two feet away, right beside

Syreeta's seat, and yet he acted as if Furo hadn't spoken. When Syreeta tapped his leg with a knuckle, he glanced down at her. 'My friend dey talk to you,' she said.

In a tone edging towards aggression, Yelloman responded, 'Wetin e talk?'

'But see am for your front nah! E get mouth, abi?'

Yelloman turned to Furo, but his eyes were lowered. He was light-complexioned, his skin tone the Semitic hue associated with the most Roman Catholic of Igbos, and in the open neck of his shirt Furo could see a flush spreading. Reluctance pulsed through his frame and his fleshy nose quivered. Furo felt a thrill of misgiving. Yelloman was over six feet tall and built like a discus thrower. Veins rippled beneath the stiff hairs on his bulky forearms; his muscled legs made his trousers look small and tight. He appeared the quick-tempered sort, a man to be treated with caution, and something about Furo had clearly incensed him.

Yelloman made a sound in his throat in preparation to speak. Like a conductor at the start of a symphony, he raised his arms in the air, and then, with sweeping gestures, his movements exaggerated as if sign talking to the brain damaged, he said to Furo, 'What—did—you—say?'

A spasm of laughter touched Furo's face but he forced it back in time. Yelloman was staring at Syreeta, who was bent double in the chair with her hands gripping her sides and her shoulders heaving. She laughed so long that Furo got embarrassed on Yelloman's behalf. Finally she straightened up, flicked a tear from her eye corner with a finger, and then met Yelloman's look of brooding. 'Abeg, Yelloman, no kill me with laugh,' she said in a choked voice. 'My friend sabe speak pidgin. No need to wave your hand like person wey dey drown.'

Yelloman's face lit up with excitement. 'Talk true? E dey speak pidgin?'

'Talk to am, you go see.'

Yelloman looked Furo in the face for the first time. His golden-brown eyes glistened like boiled sweets. He sucked on his lips, as if tasting his words, and then he fired, 'How you dey?'

'I full ground,' Furo replied.

'Hah hah – correct guy!' Yelloman barked in exultation, spreading his arms at the same time as if to throw them around Furo in a big-brother hug. But he checked himself, then glanced down at Syreeta and declared, 'I like this oyibo.'

He talked nonstop as he led Furo around the shop and guided him to the best bargains. Long monologues about Nigeria, about the meaning of man's existence as discovered through the experiences of a clothing salesman, and then questions about Furo: prying questions, eager questions, assertions phrased as questions. Where was Furo from, did he watch football, what did he think of Lagos, was he Syreeta's man, wouldn't he hurry up and start a family with her? His only daughter was six years old and already she spoke English better than her father. ('Bone that CK shirt, no be orijo. Carry the Gap one. I dey sell am for six thousand but if you buy five I go give you everything for twenty-five.') He was a self-made man, his father had lost everything during the civil war and so he had to give up school to learn a trade, but nothing spoil, he was successful as you can see, he was the owner of this shop and another in Ojuelegba, and he was widely travelled, he used to visit London every year for summer sales but had recently stopped, partly because it was cheaper to shop in Dubai and import from China, but also because those oyibo dey knack English like sey nah only them sabe the language. ('That jeans nah your own, dem make am for you, nah your size finish. Take am for two thousand.') But Furo was different, he spoke pidgin like a trueborn Nigerian, and even though his skin was white and his bia-bia was red and his eyes were green, his heart without a doubt was black. Abi no be so?

'I be full Naija,' Furo agreed, and Yelloman pounded him on the back in approval, then slashed the price of the leather slippers they were haggling over. With that last purchase Furo's budget was exhausted and, as the assistant – who had returned to receive a reprimanding knock on the head from Yelloman – began bagging his wardrobe, he took the cash from Syreeta and paid Yelloman. 'You be my personal person,' Yelloman said as he walked them to the sliding glass door. 'My gism number dey for the nylon. Call me anytime you wan' drink beer.'

Arriving at the car, Syreeta unlocked the doors before taking the shopping bags from Furo's hands and, after dropping them on the back seat, she turned back to him and linked her arms round his waist. 'Thank you,' she said, her voice muffled against his chest. She gave him a squeeze before stepping back. Her eyes shone with emotion.

'Why?' Furo asked in surprise. 'I should be thanking you!'

'I'm thanking you for what you did in there, for being nice to Yelloman.' She opened the driver's door, stuck a foot in the car, and spoke into the sun-baked interior: 'And for being you.'

Sunday evening arrived at last, and Furo, who had spent the whole day waiting for Syreeta to return from her weekend outing, now turned his attention to the TV as he supped. He watched Cartoon Network until his plate was empty, then

153

Fox News Channel as he drank his malt. In the Fox studio sat several pundits debating US debt, and the sole black man on the panel was the least articulate, the least flattered by the camera lighting, the least distinct against the blue and red of the studio's backdrop. Furo's attention soon wandered from the rigged TV show to Bola's newspaper, which had been gathering dust on the table since his visit on Wednesday. It was the Tuesday edition, the same daily Furo used to read every week for job announcements. A lifetime ago, it seemed. Returning to his seat with the newspaper, Furo began to flick its pages, his gaze scanning desultorily. Seven die of cholera; Caribbean nations plan to invest in Nigeria's power sector; Boko Haram strikes again: same old news, same recycled words, and same old faces of recycled politicians. And then – in a double-spread interview with a quarter-page photo of a soft-cheeked and heavy-lidded man – the same old problem of unemployment, but highlighted in a new way by Alhaji Jubril Yuguda, the Chairman and CEO of the Yuguda Group. Furo didn't read the interview past the opening paragraph, but the pull quote at the bottom of the page held his attention:

'We received more than 15,000 applications for our Graduate Executive Lorry Driver vacancies, but only 200 places were available . . . among the applicants were 18 PhD, 71 MBA, 680 Master's and 11,240 Bachelor degree holders.' *Alhaji Yuguda*

Several pages later, Furo was still mulling over the implications of Yuguda's words when his eyes fell on a face he thought he recognised, and as he leaned in close to read the photo's caption, his name jumped out at him. It was his photo, his old photo, a selfie of the old him. He remembered snapping it with the camera of the phone he left behind. It was a missing person announcement.

FURO WARIBOKO

Male, aged 33 years, dark in complexion, speaks English language fluently. Left Egbeda on the 18th of June at around 8:00 a.m. for an unknown location. If seen contact one Doris Esosa Wariboko (Tel: 08069834300/08143660843) or Akowonjo Police Station.

Furo lifted his head, stared sightlessly at the TV screen, and the newspaper slipped from his grasp, fluttering to the rug. His cheek muscles began to quiver and his eardrums ached from the force of the pounding in his head. He raised his hands to his neck and rubbed. His mother was searching for him. His family was spreading his name around. They had the right name but the wrong image. They had right on their side, but this was wrong. He should have known it would come to this. If anyone he knew, the Haba! people, if they saw this! Mr Obata, Arinze, the receptionist, everyone who knew his name. If Syreeta saw it! But why – why did the running never end? Because he had to settle his debts, that's why. It would never end as long as he owed his family. Theirs was a debt of semen and milk, of blood and sweat and tears. A debt he could neither repay nor escape. But he would try.

So now he had to change his name.

Furo picked up the newspaper and gazed at the face bearing his name. Tired face, tired eyes, tired mouth, and black skin: that's all he saw. That person wasn't him. He had moved on beyond that. The only problem was, even as he'd forgotten how he used to look, he didn't know what he now looked like. White skin, green eyes, red hair – black ass. Mere descriptions for what people saw, what others saw in him, and not who he was. He had to find out who he was.

It was time to see his face.

Furo ripped out the missing person announcement, and after burning it in the kitchen sink, he washed the ashes down the drain. He returned to parlour, folded the newspaper, replaced it on the table, and switched off the TV. Entering Syreeta's bedroom, he shut the curtains before pulling off his boxers and singlet. And in this state of naked grace – stripped of the past, curious about the present, hopeful about the future – he strode to the tall mirror over the vanity table and stared into the face of his new self. A face whose features had altered less in dimension than character, and whose relation to the selfie in the newspaper was as close and yet as far apart as the resemblance between adolescence and adulthood. His face had sloughed off immaturity. Then again, the unexpectedness of his skin shade, eye colour, and hair texture was the octopus ink that would confuse his hunters, as even he wouldn't have recognised himself in a photo of his new face, and so neither would his parents nor anyone who based their looking on his old image. He knew at last that he had nothing to fear. He was a different person, and right here, right now, right in his face, he could see he looked nothing like the former Furo.

Afterwards, Furo trotted off to his bedroom, spread his new clothes on the bed, and planned what he would wear on Monday. He couldn't wait for many things. But most of all, he couldn't wait to start work tomorrow. He was excited about his first real job. After he finished secondary school, he had worked for almost two years as a supervisor in his father's chicken farm, but counting eggs didn't count as a job. His next job had come after university, when he served the entire year of his national youth service teaching mathematics to junior secondary students in the sun-blasted and fly-plagued Kebbi State. That, too, wasn't a real job. He hardly showed up for class as he spoke no Hausa and his students barely spoke English, and all he remembered of that wilderness were the fun and games he'd had with his fellow youth corpers. He was still hopeful then, full of big dreams, eager to succeed. He had prospects that many of his students, who were mostly sons of nomadic herdsmen and farmyard hirelings, could never hope for. He had received an education they could only dream of. Besides, he had his parents back home in Lagos, centre of excellence, to return to. But now he knew better, and in the period since he departed Kebbi he had many times wished he'd learned from his students how to milk cows and slaughter goats and plant onion bulbs, learned a handiwork to keep his mind off his own helplessness. That, at least, unlike his stinking stint at the chicken farm, would have been something to busy himself with until he found the job he deserved. Unlike his father, he would never stop fighting, never stop moving forwards, not now, not after he'd survived the hard long years of joblessness whose only purpose was to show him how easy it was for hope to shrivel. How disappointment became a hole with an endless bottom.

That was in the past. He had a job, a new life, and it was time to choose a new name. He had been trying out names as he chose his clothes for work, but none yet sounded right, none felt like his to keep. At first he considered taking Kalabari names, and then Itsekiri, Efik, Yoruba, but he soon gave up on Nigeria. In his new life he was American and his new name would confirm that. A new name from the new world for the new him – that sounded right. Yet he was still nameless and it was already night, and Syreeta would soon return. And so he arranged his Monday clothes on hangers and put them away in the wardrobe, then cleaned his shoes and set them by the bedroom door. After placing his passport, wallet and folded handkerchief on the bedside table, he left the bedroom. In the parlour he switched on the TV and tapped the remote control till he reached a music channel showing a 2pac and Biggie video. Reducing the volume to a murmur, he settled on the settee to make his decision.

'Starting with names from A: Abe, Brad, Carl, Dave, Eddie, Frank . . .'

Frank felt right – easy to pronounce, easy to remember, and the same first letter as Furo. Good rule to apply for Wariboko. He needed a surname that would let him keep his initials.

'Wayne, West, Williams, *no* . . . White . . . *Whyte.*'

Whyte, too, felt right, felt like his, and, in a slow voice that burred in his ears, he said both as one: 'Frank Whyte.' His eyes watered as he stared at the flashing lights on the TV screen. 'Frank Whyte, Frank Whyte,' he repeated, blinking to clear his eyes.

He had found his name.

MORPHEUS

'I am not done with my changes.'

—Stanley Kunitz, *The Layers*

It didn't matter to me if I liked Tekena, but for the sake of what I wanted, I needed her to like me. And so, when I met her on that overcast Sunday afternoon, the first thing I said was, 'You're pretty.' Even as I intended to win her over with flattery, I was surprised by my reflux of pleasure, the rush of gratefulness at her acknowledgement of my appearance when she responded, 'You're pretty too.' Sunlight and water to a blossoming flower, likewise our sense of well-being is both nourished by the shine of other's eyes and the gurgle of our self-regard. Who I was as a person was more than what I looked like, but then again, how people saw me was a part of who I was.

I soon found myself liking Tekena more than her brother, whose name I didn't mention until she and I were eating ice cream at The Palms. You see, Furo had come across as a bit of a user. I know now that he was desperate, that on the day we met he was facing a predicament and had needed whatever help he could get, but something about his request to move in with me, the ease with which he asked such a thing of a stranger, had struck the wrong chord with me. His sister could be accused of taking advantage of a private mishap to build her popularity on social media, and in person I found her as chatty as I'd expected, and maybe too trusting of strangers bearing gifts, but at no point did she strike me as manipulative. Not in person, not towards me.

Thus I liked her. She was after all a recognisable Nigerian

type, not much different from me in background and social standing. We were both members of that caste of young adults who grew up in the ruins of Nigeria's middle class. We were born into the military dictatorships of the '80s and '90s; we attended the cheaper private schools or the better public ones; we read the same Pacesetter novels and watched the same NTA shows; we lived in cities. Unlike the majority of Nigerians in any age bracket, we spoke English as a first (and sometimes only) language, and our inbred accents were two to three generations old. Because of our parents, who were educated and devoted and fortunate enough to hold on to their salaried positions through all those decades of martial austerity; our private dictators, who beat their children with the same whips they used on the poorer relatives they took in as house helpers; our role models, who were so convinced of 'what was what' that they affirmed a preference for butter over margarine even when they could only afford Blue Band for our school lunch-boxes; our protectors and providers, who were neither middle class nor working class, neither wealthy enough to jet overseas on vacation nor deprived enough to cease the Christmastime pilgrimages to our family hometowns; our lifelong teachers, who instilled in us their deep-seated humiliation over the failures of Nigeria as well as their bitter nostalgia for the administrative competence of colonial rule. That was it: in Tekena's voice and gestures, in many things about her, I saw the same contradictions that had shaped me. Shame and arrogance. Pragmatism and sentimentality. Thoughtless violence and unthinking sacrifice. Red blusher and black skin . . .

The thing is, on seeing Tekena my thoughts flew to my mother. She, too, wore red blusher in my childhood memories. My sentiments about my father are less conflicted: he left when I was eight. My mother stayed to be condemned to failure in raising her son. Because the success of a man, our people say, is the father's doing. You are your father's son – you follow in your father's footsteps. Manhood and its machismo are attributed to the seed, which then follows that the failure to make a man is the egg's burden. *Your papa born you well*, they will sing to a man in praise, but when he disappoints so-and-so's expectations of XY manliness, it becomes *Nah your mama I blame*. My say is this: when you live in a worldwide bullring, bullshit is what you'll get. If they say I cannot be my mother's son, then it must be that I'm her daughter.

After we sat down in the food court of The Palms to eat our ice cream, I began asking Tekena about her brother. I lapped up all the details she gave of his disappearance, which it turned out weren't much, not enough to slake my thirst. She had awoken on that Monday morning to find he had left the house for the job interview he'd only mentioned to her when he was ironing his clothes the previous night, and since neither she nor her father had thought there was anything odd about his long absence, he wasn't missed until her mother returned from the office and asked after him. That was when Tekena went into his bedroom and found his mobile phone. And the rest, as she said, was a disaster. From Tekena's tweets I already knew that she and her parents had no inkling of the change that had happened to Furo, hence I made no mention of my meeting with him. As I uttered suitable noises of sympathy in response to her recounting of the grief his disappearance had wrought upon the household, I couldn't help asking myself, what if Furo had remained behind after he found himself transformed? This was the question I wanted answered, and one I would have to find out for myself.

There and then I decided I would ask Tekena if I could pay her a visit her at home. Before I could find an opening to put the question, something happened. This was some time later, after we'd left the food court and gone upstairs to catch a movie. We were waiting in line to buy our tickets at the box office when a man walked up to us. I had seen him coming, and I suspected he was trouble, though I'd thought his trouble was my companion's to rebuff. I was wrong. It was me his potbelly was jiggling towards. He had an enormous one, which he carried with as much pride as the tablet-sized smartphone clutched in his left hand. He looked to me like some local government chairman, one of those gruff-voiced goons who had moved on from extorting bus conductors and now made their money in ballot-box bullying. I was already irritated by the way he smirked at me, and I was tense on account of how close he was standing, but when he said, 'I like your hair o,' raising his hand at the same time to stroke my locks, the violence of my shudder shocked me as well. I sensed Tekena's look of vicarious horror before she struck his hand away and said in a furious tone, 'Leave my girlfriend alone!'

Crudity is a disease that money exacerbates rather than cures. And that man was an exemplar of the condition. Leave my girlfriend alone, Tekena said. A statement that left no wriggle room. A less vulgar man, if he were still intent on wooing a woman whose animosity was so evident, would have first apologised for his forwardness, and then he might have offered one of those flattering lies or I've-seen-you-before lines that constitute the arsenal of impromptu courtship speech. Not our man. He was too hippopotamus-skinned.

His own response was rank aggression. 'Which kin' girlfriend?' he sneered at Tekena, and when she threw him a glance that told him to go and die, he said with a filthy laugh: 'Una be lesbo?'

Tekena, for all her playfulness on Twitter, was a Lagos pikin. She could give as good as she got. Brinkmanship, one-upmanship, fuck-that-man-up-ship – these were acquired skills in a city where even beggars cursed you out at the drop of a coin. Thus the overboard-ness of her response, which she began by hooking an arm around my waist in a suggestive manner before saying to the man: 'And so what if we're lesbians? How does that concern you? Abi you think sey if we want man nah you we go come meet? You, ke? With this your big belleh that can even crush a cow?' These words were delivered in a tone of sweetened poison, and for some seconds after she spoke, the man was as stunned as I was. He recovered first, and opened his mouth to bellow, but thinking better of it, he walked away. 'Smart move!' Tekena called out after him.

A woman defended me from what I used to be.

Womanhood comes with its peculiar burdens, among them the constant reminder of a subordinate status whose dominant symptom was uninvited sexual attention from men. I hadn't foreseen this fact of my new identity. Bus conductors whistled at me on the street; drivers pulled over to offer me rides to bars; and when I went shopping for my new wardrobe in Yaba market, the touts grabbed at my hands and laughed off my protests. All manner and ages of male called me fine girl, sweet lips, correct pawpaw, big bakassi. Landlords wanted to know if I would soon marry, if I had children, if my father or my boss would stand surety for me. A woman is not expected to live alone, to walk alone in peace, or to want to be alone.

Pity the man who never becomes the woman he could be.

It was early yet in my journey to the far reaches of my identity. Like those before me who had transitioned into otherness, I was finding out that appearances would always be a point of conflict. Male or female, black or white, the eye of the beholder and the fashion sense of the beholden, all of these feed into our desire to classify by sight. The woman and the man: stuck together in a species and yet divided by a gendered history going back to the womb. But in this war of the selves, I had switched sides. Despite the snake of maleness that still tethered me to the past, I was more than man, interrupted.

I was whoever I wanted me to be.

When Tekena and I emerged from the movie theatre, I told her I planned to be in Egbeda on Saturday (a small lie) and asked if it was OK to stop by her house for a quick visit. She gave her consent with expressions of genuine pleasure, and the next weekend, shortly before midday on the last day in June, I knocked at her gate. She came to open it and we went into the sitting room, where I spotted those two objects of my rampant curiosity: Furo's mother and father.

Monima Wariboko was a former civil servant who now owned a chicken farm. He was sixty-four years old and had been married for thirty-five of those years. The first time I saw him, he was slouched in an armchair that occupied prime position in front of the TV. He was a big-boned man, larger in stature than his son, and yet, sitting there, hypnotised by the TV, he seemed the smallest person I had ever seen. He was thoroughly broken. This was apparent from the slackness of his lips when he raised his head to accept my greeting, and that wheezing voice, that exhausted way of speaking, so disheartening to hear in a person who wasn't Marlon Brando. He was unclothed except for an old wrapper of his wife's, a colourful wax-print fabric, which he wore around his waist and knotted under the Gollum swell of his belly. He resembled a fisherman straight out of a daguerreotype, a wastrel who hadn't netted a catch for years and yet fatted himself on the cassava from his wife's farm, and then went to pose for the camera because he was the only one not at sea when the colonialists came calling. He annoyed me on sight.

That's how I felt the first time I saw Furo's father, but later, upon reflection, I picked out the nettles from my eyes. Yes, he was indeed a broken man, housebroken and heartbroken, and a broke ass, too, but he had stuck around. He was a father figure to his children, a weak father for sure, but a father they could see. He was good friends with his daughter, who clearly loved him dearly. He didn't assault his wife or embarrass her with roadside sexual affairs. He didn't remain in the civil service to do nothing and embezzle money. He established his own business through honest work and gave his best at running it, and though his best ended up ruining it, at least, on the day his coffin is lowered into the ground, someone can say in truth, 'Here lies a good man.'

Tekena introduced me to her parents as a new friend she had met on Twitter. After responding to my greeting, her father had turned his attention back to the TV, and so it fell to her mother to ask what Twitter was. While Tekena explained, I studied this woman. She was lying on her side on a sofa with her head resting on the armrest, and she was so petite she didn't have to bend her legs to fit them within the sofa's length. Going by the bellicose nature of Tekena's tweets about her mother, I had foreseen a more imposing figure, matriarchal certainly, maybe the market woman type, with iroko trunks for limbs, a buffer of a bust, and a rock-boulder backside. Doris Esosa Wariboko née Osagiede was anything but. Perhaps because of her diminutive build, she had aged rather well. At fifty-eight, she looked in her forties. Despite having borne the load of two children, her belly showed few signs of sagging. Her bare legs were smooth-skinned, her face was devoid of wrinkles and sun patches, and she wore her hair in neat dreadlocks, the roots so black they were obviously dyed. It was her hair that decided my mind about her.

All children of living mothers hold this truth to be self-evident: your best friend's mother, your spouse's mother, your mother's mother, someone else's mother is always the better mother. Show me the man who wants the mother he has and I'll show you his Oedipus complex – and yet, if I were Furo, I would want my mother to be that woman sprawled on the sofa. But he also left her behind the same as he abandoned his father, his likable sister, his past entire. Meeting Furo's mother didn't take me closer to his story; no, rather, it made me question my questions. (Question: Would Furo's family have accepted him for what he'd become? Answer: No white man has ever been lynched in Lagos.)

Before Tekena led me off to Furo's bedroom, her mother and I shared a moment over hair. I brought up the topic, and I did so because I wanted to hear her speak so I could sound her mind. It also seemed the safest subject I could raise with a woman who was grieving the loss of her child. So I told her she had good hair. She said thank you, at the same time glancing at me with those fierce eyes from which the laughter had only recently been banished. I tried again, saying excuse me Ma, but I would like to know what she used on her hair that gave it such body. That was when she noticed mine. 'Come,' she said and sat up. I approached her, and then, in obedience to her gesture, I knelt at her feet and placed my head in her lap. As her fingers worked through my locks, I felt a dagger thrust of compunction over the knowledge I was keeping from her. Blast the novel. No story is worth the human suffering that vivifies it. *I know who your son is*, I wanted to say into the sadness of her cocoa smell. *I know that he's alive and well. I know why he left.* But I bit my tongue until she said, 'You use shea butter. That's good. I use coconut oil, but your hair's too strong for that.' After speaking, she retracted her hands from my hair and, clasping my chin, she lifted my face to look into it. As our gazes met, I endured the most deceptive moment of my life. I felt like sobbing with relief when she said at last, 'Talk to your friend. Those oyibo hairs she keeps putting on—' Tekena raised her voice in protest, and so her mother left the statement unfinished, but I got the point. All those nuggets I had hoped to excavate from Furo's story, those subtexts of self-identity and self-deceit, of a continental inferiority complex, of the widening gyre of our parents' colonial hang-ups, all of these were destroyed by a mother who showed up my fraudulence in a few quiet words.

I found nothing in Furo's bedroom. There was a small thrill in being the only one who knew this was the chamber where he had woken up to his new self. And for some seconds I even thought I got some insight into his personality from how clean his bedroom was, everything in its place, his clothes hung in the wardrobe, his desk arranged, his bed made, but that crumb was lost to me when I asked Tekena if anyone had cleaned the room since his disappearance. His mother, I was told, cleaned it every day in readiness for his return.

Right there in that bedroom, posing beside Tekena as she snapped a selfie to post on Twitter, I realised I needed to speak to Furo.

FRANK WHYTE

'For the black man there is only one destiny.
And it is white.'

—Frantz Fanon, *Black Skin, White Masks*

The soreness in Furo's buttocks was a minor irritation when he opened his eyes on Monday morning. A bigger worry was his new job, all the unknowns that could go wrong on his first day. But as much as he dreaded this new adventure, he was also excited by it. Yawning widely to clear his head of sleep, he sat upright in bed and threw open the doors of his mind to the sounds scrabbling beyond the darkness of the bedroom. He could hear Syreeta knocking about in the kitchen; she was becoming flatteringly domestic. And she had offered, last night, as they lay in bed, before she turned to him with her 'fuck me' sigh, to drive him to the office this morning. It was she again, sounding just like his mother, who had suggested that they set off early to avoid the Monday traffic. Furo was surer than ever of how she felt about him, but still, just to be safe, now that the two weeks were up, he would ask if he could stay on longer at her apartment. Later today, he thought, when he returned from work, he would ask then. At this, his first decision of the day, he climbed out of bed.

After a rushed breakfast of toast and boiled sausages, Furo and Syreeta left the house at five thirty. The sky was deep purple; the moon was still out; dew dripped from the leaves of the looming trees in whose branches roosters roosted. As they tramped past the silent houses, the crunch of sand beneath their shoes sounded like ghouls in conversation. The estate streets were deserted except for clusters of sheep bedded on the tarred road leading to the gate. Syreeta had to zigzag the Honda around the motionless shapes, and when the headlights stilled against the closed gate, the guard, swaddled in blankets and rubbing his eyes with the heels of his hands, shuffled from the shadows and shone his torchlight into the car before crossing to unlock the gate. Syreeta sped through with a scream of rubber.

The roads were clear through Victoria Island, across Third Mainland Bridge, and down the endless stretch of Ikorodu Road, but, as the sky brightened under the sun's approach, they drove into heavy traffic at Maryland Roundabout. At first sight of the congestion Syreeta cursed, and as the Honda slowed, Furo stared out the window at the stagnated cars and thought about the last time he had passed this way. On foot, homeless and broke, and headed for The Palms. He owed Syreeta much more than he could tell her. 'Sorry about the traffic,' he now said to her. 'Hopefully you won't have to drive me tomorrow. I should be getting my car today.'

She took a moment to respond. 'I still think that salary is too small.'

The previous night, after lovemaking, they had had a conversation about Furo's job. Syreeta felt that his status, his oyibo-ness, had been taken advantage of. She argued that he was worth way more than eighty thousand and a company car, and when he sighed with indifference, she told him that the first job she'd got out of university had paid two hundred and fifty thousand. She was also given a car, the Honda. At this offered scrap from the mystery of her life, a history she had guarded thus far with utter silence, Furo's interest sat up and woofed. She had to be, and if he had thought about it, he would doubtless have concluded that she was, but it had never occurred to him that Syreeta was a graduate. After he blurted out his surprise, she laughed before saying how could he think she wasn't, and then she told him that she had a degree in accounting from Unilag, and that she had done her youth service at the National Assembly in Abuja, where she was retained afterwards, though she gave up that position when her benefactor lost his senatorial seat in the last elections. She capped her testimony by repeating that Furo could do better, to which he responded with some heat: 'Our situations are different. You're a woman.' A kept woman, he meant, and Syreeta caught his meaning in his tone. She shot back: 'And you're a white man. You don't have to fuck anyone for favours.' Then she turned her back and ignored him until he fell asleep.

But now she was smiling as Furo replied with caution: 'Maybe the salary is small, but it's all I have.'

'Until something better comes along,' she said.

'Yes,' agreed Furo.

'That's the spirit. Something better will come, very soon, you'll see.'

When the Honda pulled up at the gate of Haba!, Furo said his goodbyes to Syreeta, then clambered down from the car. He felt like a cosseted child on the first-ever day of school, a feeling of abandonment and peril that grew stronger as Syreeta drove off with a cheery wave. It felt too easy to call her back, to climb back into the coolness of the car and be driven home to finish his sleep, and then watch TV, eat her cooking, do anything but worry about work, money, responsibility. It felt too easy to give up what he had wanted for so long – a money-paying, office-going, real-life job. Not easy enough, he told himself, and striding to the closed gate, he nodded at the maiguard who emerged from the gatehouse at his knock, then said in answer to the old man's polite question, 'I work here.'

*　*　*

Following their start-up meeting, which lasted about an hour, Ayo Abu Arinze showed Furo around the office, and during the tour he delivered a running commentary on the internal workings of the three-year-old company, its mission and vision, rules and regulations, the anecdotal history. 'Work starts at eight and ends at five, but the office is locked up around ten, so you can stay until then if you want . . . what we sell, in a nutshell, is self-education . . . lunch hour is between noon and one . . . I was a senior manager in the telecoms industry before I resigned my job to start this company . . . every word in a Haba! proposal must be spelled correctly, no text message spellings, that is a rule . . . Nigerians must start reading serious books, whether for work or for pleasure, that's my vision . . . the red button on the dispenser is actually cold water and the blue is hot,' Arinze said as he led Furo into office after office and presented him to the staff as Frank Whyte, the new head of marketing.

Sales, Accounts, Human Resources, Information Technology, and Marketing: the five departments of Haba! The sales department comprised two staff members, one of whom had been employed on the same day as Furo. The senior sales manager and department head was a bejewelled, hijab-wearing, boubou-clad woman called Zainab. She beamed a fatigued smile at Furo, and when, to the clatter of gold bangles, she raised a hand and patted her belly, he saw she was with child. The new salesperson was a plump, stylish woman whose name was Iquo, and after Furo was introduced, she spoke in a confident tone of voice, her words directed at Arinze: 'I remember Mr Whyte from the interview day. I also want to thank you, sir, for granting me the opportunity to work for this great company. I promise to give my best, sir.' She sounded easy to boss around. This intuition of Furo's was strengthened when she stood up from her desk and rushed towards the door as he and Arinze turned to leave, but Arinze waved her back and said, with a cool glance at her eager face, 'I can get the door myself. One more thing, please don't call me "sir".' The next-door office was the IT department, and it held one person, Tetsola. He was a wide-shouldered and long-limbed man who sat hunched over a white-tiled ledge in the dim cubbyhole that was crammed with dismembered computers and discarded compact discs and tangled rubber cables. His office, which shared a wall with the lavatory, had been converted from a bathroom, and perhaps for this reason, because of the mouldering smell that seeped from the peeling walls, he remained silent when Furo was introduced. He dipped his head at Furo's hello, and then shuffled his feet in their outsized sneakers as Arinze described his duties and praised his work to Furo, but he refused to say a word. After emerging from the IT office, as they made their way downstairs, Arinze told Furo that he himself handled the company accounts, hence his office doubled as the accounts department, while the HR department was staffed by two people, Obata and Tosin. Obata was the head of department, but it was Tosin who managed the support staff of two drivers and one gatekeeper. She also served as his personal assistant.

'Meet the amazing Ms Amao,' Arinze said as they reached the reception desk. 'Tosin has been with me from the very beginning . . . she and I opened this office together as the only staff. You could say she's the face and voice of Haba! Anything you need to know about the business, about how we started, or where to get ink for the printer, or how to requisition books from the store, Tosin's the person to ask.' And to Tosin he said, 'This is—'

'I know, Furo Wariboko,' Tosin interjected.

'Oh yes,' Arinze said with a low chuckle, and then nibbled

his lower lip. Finally he spoke. 'From now on he will be known only as Frank Whyte.'

During their meeting in Arinze's office, Arinze had expressed astonishment at Furo's decision to change his name. In response to his cautious questions, Furo explained that Frank was his Christian name and Whyte was his *furo ere*, his family name, the English version of his family's compound name. Many Kalabari families still retained this legacy of the slave-trading days when the chieftains answered one name in the clan and another to the white customer, the European sailors, who had no interest in learning their names and thus, partly in mockery and partly from necessity, addressed them by English nicknames. Hence it became that Fyneface was Karibo, Yellowe was Iyalla, Black-Duke was Oweredaba, Bobmanuel was Ekine, Georgewill was Otagi, Harry was Idoniboye-Obu, and, according to Furo, Whyte was Wariboko.

But Whyte was not Wariboko. Furo wasn't worried about this fabrication, his first to his boss. He had no fear he would be caught out. Ayo Abu Arinze was Yoruba or more likely Igbo, or even of mixed ethnicity, with some Hausa thrown in somewhere – his three names together were confusing, but his surname was Igbo – and more to the point, he wasn't Kalabari, so it was unlikely he would know the secret history of Kalabari names. Yet Arinze was Nigerian enough to know that the whitest names in the country came from Furo's parts, the Niger Delta. Besides, he was pleased at the reason Furo gave for making the change. Because, as Furo said, Whyte would be easier for Haba! customers to pronounce and memorise, and, furthermore, it would remove the distraction of a white man bearing a black name. Such dedication to duty boded well, Arinze said, and he agreed with Furo that no one in the office need be informed of his old name.

From the lobby Furo and Arinze went back upstairs to Obata's office. Obata was typing on his laptop, and he looked up from the screen as they entered, then pushed back his chair and rose to his feet. He greeted Arinze in a genial tone and nodded at Furo like an old enemy, and then, apart from a sidelong glance at Furo's face, he showed no emotion as Arinze informed him of the name change. When Arinze finished speaking, he asked:

'What name should I use in his employment file?'

'Frank Whyte, of course,' Arinze answered.

'And his salary account? Will that be opened under this name?'

'That's a good point,' Arinze said. He turned to Furo. 'What do you suggest? Your new passport bears your old name. We'll need new ID to open a bank account.'

Furo pondered on this snag before he said at last, 'I'll make the change official. I'll get a new passport. Is it possible to pay me in cash until I bring the passport?'

'That we can do,' Arinze said. 'Tell you what, Obata. Don't open a file for him, not yet. For tax purposes let the records show that he's on a three-month internship in marketing, and put down his salary as marketing expenses. Frank, you'll have to bring your passport before the end of three months, by the end of September. Then we'll make your position permanent.'

'I'll get the passport this month,' Furo said. And he added: 'Thank you, Abu.'

'Perfect,' Arinze said. 'Now let me show you to your office.'

After Arinze left him alone, Furo strode around his office, acquainting himself with his new status. The austere, white-walled room was furnished with a wood-laminate desk, a steel-legged plastic chair, a foot-flip trash can, an air conditioner whose remote control was the only item on the desk's surface, and a single-tiered pinewood shelf that was affixed to the wall across from the desk. The shelf was lined with books whose spines bore titles such as *The Rules of Wealth* and *Defying the Odds* and *The Leader Who Had No Title*. Adjacent to the shelf was the room's only window, underneath which stood two cardboard boxes, and when Furo opened their flaps, he found that both were packed full of new-smelling books. After closing the boxes, he rose from his squat, then raised his hand to the window and wedged open the slats of the venetian blind. He gazed through the glass into the front of the compound, where he saw that four cars were parked, a black Mercedes jeep and three sedans. The jeep had to be Arinze's, and since he couldn't hope for that, Furo imagined that the least punished-looking of the sedans, a red Kia, was his.

His fantasies were interrupted by a knock on the door. He edged away from the window before calling out, 'Come in,' and the door swung open to reveal Tetsola, the IT man, at full size. He looked seven feet tall. When seated in his office he had appeared uncommonly large, but then Furo had also felt Brobdingnagian in the cramped space. What he now felt was embarrassment at his own puniness; and some confusion over his gut-deep stirrings of inadequacy. Everything about Tetsola – his basketballer limbs and those heroic shoulders, but also the commando jut of his chin – were exaggerations of the human form. *The stares he must draw,* Furo thought with a rush of resentment as unexpected as it was strong. He knew very well how it was to be stared at by everyone; he knew the price he paid for the loss of his anonymity. Yet he still envied Tetsola for standing out from the crowd. Or, nearer the truth, standing above it.

'Come in,' Furo said again, to break the cycle of his thoughts.

Tetsola ducked into the doorway and loped forwards. Standing closer, he towered over Furo like a father figure. In his raised palm was balanced a black Zinox. Furo guessed that the laptop was the reason for the visit, and he waited for Tetsola, who was glancing around the room with a smile that showed his bovine teeth, to confirm this, and just as he began to speculate that his visitor might be mute, Tetsola confounded him by saying in the wrong voice, a voice right for an eunuch but too feeble, too squeak-squeak, for a giant's maw: 'I've brought your lappy.'

For the next half-hour, while seated at his desk and facing the laptop screen, Furo listened in mute wonder to that nasal tone as Tetsola ran him through all his improvements to the laptop. He had upgraded functions, partitioned hard discs, and installed the latest versions of the best programs for any task Furo would ever need to perform on a machine of such limited processing power, limited not because the Zinox was bad, but because, didn't Furo agree, Mac was the greatest. Much of this geeky lecture, on account of the terminology as well as the R2-D2 inflections of Tetsola's voice, was unintelligible to Furo, and the torrent of information only succeeded in making his buttocks sweat. He kept adjusting himself to find a less pinching position in the chair, but he kept on listening, he kept on looking, he wanted to understand everything there was to know about the first computer he could call his own.

At long last Tetsola announced his duty ended and exited the office. Alone with the laptop, Furo opened a browser and signed into his Yahoo mailbox. It was over two weeks since he'd last been online, and though he suspected – or, rather, knew – what awaited him there, he still had to see for himself that he was right. He was, of course: there was indeed something to see: a digital influx of panic and grief. His mailbox had three hundred and seventeen unread emails, many of them newsletters from the job-listing websites he was subscribed to; but he noted one email from his mother, several from his father and his sister, and countless Facebook and Twitter notifications from friends, relatives, and total strangers. He was tempted to dip into all these messages addressed to someone he no longer was, but he realised the cruel folly of that action, as already he could feel his resolve crumbling under the weight of the subject line of his mother's email, sent on 22 June, which read: 'MY SON WHERE ARE YOU???' Furo's struggle with himself was rife with sighs, and in the end, by the simple trick of averting his eyes from the screaming caps, the hook-like question marks, the words fatted on desperation, he succeeded in withstanding the Pandora pull of his mailbox. He did not succumb to his mother's email nor to any of the others, not a single one. Instead, upon returning his gaze to the screen, he opened the mailbox settings, scrolled down until he found the option he sought, and deleted his account.

Logging into Facebook, he found the message icon red with alerts. As for the friend requests, they ran into hundreds. His wall was taken over by postings about his disappearance, ladders of comments in unreadable net lingo, sunny emoticons depicting horror, and video clips of green pastures and floating clouds set to cantatas. Also photos. It seemed every group photo he had ever appeared in was tagged on to his wall. By long-forgotten relatives, unrecognisable childhood playmates, and unknown people whose names he found impossible to pronounce. Chinese names with their Xs, Russian names spelled in Cyrillic; and the trendy idiocy of misspelled Nigerian names, those Yehmeesees and Kaylaychees; and also names that seemed like *noms de guerre* for child stalkers. It was alarming: the scale of the uproar, the scope of his celebrity. All this time the whole of Facebook was searching for him and yet he had no idea, he hadn't heard a thing.

Getting off Facebook was a hassle, as the deactivation process was so well hidden that he was forced to Google it and follow the instructions he found in a *Vice* article. Facebook defeated, he turned his avenging fury on the newest and least utilised of his online platforms, his Twitter account. He signed in to find a string of mentions from @pweetychic_tk, whom he suspected was his sister and thus didn't read her tweets before deleting the account. Then he picked up the notepad sheet on which Tetsola had scribbled 'frank.whyte@gmail. com' and 'habanigeria789', his official email address and his temporary password. He logged into the brand-new mailbox and changed his password without trouble, then read his first email, a welcome from Gmail. He was busy with customising the look of the mailbox when he heard from down the hallway the approach of feet, and sure enough, the footsteps stopped at his door. 'Come in,' he said in response to four loud knocks, made with a fist.

He recognised the shoes first. The pointed toes, the age-softened oxblood leather, the carelessly knotted laces. Then the face with its prominent cheekbones and that stuck fruit of an Adam's apple. It was the man he had met on the day of his interview, the one who spat as he spoke, whose brother was married to a white woman in Romania. Or was it Poland?

'*You!*' they burst out together, their gazes meeting across the room. The man broke the look as he turned to close the door, and then, covering the distance to the desk with quick strides, he said with a grin, 'Didn't I say you would get the job! So you are my new oga?'

'You work here?'

'Yes now, I'm the driver. MD has told me I will be driving you from today.'

And all this time he had assumed that the man was a job seeker whose interview with Obata hadn't gone well. Now it made sense, the help the man had offered that day. It was also apparent that Obata was a pain not only to him.

He said to the man, 'So you're my driver?'

'Yes o,' the man replied. 'See how life is.'

'What's your name?'

'Victor Ikhide. But all my friends are calling me Headstrong.'

'I won't even ask why they call you that,' Furo said with a snort of amusement. 'Ehen, before I forget, now that you're here—' He rose from his seat, crossed to the window, and pried open the blind. 'Come and see. I want to ask you something.' When Headstrong joined him, he tapped the glass in the direction of the parked cars. 'Which of those cars is mine?' he asked, and Headstrong replied, 'It's the First Lady.'

The First Lady was a 1989 Toyota Corolla, this one ash-coloured, sagging with age and bruised around the edges, the roof hatch puttied shut. The model, which was popular in the late nineties, was considered a woman's car, hence the nickname given it by Nigerian mechanics. Of all the cars in the compound, the First Lady was the one Furo least wanted – and now, for the first time, he thought that perhaps Syreeta was right. He deserved better.

Headstrong sensed the disappointment in Furo's silence, but he misinterpreted it in the best light. 'Don't worry,' he said. 'It's a strong car, it won't break down. I'm the one that is servicing all the company cars. The engine of that one is still good. Where do you live?'

'Lekki,' Furo muttered, 'behind The Palms.'

'Ah, I see! No wonder MD assigned me to be driving you. I live near that side, in Osapa London. It's a long drive to Lekki, I won't lie, but the car can handle it. Cool your mind, oyibo!'

Furo turned away from the window. 'I have to get back to work. I guess I'll see you at five.' He walked to his desk but remained standing until Headstrong had opened the door, and then he called out, 'One more thing. My name is Frank. Don't call me oyibo.'

'Yes o, Oga Frank,' Headstrong said, and laughed as he slammed the door.

The rest of the morning passed in a loop of the new familiar. Knocks on his door, getting-to-know-you chats with Mallam Ahmed (the gatekeeper-cum-storekeeper-qua-handyman) and Iquo (who gushed about his office and special status for so long it became obvious they would never be friendly), and a quick visit from the taciturn Obata, who brought along a camera to take a photo for filing purposes; then the hours he spent alone, pacing the square of the room and staring out the window, through which he witnessed the arrival of the Haba! delivery van, this followed by another knock on the door and the entry of the second driver, Kayode. He was a socks-and-necktie man, a softer-spoken fellow than Headstrong; and no, he had no nickname, he said with a surprised look when Furo enquired. After Kayode left, Furo returned to his desk, where the only work waiting was the task he had set himself to, of browsing the internet in search of book-marketing tips from online experts whose free advice seemed one way or the other to involve the Amazon website. He was still on his laptop at sometime past midday when Tosin knocked on his door and invited him to lunch, but he declined, he wasn't hungry, he thanked her for asking, and when she turned to leave, he snuck a look at her narrow waist, her flared hips, her musical sway, and said to himself what a great place Haba! was, such beautiful people, so warm, so welcoming. He looked forward to knowing Tosin better.

Shortly before five Arinze stuck his head into the doorway and asked Furo if he had met his driver, if he had seen his car, and then told him that the car was Haba! property and should be treated as such, that after work it should be parked at Furo's house, never at the driver's. 'Victor can't be trusted,' Arinze said. 'Give him an inch and he'll use your car as a taxi.' Advancing into the office, he handed the car key to Furo and told him to always make sure to collect it from the driver after he was dropped off. And finally he asked, 'Are you happy with things so far?'

'I am,' Furo replied.

'Perfect,' Arinze said. 'I have a client for you. Let's meet in the morning, at nine, my office.' A pause, a nibbling of the bottom lip, and then: 'Have a good day, Mr Whyte.'

Furo departed his office at five sharp to find Headstrong perched on the bonnet of the First Lady, and after handing over the car key he slipped into the front seat, then slammed his door in echo of the gale force with which Headstrong had closed his. While Headstrong poked at the ignition, Furo noted that the car had neither radio nor air conditioning; but the engine started without any trouble. Headstrong swung out of the car park and sped forwards over the bumpy ground, as rough a driver as expected. Again, as Furo feared, Headstrong began to talk as soon as they hit the road. In a podium voice, with frequent glances away from traffic, he went on about this and that but all related to his goal to travel overseas, anywhere was good so long as it wasn't Africa, though South Africa wasn't bad, there were white people there, and didn't Furo think that black people were their own worst enemy, if not, then how come suffering followed the black man like flies follow shit; but Furo should know, he lived in Nigeria, he could see for himself – and how come he had a Nigerian accent, how long had he lived in this rubbish country?

'All my life,' Furo answered in a voice sunk low by fatigue.

That was what it felt like to him, that all his life would be spent listening to the prattle of a man he must ride with five days a week, in traffic and in a car that lacked even the comfort of a radio. On entering the car, he had shunned the back seat, the owner's corner. Sitting in front had seemed the right thing to do, as much for the view as for the sake of the driver's feelings, but that decision now proved a blunder. Seeing the superabundance of saliva that Headstrong secreted, clearly in his case for lubrication, he was genetically equipped to talk for ever. These churlish thoughts of Furo's were presently interrupted by a loaded silence, into which he ventured:

'What did you say?'

'But how come?' Headstrong repeated.

'How come what?'

In a tone of exasperated emphasis, Headstrong said, 'How come you've lived in Nigeria all your life? Why haven't you left?'

'Because I like it here,' Furo said.

And yet, and yet, even through all the painful years? The migration stories were always there, floating around like redemption songs in the rundown auditoriums and overflowing hostels of his university. He knew countless people who had chosen that path. Professors, students, even a girl in

187

second-year zoology whom he had fancied from afar. Some had left from university and the others had gone in droves in the years after graduation, westward-bound through air and over water and across the Sahara sands. And yet, and yet, he had never been tempted, never thought of migrating, of seeking asylum in the sunless paradises of the world. Not then, not now, not yet. He knew why he remained, but Headstrong would never believe him, especially if he told him everything that he couldn't. Some are born to love a mother who devours her young, a nation that destroys her own, but not Furo. He had never loved enough to be disheartened.

Headstrong regained his voice. 'Either you're joking or you're mad!' he burst out. His tone was shrill, and he kept looking away from the road as he addressed Furo, he kept showering spit in his direction. 'Nobody can tell me that they like living in Nigeria. Except that person doesn't have any sense at all, at all. Even if you have all the money in the world – you see that pothole, you see what I mean, where are the good roads? You don't know what you're saying! OK, let me ask you this one, what about light? You like NEPA, abi? Is it because you have money to buy generator? So what about petrol? Tell me now, how can you run your generator when fuel scarcity is everywhere? And what of armed robbers? What of kidnappers? Ah, OK, what of Boko Haram? You like them too? Police, nko? Apart from standing on road to be collecting money from innocent people, what work are those ones doing? Or even . . .'

On he went, his voice flailing at Furo.

Furo's position was now unbearable. His skin crawled from drying spit, his buttocks ached with renewed malice, and a deep flush was burning across his face. Other commuters were staring into the car, as startled as he was by the spectacle of the oyibo being screamed at by his driver. He had to do something to regain control, to restrain Headstrong's belligerence. No longer would he stand for the micro aggressions and blatant rudenesses he had gotten from Headstrong ever since the first day they met. He was the boss here – he wasn't mates with this ordinary driver. Even Arinze wouldn't talk to him this way. Neither would Syreeta, the only person he owed anything to. Headstrong was out of bounds and needed putting in his place.

'Shut up!' Furo yelled at the top of his voice. In the stunned silence, he took several deep breaths before saying in a threatening tone, 'Look here, Mr Ikhide, I've had enough. What gives you the right to speak to me that way? You're my driver, just stick to your job. In fact, another word out of you and I will report this matter to the MD!'

'I'm sorry,' Headstrong murmured without looking over. His balled hands tightened their grip on the steering wheel as he added: 'Please don't tell MD.'

'You talk too much, it has to stop,' Furo said, stern-voiced. There was more he wanted to say, especially about the spitting, but already he was growing weary of playing boss, and so he finished in a softened tone, 'I'll forgive you this time, but watch yourself.'

By the time the car arrived at Oniru Estate Furo was wondering if perhaps he had been too harsh. Since the telling-off, Headstrong had remained silent and fixed his attention on the world in front of the windscreen, and Furo now regretted the loss of ease between them. But he resolved that the quiet was worth the tension, and after Headstrong, following his instructions, parked the First Lady behind Syreeta's Honda, then got down, locked the doors, and handed over the key, all of this done in silence, Furo claimed the final word: 'Report here tomorrow morning by six o'clock. You have my number, call me when you arrive.'

Furo planned that night to inform Syreeta of his name change and then borrow money from her to make another passport, but he was exhausted from his first day of work; and, also, they had so much to discuss already – his first-ever office, his disappointing car, his early impressions of his colleagues, his very own laptop which needed a carrying bag, his masterful handling of the driver's impertinence; and not forgetting his wish to stay on longer in her apartment, a question to which she responded yes with reassuring promptness – that in the end he decided there was no hurry, it could wait, he didn't need the passport anyway until September; and, again, in spite of his fatigue, he would rather make love to her than explain why he'd adopted a new name; and so, perhaps because she had missed him all day, but certainly, on his part, because his confidence was raging from his improved circumstances, Furo and Syreeta fucked relentlessly that night.

At the nine o'clock meeting on Tuesday morning, Arinze gave Furo a crash course in sales. Lesson over, he handed Furo his company ID card, a pack of business cards, and a bundle of branded bookmarks that Furo was to present to clients as gifts. The business cards – a simple design of green text on a white background, with 'Haba! Nigeria Ltd' stamped on the flip side – bore Furo's mobile number underneath 'Frank Whyte' and his email address underneath 'Marketing Executive'. Seen in print, his name felt the more his and his title gave him purpose. His plastic ID card displayed a colour photo of an unsmiling man with a buzz of carroty hair and eyes the colour of sun-warmed seawater. It was a face that startled Furo less and less.

After the meeting ended, Furo returned to his office and summoned Headstrong to lug down the carton of sample books that Arinze had selected. To aid Furo in his sales pitch, Arinze had printed out a memo whose first three sheets had the books' descriptions, snippets of promotional reviews, their list prices and discount ratios. On the penultimate sheet were details about the client company and its owner, Mr Ernest Umukoro; while the last sheet contained some FAQs about Haba! as well as Arinze's answers, which were in red. Armed with this information, Furo set off for Gbagada, where the company was located. The company name was TASERS, Total Advertising Services. It employed forty-six people, the memo said.

On the drive down, Furo sat in the back seat with the carton of books beside him, and as the silent Headstrong steered the car with steady hands and a ramrod neck, Furo looked through the books. There were twelve titles, two copies of each, twenty-four books in all. He found some titles he had heard of before, even seen vendors flogging in traffic. One such was *Execution: The Discipline of Getting Things Done*. Another was *The 7 Habits of Highly Effective People*. Furo knew *The 7 Habits* well, his father owned a copy whose tattered cover used to be a constant sight around the house, and over the years as Furo searched for a job he had picked it up many times with the intention to read but hadn't ever gotten around to achieving this. Apart from the pain in his neck, his scepticism was blameworthy for his inability to dig into that marker-highlighted bible of his father's. His highly ineffective, chicken-farming father. A man as blind to his ironies as those book vendors who sweated while wearing

T-shirts emblazoned with the slogan *My money grows like grass*. At least the vendors were disciplined in their execution, they got things done. More to the point, they weren't sold on the books they were selling.

Returning *The 7 Habits* to the carton, Furo resolved again to read it – if only the pain in his neck would allow him. At this thought, he jolted forwards in his seat, raised his left hand to rub his neck, swung his head side to side and worked his jaws, then clamped his mouth shut and composed his face as Headstrong cast a startled look in the rear-view mirror.

The pain in his neck was gone.

TASERS was on the top floor of an eight-storey building whose elevator didn't light up when Furo jabbed the buttons. In a far corner of the lobby the uniformed porter was playing a game of draughts with a rifle-bearing police officer, and when Headstrong, at Furo's command, walked over to the porter to ask if the elevator was ever coming, the man raised a hand and pointed out the staircase without looking up from the draughtboard. Furo crossed to the unlit stairwell, waited some seconds for his vision to adjust to the shock of darkness, and then, as the sound of Headstrong's footsteps approached behind him, he set off at a sprint. But five floors up he ran out of breath, staggered huffing on to the landing, then hunched over to find his wind. He was in that position when Headstrong arrived with the carton of books balanced on his head and his mobile phone held out before him, its screen lighting his path. He continued on with his light and load, the echo of his foot-steps fading above Furo's head. Furo waited for the sweat on his face to dry before he resumed his ascent, and as his heavy feet delivered him on to the last-but-one floor, Headstrong jogged past on his way down.

At the stairhead, the door marked TASERS was ajar. Through the gap Furo sighted the carton of books on the reception counter. The flaps hung open. Standing close by was a woman whose sleek black hairpiece was styled like a geisha's hairdo. She was holding one of the books, flipping through it, but as Furo pushed past the door, her hand stilled in the splayed pages, and she turned around. Furo halted, said good morning, and after the woman returned his greeting, he said: 'I'm here to see Mr Umukoro. I'm from Haba! Nigeria Limited. My name is Frank Whyte.'

The woman cocked her head and asked, 'What of Mr Arinze?' she asked.

'He sent me,' Furo replied. 'I'm the new marketing executive.'

The woman's face cleared. 'Marketing executive,' she said, drawling the words and nodding slowly. 'It seems Haba! is moving up.' She extended her hand to the open carton, placed the book in it, and after closing the flaps, she said in a tone that strove to be casual, 'Your boss usually comes himself. You know he has been trying to sell us books since last year?' At Furo's silence, she gave a small smile and said, 'I'll tell oga you're around.' She strode to a glass-panelled door, buzzed it open and stepped into a long passage, and some time later, through the closed door, Furo heard another door open. He turned away from the door and swept a glance around the reception area, but his mind was elsewhere. In light of the information he'd just got from the woman, that Arinze himself had been to TASERS to sell books – a detail he neglected to mention during their meeting – Furo realised he needed a fresh strategy.

What had Arinze told him this morning? *Know your strategy beforehand.* Because of what he now knew, what he'd just learned, that was a fail. *Convince the client that what you're selling is what he needs.* But Arinze, over several visits, hadn't succeeded in that. *Once you get the client talking, the sale is halfway made.* That was it. Furo could feel the seismic tremors of an idea taking shape in his mind, and decided to plant his trust in the impromptu. He would forego any introductions other than a greeting and the handing over of his business card, following which he would spread out the sample books and then ask the client which of the titles he had read. With this new strategy, Furo thought he stood a chance of getting the client talking; and when the door swung open, after the woman announced that oga was ready to see him, he reached for the carton of books, but she said no, leave it, I insist, I'll have someone bring it in. Without his conversation starter his plan was a non-starter. And so he told the woman not to bother, but she marched forwards and nudged his hand away from the carton, shook her head at his protestations, and said in a firm voice as she guided him by the elbow towards the door: 'There's no way I'm letting you carry that heavy load.'

Furo was ushered into an office whose every surface seemed laden with plaques and trophies, the walls covered with framed certificates and photographs of staff receiving framed certificates. Daylight filtered through the blue window screens and gave the room the atmosphere of a stained-glass chapel. The air was thick with the smell of dusty rug. 'Take a seat,' the woman whispered before withdrawing. An enormous man in white shirtsleeves, a red bow tie, and yellow-polka-dot braces was hunkered down behind the desk facing the door. When Furo halted at the desk, the man glanced up from his iMac screen and nodded at him to sit before returning his gaze to the playing video, which sounded like a sports car advert, a husky male voice waxing beatific about curves and balance. After the video reached its end, the man turned his cold eyes on Furo and said, 'So Abu sent you.' Furo recognised his voice from the video.

'Yes – yes – good morning – sir,' Furo replied with a stammer. He drew a calming breath, and reaching into his breast pocket, he pulled out a business card, then stood up from the chair and leaned over the desk with the card extended. But Umukoro refused the card with a sharp shake of his head, and then gestured at him to sit back down. 'I know why you're here,' he said. 'Start talking.'

Furo's thoughts scattered in all directions. His improvised strategy was based on the sample books. He had nothing to say until the carton was brought in. As he tried to collect his thoughts, he began recalling all the things he should have done. He should have been less eager to avoid the hostility that brimmed in Headstrong's manner. He should have come up the stairs with him. He should have stopped him from going back downstairs. He should have ignored that bad-luck receptionist. He should have phoned Headstrong to come up again and do the carrying. He should have insisted on carrying the carton himself. Or at least picked out some books – he should have thought of that before. And now this fatty bum-bum was waiting for him to sell books he should already have read, books he knew nothing about except – the memo sheets!

He shouldn't have forgotten them in the car.

Umukoro's voice stabbed the air. 'How long have you worked for Abu?' In a feeble tone, Furo responded, 'I started yesterday,' and Umukoro's lips closed in a smile that turned his face sinister. At that instant Furo knew he had squandered any chance of succeeding where Arinze failed. Thus his surprise when Umukoro said, 'I want to discuss something else, but first, let me tell you, Abu has come here many times to sell his books. The last time he came, I told him I would buy some books the next time he dropped by. But you're not Abu.'

Sitting up to the pull of his ears, Furo spoke earnestly, 'I'm his representative, sir.' Whatever else he would have said was forsaken when three soft knocks sounded on the door, which then swung open to reveal the receptionist. She stepped inside and held the door open for the porter who had been playing draughts in the lobby. He shambled in bearing the carton and set it down by Furo's chair. After the door closed behind them, Furo tried again. 'Let me show you the books I brought. I'm sure you'll like them. Mr Arinze selected them himself.' He bent over the carton and took out four books, two in each hand, then spread them on the table. Bending down again, he reached for *The 7 Habits*. 'This book changed my life,' he said with an abashed grin as he straightened up. 'I don't know if you've read it yet—'

'Save your breath,' Umukoro said brusquely.

Furo's disappointment showed on his face. And yet, as he tossed *The 7 Habits* into the carton, he wondered what Umukoro wanted to talk about.

'You know my business is advertising.' Umukoro stared at Furo until Furo kenned he was awaiting acknowledgement. 'I work mostly with multinationals,' he continued after Furo nodded, 'and most of their local branches are headed by foreigners. You white men like to do business with your kind.' He dropped his gaze to the books on the table and a spasm of distaste curdled his face. 'How much is Abu paying you? A hundred thousand per month? One fifty? I'll double that. And I guarantee you'll learn more about marketing than a bookseller can teach.' He smiled his sinister face again. 'Are you interested?'

'Excuse me?' Furo said.

'I want you to work for me.'

Furo's first instinct was to refuse. He was tempted by the money on offer – with three hundred thousand naira he could do anything, go anywhere, be anybody – and yet he knew he couldn't bear to work under Umukoro's weight. The man looked like a butcher and sounded like a moneylender. He gave off an aura of heartfelt arrogance and easygoing nastiness. Moreover, he wasn't the sort that Furo could ever call Ernest. After one day of working at Haba!, Furo already felt needed there; and he trusted Arinze's intentions. Across the desk, in those unblinking eyes that were narrowed by their fleshy pouches, in that huge belly of a man who had swallowed his ego, Furo sensed that Umukoro saw him as no more essential than cake icing. He wanted but didn't need him, and if ever he felt the need, he would throw him over with the same ease that he now offered to take him up. Syreeta was right, he deserved better. But this wasn't it.

Furo spoke. 'Thank you for the offer. Let me think about it. I'll get back to you.'

'No you won't,' Umukoro said. By the steady creaking of his chair and the quivering of his papal dewlaps, Furo guessed Umukoro was swinging his knees. The creaking stopped, his face froze over with indifference, and raising his hands to his computer keypad, he started typing as he said to Furo: 'You've wasted enough of my time. Show yourself out.'

Furo arrived in the reception to find the receptionist engaged in a conversation with a man and a woman, both fashionably dressed, the man wearing a double-breasted suit of blue worsted, the woman a pearl-grey silk blouse and a pleated wool skirt. The ease of their postures, the relaxed cadences of their voices, marked them out as employees.

Their voices dropped off as Furo approached the counter, and when he set down the carton to catch his breath, the woman asked the receptionist, 'Are these the books?' The receptionist said yes, after which the woman threw Furo a sideways glance before asking, 'Can I see them?' Without a word, Furo peeled open the flaps and stepped away from the carton. The woman reached in and pulled out *1001 Ways to Take Initiative at Work*. 'I haven't read this one,' she said to Furo. 'Is it any good?'

'Yes,' Furo replied, and edging forwards, he stuck his hand into the carton and took out *The 7 Habits*. 'I also recommend this one,' he said, and held it out.

'Isn't that Stephen Covey?' said the woman as she accepted the book. 'I read it a long time ago. I've read most of his books.' Her words drew the attention of her male colleague, who came up behind her and peeked over her shoulder. She passed the Covey to him, and then waved the *1001 Ways* at Furo. 'How much is this?'

The question caught Furo unawares. His self-esteem was scalded from his futile meeting with Umukoro, and though he'd been willing to play along with the woman's interest, he hadn't expected the game to end in serious talk. At the mention of money, he now felt the oil slick of misgiving as he realised that the book prices were on the memo sheets in the car. He'd seen the prices, and had even checked to confirm that they were given for all twelve titles, but he hadn't memorised the figures, hadn't thought he needed to. His newness on the job was showing up in too many ways, and his frustration at this proof of his ordinariness, his annoyance with himself for committing the same apprenticeship errors as anyone, nagged at his faith in his innate ability to think himself out of a straitjacket. While he struggled to keep his face from betraying his confusion (over the price) and dejection (from his identity crisis) to the woman awaiting her answer, his mind, that Houdini, rose to the rescue, as he remembered that he had seen the price of *The 7 Habits* scrawled in pencil in the top right corner of the title page. He was sure he had, he knew he had, it looked like a price, and he hoped the same had been done for all the books, as he couldn't risk losing this opening by going downstairs for the memo sheets. And so he said to the woman with a confidence he didn't feel, 'The price is on the first page.' She opened the book, stared at the page for suspenseful seconds, and when she said, 'One five, that's not too bad,' Furo beamed a super-ego smile before proclaiming:

'That's the cheapest you can find it anywhere in Lagos.'

He had no reason to doubt this claim. And what did it matter if it was bogus, he was doing his job. He was sure there was some jargon from Arinze to apply as appropriate, but he was too busy in the trenches to remember principles. Besides, he had caught the woman stealing glances at him. Lie or no lie, the sale was looking like his to make. When Furo spoke again, his tone was soft with coaxing. 'I'm sure your decision won't be influenced by price,' he said to the woman, and flicked his eyes over the front of her blouse. 'From your sense of style, anyone can see that you recognise quality.'

The woman took the *1001 Ways* as well as four other books, and while she was away in her office fetching the money, Furo convinced her male colleague to buy *The 7 Habits* and talked the receptionist into placing orders for two books to be delivered at the month's end. The other woman returned with cash and three colleagues, all female, and after Furo asked the new women for their names, before he distracted them with the play of his eyes as he spun his salesman yarn, he told Yemisi and Felicia and Enoch – the woman and the receptionist and the man – to spread the word of his presence to the rest of the TASERS staff, all forty-something of them. For that was his bright idea, his face-saving stratagem: to sell off the sample books and collect individual orders. To show everyone and their mother that his long years of unemployment had been a wrongful imprisonment, that he goddamn well deserved his freedom at Haba!, and that Arinze, in granting him parole to prove himself, had indeed made the right judgement.

Through the open French windows, sunlight breezed into Arinze's office and threw wavering shadows across the glass desk, rainbow-coloured patterns that drew Furo's eyes as he narrated all that had happened on his visit to TASERS. Arinze listened without speaking until the end of the report, at which point he stated in commendation: 'That was quick thinking.' After accepting the sales cash and receipt duplicates from Furo, he instructed him to hand over the pending orders to Zainab, the head of sales, for follow up. Replying he would do so immediately, Furo rose from the desk and walked to the door, then turned around when Arinze said in a brooding tone, 'So Ernest tried to poach you?' Furo stood silent as he had nothing more to say on that topic, which seemed to be a touchy one for Arinze, who confirmed this by now saying: 'And that's supposed to be a friend. We learn every day.'

Upon entering the sales office and finding it empty, Furo deposited the pile of order forms on Zainab's desk and left her a note explaining their source, then made his exit. As he pulled the door closed, Tosin appeared at the top of the stairs.

'Hey, Frank, wait!' she called out. 'It's you I'm coming to see.' Though her stride was hurried, the relaxed swinging of her arms assured Furo there was nothing to worry about. A laptop bag dangled from her shoulder on its too-long strap and bumped against her thigh with each step she took. She was smiling as she reached him and said, 'It's lunchtime.' Then she waited, her silence loaded. Her tacit invitation reminded Furo he hadn't eaten breakfast that morning, because Syreeta was still sleeping as he prepared for work. He also remembered that it was Tuesday, Bola's day. Syreeta would be out when he got home. There would be no dinner unless he cooked it.

'Lunch sounds good,' Furo responded. Sweeping his arm in the direction of the staircase, he said, 'After you.' Instead of leading the way, Tosin unslung the laptop bag and held it to him. 'I saw you didn't have a bag to carry your laptop yesterday. I don't need this, you can use it,' she said. Furo stared at her; he made no move to accept the gift. 'If you want it,' she added in a voice that cracked under the weight of being casual, and the bag, the hand that held the bag, trembled in front of Furo. He reached out and took the bag.

'This is nice of you,' he said, his voice heavy with feeling. 'I'm really grateful.'

'It's nothing,' Tosin replied in a bright voice, and spinning around, she skipped forwards. Furo fell in step beside her, and when he glanced at her radiant face, he was struck by the sensation that he was reliving a happy memory.

They went to a fast food restaurant, Sweet Sensation, where Tosin told him about herself and he asked her about Obata; they sat alone at a window table and chatted until the jostle at the food counter was a little less hectic than it

201

had been on their arrival; she asked him how he liked Arinze and he told her very much; they rose together from the table and walked side by side to the food counter to place their orders, his for that staple of local fast food menus, jollof rice and fried chicken, hers for that precursor of farting jokes, beans and boiled eggs. It wasn't so much that she favoured beans than that she had grown tired of eating the same fare every day, rice and rice and rice, whether jollof or fried or just plain white. She told him this on Wednesday after she ordered beans again at another fast food restaurant, and when Furo asked if there was any buka around where they could eat eba and soup, she said there was. She admitted she had avoided leading him to such places because she wasn't sure if he ate such food, and she promised to take him there the following day. On Thursday Furo arrived back at the office from his sales excursions two hours later than Haba! lunch-time, and halting at the reception desk, he started to apologise to Tosin for missing their buka appointment, but she told him there was no need to, she hadn't been to lunch yet, she had waited for him. At this disclosure, Furo hurried upstairs to drop off his laptop bag and sample books, and coming back down, he found Tosin ready to go.

They were across the road from the buka before Furo recognised it as the place he had visited all that time ago, the roadside buka where he had eaten on the day of his Haba! interview. The same curtained shed where a fight had broken out between the food seller and her customer, the same food-is-ready spot where he hadn't paid for his meal. Hadn't yet paid, and hadn't paid only because the fight had given him no chance, but now, at the first chance he got, he had come back to pay – that would be his story for the meat-gifting food seller with the red hair. In actual truth, if he had known beforehand that this would be where they were headed, he might have found a reason for not coming along, but now that he was here, it was the right place to be. Holding that thought in his mind, the karmic rightness of his unintended actions, he followed Tosin across the busy road and through the dusty curtains of the buka.

The buka was vacant except for the food seller, who now had blue hair. A bright blue hairpiece with silver highlights, it was glued along her hairline, smooth as crow feathers across her scalp, the ends gathered into pigtails that rode her shoulders. Dancehall queen-coloured, Swiss milkmaid-styled. Despite the new hair, it was the same woman who jumped up from her bar stool with an exclamation of recognition. Of course she remembered him. She was very sorry for what happened the last time, no mind that idiot. No, no, no worry, forget the money, forgive the past. These sentiments were gushed out after Furo approached her with banknotes clutched in his outstretched hand and said, 'I was here some weeks back. I couldn't pay that day because of the trouble with that man, the one who insulted you. I just remembered. Here's your money.'

Tosin, too, wasn't a stranger to Mercy's buka. After her bewilderment was dispelled by Furo's explanation, she greeted the food seller by name, then complimented her on her hairpiece, and asked after Patience, her eldest daughter, who sometimes assisted her mother in manning the establishment, but did so less these days as she had entered university, a fact her mother offered in a tone so full of pride that Furo even smiled. Pleasantries dispensed with, Tosin asked for oha soup with pounded yam, a meal which Furo, upon her recommendation, joined her in ordering, to Mercy's expressed delight. And then, while the food seller busied herself in dishing out the food, Tosin leaned across the bench towards Furo, closer than they had been in three days of lunching together, near enough for her woman smell to tickle the hairs in his nostrils, and placing her hand on his knee, she said in a voice husky with admiration: 'You're so real. I like that. I like you.'

'I like you too,' Furo said.

On Friday morning, as Headstrong banged his fist against the car horn, Furo looked up from the book he was reading – *The Five Dysfunctions of a Team* – and stared out the windscreen at the closed gate. He saw at once what it was that angered Headstrong. The maiguard, Mallam Ahmed, was standing beside the gatehouse with his back turned to the gate. He was engaged in heated discussion with Obata and another man who sat in a battered wheelchair. The stranger wore a candy-green muscle shirt and the empty legs of his tracksuit trousers were knotted at the ends. His Popeye arms waved above his head in rage.

'I'll get the gate,' Furo said to Headstrong, and alighted from the car, walked to the gate, and shouldered it open. After the car gunned through, he headed for the quarrelling men. He halted beside Obata, who fell silent and shot him a scowling look, then swung back his face and resumed his stream of insults.

Arinze, it turned out, was the ghost in the gathering. Though his name didn't once pass Obata's lips, Furo soon realised that Arinze was the person Obata was most angry at, the one he blamed for what had happened. Mallam Ahmed, out of deference for Arinze, only alluded to him in the most roundabout ways, but at no point in his stumbling defence of his own involvement did he fault Arinze for what had happened. The man missing his legs – the maiguard called him Solo – was the only one who said Arinze's name aloud. And so Furo put his question to Solo.

'Wetin happen?'

All three men raised astonished faces. It was Solo who voiced what they were thinking. 'You sabe pidgin?' he asked in a tone of disbelief, and at Furo's nod, he grasped his wheels and rocked the chair forwards. He began to speak, his voice subdued at first, but it rose in passion as Furo responded, and then surged higher as Obata tried several times to interrupt. By the time he wove his story to an end, his wheelchair was rattling from the force of his emotion.

'But why this oga go come dey threaten my life with police?' These final words ejected from a mouth that remained open in a rictus of righteousness, Solo flung out his muscled arms and glared upwards at Obata, who saw a chance to get a word in.

'You're a liar!' he yelled and shook a finger at Solo. 'Just imagine, you tout, you handicapped criminal, telling me that cock-and-bull story! You're a bloody idiot!'

'See me see wahala,' Solo said and swung his frantic gaze to Furo's face. 'Oga oyibo, I think you see as this man dey curse me?'

'Only curse?' Obata retched up a laugh. 'I haven't started with you. If you don't produce your gang today,' and here he sucked in air through his teeth, 'you'll see what I will do!'

'So what will you do?'

Obata whirled to face Furo. 'What?'

Furo maintained a civil tone. 'Insulting this man is not getting us anywhere. You say he knows where the others are. Fair enough. So what's your next step?'

'And how is that your business – Furo Wariboko?'

Furo felt his ears grow hot. His chest burned with loathing. He opened his mouth to release the steam building in him, then closed it as he realised the risk that arose from squabbling over that name. He wouldn't let Obata trigger him into ceding control. He had everything to hide and nothing to prove, so Obata was rigged to win that shouting match. Right from their first encounter, Obata hadn't bothered to hide his hostility towards him, and though he was prepared to resist all salvos from that quarter, he couldn't restrain his vexation at the steady sniping he had endured from Obata all week long. The suspicious glances Obata gave him in passing; the snide remarks Obata uttered within his earshot about the treacherousness of oyibo people; the refusal of Obata to speak his name in his presence; and now, in a marked escalation of their secret war, the broadcasting of that name that had the power to demolish everything that was Frank Whyte. Furo was maddened by Obata's sneak attack, but he wasn't mad enough to respond with shock and awe. When he spoke, his voice was cold as iron.

'Abu gave you clear instructions about my name. Please follow them.' He paused, marshalling his thoughts. 'The language I've heard you use with these men is inexcusable for someone in your position, and in fact, your attitude regarding this matter is unprofessional.' In the charged silence, Furo shook his head at Obata. 'I'm an executive of this company. It is within my right to tell you when your actions reflect badly on us. You can't go around insulting people. Do that in your house if you must, but not at Haba!'

'Tell am o!' Solo exclaimed. Even Mallam Ahmed appeared to have picked a side: he turned his face aside to hide the smirk ghosting across his po-faced demeanour.

For an instant Furo assumed his words had caused an

effect opposite to what he wanted, but Obata was more dependable than sweating dynamite. His eyes got redder and rounder as his outrage grew; his throat worked silently as if from bitterness; and then his stillness shattered. His yells flew at Furo like bursting shrapnel.

'See this man o – you shameless impostor! What do you know about Haba!? You just joined only which day and already you're growing wings. I don't blame you sha. It's oga I blame for employing a common fraudster.'

Furo's smile was a poster image of cordiality. 'Are you done?' he asked Obata.

'So you find me funny?'

'Just tell me when you're finished.'

Obata raised his arm and jabbed Furo in the chest with a stiffened finger. 'Idiot oyibo, I've just started with you! By the time I'm finished you won't have a job.'

'Thank you,' Furo said. He turned to Mallam Ahmed. 'Go and call the MD. Tell him I said he should come now-now.'

'Yowa,' said Mallam Ahmed and headed off, his rubber slippers slapping the ground.

Obata was stunned into silence. He licked his lips to wet them. He cast up his arms and let them drop to his sides. He exhaled in loud spurts. Swinging his gaze between Furo and the departing man, he reached a decision. His voice sounded trapped when he called out, 'Ahmed, wait first.' Mallam Ahmed marched on, and when Obata spoke again, a note of panic sounded in his throat. 'Ahmed, can't you hear me? You're under my department, you take instructions from me. I'm giving you a direct order. Stop there!'

Mallam Ahmed halted, turned around, and retraced his steps. Throwing a regretful glance at Furo's feet, he said, 'Nah true e talk. I no fit disobey order.'

'No problem,' Furo said brusquely. He looked at Solo. 'Wait here for me.'

'Frank,' said Obata.

'No go anywhere,' Furo continued as Solo nodded assent.

'Frank, listen to me,' Obata said with urgency, and placed a gentle hand on Furo's arm.

'I dey come,' Furo finished, and as he made to move forwards, Obata's grip tightened on his flesh. 'Get your hand off me!' Furo snapped at him.

'Please, just listen to me,' Obata said and dropped his hand. 'I was out of line.'

'That's not good enough,' Furo said. But he waited.

Obata coughed to clear his throat. 'I lost my temper. That's not an excuse. It won't happen again.' And then he muttered, 'I'm sorry.'

Furo raised his gaze to meet Obata's hate-moistened eyes. 'I'll be frank with you,' he said. 'I'm still unhappy about the way you treated me the other day, on the day of my interview. But I won't take your insults any more. The way you spoke to me today is totally unacceptable.' At Furo's stern tone Obata's eyes had fallen, and so Furo now finished in a softer voice. 'I won't report you this time, but the next time you insult me, or refer to me by that name, I will tell Abu that either you leave this company or I do. I hope we're clear?'

Obata nodded before saying in a gruff, unsteady voice, 'We're clear. I wash my hands. You can deal with this,' and he waved his arm at Solo. 'It's your department anyway.' He spun around and walked with long, quick steps towards the office building. Furo looked away from the retreating form when Solo said with a low chuckle, 'Power pass power. See as that one been dey shine eye for me. Now whitey don tell am word, e no fit talk again. Oyibo, you be correct guy.'

'My name nah Frank, no call me oyibo,' Furo said in a curt voice. After again asking Solo to wait, he stepped away. As he approached the parked First Lady, Headstrong, who had been watching all this time from his perch on the car's bonnet, stared at him in a manner that seemed to grow less unfriendly with closing distance, until his gaze dropped when Furo reached him, and he held out the car key in silence, then pushed off the car and trod in the direction of the gatehouse. Furo locked up the car after collecting his laptop bag and the dog-eared copy of *The Five Dysfunctions*. He strode into the office building, glanced at the unoccupied reception desk, then sprinted upstairs and headed for Arinze's office. He tapped once before opening the door to find Arinze talking to Tosin; but, as he made to withdraw, Arinze said, 'No, Frank, we're done here, come on in. I have some exciting news. Have you just arrived? I've been looking for you.'

'I was downstairs,' Furo responded. He smiled at Tosin as they passed each other, and then took the seat she had vacated. 'I just met Solo.'

Arinze looked perplexed. 'Who is Solo?'

'He's one of the special vendors.'

Delight deposed confusion in Arinze's features. 'Where is he? Is he still around?'

'He's waiting downstairs.'

'Perfect! I'll see him after our meeting,' Arinze said. He hunched forwards and began rolling a pen along the desktop, and after he grew tired of this dissemblance, he settled back in his seat and spoke in an eager voice. 'You've heard about my little project – the special vendors?'

At Furo's yes, he pressed on: 'So, what do you think?'

'It's a brilliant idea,' Furo said.

And he meant it.

Going by what Furo had gathered from Solo's story: exactly a week ago, Arinze had sent Mallam Ahmed to the National Stadium in Surulere to scout for unemployed, wheelchair-bound men who were willing to earn some money by selling books, and after Mallam Ahmed returned with Solo and three others, Arinze met with them and determined he would try them out with ten titles each, after which, based on their success at selling the books, he was ready to hire them on commission and also brand their wheelchairs with promotional stickers and then arrange for the delivery van drop them off every morning at the busiest spots in Lagos. *Haba! Special Vendors,* Solo said he had called them.

Arinze spoke. 'I'm really glad you like the idea. It wasn't easy convincing Zainab to support me on this one, and as for Obata, he was dead set against the project. But I mean, just imagine the potential! The branding benefits, of course, not the money. We'll never make money selling books to individuals, not in this country.' He paused, wrinkling his brow. 'You say there's only one of the special vendors downstairs? That's strange. I hope he brought good news. I gave them some books last Friday, and they were supposed to report back on Tuesday, but we didn't hear from them. And now only one shows up?' He pushed back his chair and stood up. 'Tell you what, Frank. I'm sorry, but can we postpone our meeting to eleven? I have to see this man now.'

'Eleven's fine,' Furo stated, and rising with a rush of pity, he trailed Arinze to the door, walked behind him down the hallway, and stopped at his office as Arinze continued towards the stairs. He couldn't bring himself to tell him what had happened. That early this morning, before the start of work, Obata had dispatched Mallam Ahmed to the National

210

Stadium to search for the missing men among the sunrise crowd of sportspeople and fitness freaks. For nearly two hours, everybody the maiguard questioned had denied knowledge of the men's existence, and when Mallam Ahmed finally found Solo – in a huddle of wheelchairs under the shade of a fake almond tree, some of the men bench-pressing, others puffing spliffs – the first thing Solo said was: 'Police don seize de books o.'

Eleven sharp, Furo returned to Arinze's office to find it empty. He stopped in the doorway, wedged from front and back by his surprise at the absence – an absence which to Furo was out of character for Arinze, who was the type that always kept his word. Furo was mistaken in this instance, as he discovered when a disembodied voice floated in through the French windows, making him flinch in shock. 'I'm over here.' It was Arinze.

Furo stepped out through the French windows. It was his first time on the balcony, his first sighting of the backyard scenery, and his umpteenth experience of the particular disorder that attended everyman solutions to everyone's problems. As he took in the skyline, his gaze was captured by the battalions of plastic tanks mounted on towers of rusted rigging, each tank a sole source of water in the compound where it was stationed. And the rears of the fortressed houses, their concrete fences crowned by glass shards and metal spikes and razor wire. Also vying for attention was the sound and the smoky fury of countless generators. The nerve-grinding roar of individual power generation was as much a consequence of every-man-for-himself government as the lynch mobs that meted out injustice in public spaces. Private provision of public services had turned everyone into judge and executioner and turned everyone's backyards into industrial wastelands. Every man the king of his house, every house a sovereign nation, and every nation its own provider of security, electricity, water. Lagos was a city of millions of warring nations.

In the far corner of the balcony, Arinze was stooped over the railing with his forearms dangling out. When Furo drew close to him, he spoke without looking up, like he was resuming an old conversation. 'The most painful thing is the constant disappointment. Everything in this country prepares us for that feeling. One disappointment after another . . .' His voice trailed off, and Furo grunted to show he was listening, and then snuck a glance at him. Bitterness showed in the squeeze of Arinze's lips, but his voice was untouched when he spoke again. 'I've scrapped the special vendors. It was a failure. I should have known better.' He bit his bottom lip, then straightened up from the railing and turned to Furo. 'Let's get to work.'

Once inside, they took their seats at the desk, and Arinze read through sales data on his computer screen before declaring satisfaction with Furo's performance. Furo had visited seven companies in four days, sold ninety-one books, and brought in orders for about three hundred. 'Not bad for your first week,' Arinze said in a tone of approval; but the next instant, in a voice veered on the businesslike, he instructed Furo that he was only to go out for marketing assignments on Monday of the following week, because on Wednesday they would be travelling to Abuja for a crucial meeting, and it was essential that Furo prepare for it.

'Who are we meeting?' Furo asked.

'Alhaji Jubril Yuguda.' Arinze must have seen recognition in Furo's face, because he nodded once and then said in a voice as soft as a prayer: 'The big man himself.' Giving up all pretence of concealing his exhilaration, he leaned forwards on the glass surface of the desk, his presence looming with the parallax creep of his reflection. 'You must have heard of Yuguda's project, it's been all over the news: the lorry driver employment scheme. OK, perfect. It kicks off this month, the seventeenth. One of the project objectives is to give the drivers some business training, so that they can set up their own SMEs. That's where we come in. Yuguda wants books. Lots and lots and lots of business books.' Arinze's tone kept dropping lower as the books piled up on his tongue, until finally, under the weight of all that hope, he sank back in his chair. 'It's the big time, Frank,' he said, his anxious gaze holding Furo's. 'It can change everything for us.'

The one o'clock sun was the fiercest it had been since 19 June. It was a sweating Furo, irked by the slow progress of Iquo and Tosin as they headed back to the office from lunch at the buka, who finally found refuge in the reception's coolness from his dread of sunburn. He left the chatting ladies at the foot of the stairs, and as he walked down the hallway towards his office, he met Kayode emerging with the crash of flushing water from the lavatory. Over the past week Furo had been validated in his impression that Kayode was the opposite of Headstrong, as since their brief exchange on his first day of work the driver hadn't spoken to him again. For this reason, a niggling curiosity, Furo halted by Kayode, greeted him in a cordial tone, and said the first thing that came to mind: he asked him if he knew where Headstrong was. Kayode kept his gaze on the floor as he shook his head no, all the while maintaining his grip on the lavatory doorknob. 'If you see him, tell him to come and see me,' Furo said, and then turned towards his office with the eerie suspicion that Obata was spreading evil gossip around the office.

Furo was Googling the Yuguda Group when a knock sounded on his door. 'Headstrong,' he called out distractedly, and as the door opened to admit Tosin, he exclaimed, 'Hey beautiful!' He was rewarded with a supernova smile. Tosin flitted across to his desk, rested her hips against the edge, then cast a glance at his laptop screen and said, 'What are you up to?'

'Some research on the Yuguda Group. I'm travelling to Abuja with Abu on Wednesday. We're meeting Alhaji Yuguda.'

'I know. That's why I'm here. I was instructed to book your flights. I want to confirm what name you'll be travelling under.'

'Oh,' Furo said, and his tone supplied the missing 'no'. He had just realised he would need ID to fly, and since the only official document in his possession belonged to Furo Wariboko, he would be forced to travel under that name. That was the last thing he wanted, this pulling back to a place he had left behind. This resurrection of a self he had buried. All these questions and challenges from HR, from Obata and even Tosin. While thinking these thoughts, Furo had risen from his seat, and he tramped around the office until he saw Tosin watching him. Reaching a quick decision, he stopped in front of her and said, 'Can you give me some time? I'll let you know by Monday.'

'We have to book early,' Tosin said. She paused before adding, 'I'll wait till Monday.' And finally, in the gentlest of voices: 'I hope I'm not prying, but which name is really yours?'

Despite her stated hope, she was prying full steam ahead.

Furo was attracted to Tosin, he had admitted that already. He knew the feeling was mutual. Since they'd begun lunching together the signs of her affection had grown stronger with passing days and lengthening conversations. From the start he had shown his enjoyment of her company with light flirtation. Not today though, and not, as she might think, because of Iquo's presence, but because yesterday, while making love to Syreeta, he had imagined Tosin in her place. The guilty sting in the tail of that fantasy had stunned him back to his senses. Tosin was not Syreeta. Not Syreeta who asked no questions, not even about his buttocks; who revealed nothing about herself, not over food or in bed; and with whom it felt good to be bad.

Furo spoke, his tone cutting, 'My name is Frank Whyte.' He averted his face from the mercury surge of hurt in Tosin's eyes, and then he walked the long way round his desk. Standing beside his chair, he said, 'You'll have to excuse me, I need to get back to work,' and when the door closed behind her, he relaxed his features with a sigh, then sat down, picked up his phone, and searched through the contacts until he found the number he'd stored as *Passport Deji*. The call was answered by the voice he recognised. 'Afternoon,' Furo responded to the man's hello, and then began his introduction: 'I'm the guy—'

'I remember,' Passport Deji cut him off. 'You're the oyibo who get Nigerian name.'

'That's right,' Furo replied, and then he said he had changed his name and he needed a new passport by Tuesday at the latest. He ended with the question that was burning a hole in his pocket: 'How much will it cost me?' Passport Deji was silent a long time. 'It's not possible,' he said at last, his voice doleful at the loss of business. 'Not in Lagos. Your fingerprint have already enter immigration computer. You must go to Abuja. That nah the only place where you fit do a new passport with another name.'

After the call, Furo chuckled through a long list of paraprosdokians – phrases with unexpected endings, such as (1) Money can't buy happiness, but it sure makes misery easier to live with; (19) You're never too old to learn something stupid; and (37) If you're supposed to learn from your mistakes, why do some people have more than one child? – which were in a chain email forwarded by Tetsola, until three o'clock came and went. Afterwards he tried to make up for his misuse of office time by spending the next hour reading up on Yuguda's business, but by five o'clock he was sugar-sick from gleaning details in online tabloids. He had Monday and Tuesday to continue his research, and so he gave up for the day, and shut down his laptop, and was reaching for his bag when the door to his office flew open. The startled leap of his heart hauled him to his feet, but he regained his calm when Zainab said from the doorway, 'Thank God I caught you! Please, Frank, I have a favour to ask.' Releasing her grip on the doorjamb, she placed her hand on the bulge of her belly, and gulping air like a blowfish, she shuffled into the office on legs bowed by the weight of life. Furo hurried round his desk to meet her halfway. This was the first time she had entered his office, and because of the straight cut of her satiny jellaba, it was also the first time he had noticed how advanced her pregnancy was.

'Do you want to sit?' he asked as he took her elbow. In response she shook her hijabed head, then leaned against him, and as he led her towards the table he said, 'I hope the baby's treating you well? Is this your first?'

'Ah, no, my third,' she answered with a fatigued smile, and rested her haunches against his desk. 'But this one is giving me more trouble than the boys. It's a girl.'

'How many months?'

'Almost eight. I'll do my CS in August, after Ramadan ends, Insha'Allah.' She fell silent to catch her breath, and then glanced around his office with interest before she said, 'Let me not keep you. The favour I want to ask is, we just received an order for fifty books, but the customer wants us to deliver them today. He's in Lagos Island, near Awolowo Road. Your driver told me you pass there on your way home. Can you please drop off the books for me?'

'Of course, no problem, I can do that,' Furo said.

'O se o, Frank.' She reached out and patted his hand. 'Do you speak Yoruba?'

'I don't.'

'Ah-ah, why not? Your girlfriend hasn't taught you yet?'

Furo gave a chuckle at the fishing in her question. 'I don't have a girlfriend,' he said.

'But still,' Zainab stated in a voice from which dangled something hooked. 'You can't stay in Lagos and not speak Yoruba. I'll teach you myself. In fact, you should have a Yoruba name by now. I'll give you one—' She fell silent, a squall brewed in her face, and she clamped her lips in pain as her hand rubbed her belly in commiserative circles. After her sigh of release indicated the spell had passed, she smiled a sweaty smile, and jerking her thumb in the direction of her bump, she quipped, 'I can't teach you anything until this one has come.'

Neither her suffering nor her jesting could quell the irritation Furo had felt at her suggestion of giving him another name, and so he said in a dour tone: 'Take your time. I'm not going anywhere.'

Zainab searched his face, then heaved up from the desk and toughened her voice. 'I'll give your driver the books and the delivery address,' she said. 'The customer will sign the invoice. I'll collect the duplicate from you on Monday. I appreciate the help.' Placing her hands on her belly, she clutched it like a dance partner, and then started towards the door, leaving behind a trail of pheromones that hinted at reproach.

With Zainab gone, Furo packed up his laptop, exited his office, and then halted for an awkward moment at the top of the stairwell and adjusted the bag on his shoulder in readiness to see Tosin, whose voice he could hear below. The first thing he sighted on reaching the bottom step was Headstrong in front of the reception desk. His arms rested on a carton that stood on the desk, and he was listening to Tosin, who was seated. The hum of their voices continued without pause as Furo strode past the desk. He had unlocked the car and was waiting in the back seat by the time Headstrong emerged from the building, the carton in his arms. The entrance door closed in slow motion, pulled back by its own weight, and then it squealed open again as Tosin came through with her handbag in one hand and a carryall in the other. While Headstrong headed for the back of the car to stow the carton, Tosin startled Furo by catching his gaze. Making a beeline for the car, she halted beside the window by which he sat, her silent form blocking the light.

'Hello,' Furo offered. His voice came out squeezed. 'Hello too,' Tosin responded, and as she let the silence do the rest of her talking, he decided to try again. 'Are you travelling?'

'No. I'm spending the weekend in Ajah.'

Furo almost giggled with relief. 'That's my direction. I can give you a lift.'

'I can't thank you enough,' Tosin said drily. When she took a step towards the front of the car, Furo said, 'Hold on a sec,' and throwing open the back door, he leapt out. 'Let me have that,' he said, and grabbed the carryall from her hand. After she climbed into the back seat and scooted over for him, he placed the carryall between them, and then pulled the door shut. At that instant, as if at a sign, Headstrong banged the boot closed.

From the moment the First Lady sped through the gate and Furo stuck his head out the window and shouted bye-bye in response to Mallam Ahmed's waving, nobody said a word. Headstrong stared ahead, Tosin stared at the driver's backrest, and Furo stared at nothing. But nothing soon became that beast of metal and rubber, of bellicose honks and hydrocarbon fumes: a traffic jam at Olusosun. This go-slow was unlike any other, because it crawled past a terrain which stank to the carrion bird-darkened heavens. On those days when the road was clear, cars sped up when approaching the scandalous sight: a range of craters dotted with blazing fires and strewn with galactic garbage. But today, as Furo grabbed for the glass winder, he saw car windows shooting up everywhere. For all commuters unlucky enough to pass by Olusosun, closed windows and breakneck speed were reflex actions, futile efforts against the stink that rose on plumes of smoke from the largest dumpsite in Lagos.

The traffic jam evaporated at the mouth of Third Mainland Bridge. As was usual at this hour, the bridge was free-flowing in the direction of Lagos Island, while the opposite lane, clear of traffic in the mornings, was now gridlocked. Lagoon breeze fanned across the bridge, and as the First Lady hurtled singing into its path, Tosin broke the silence. 'Frank,' she said, and when Furo turned towards her: 'How do you manage with all the stares?' Furo's expression announced his bafflement. 'The other cars, in the go-slow, people kept staring at you.'

'Oh, that.' Furo snorted in dismissal. 'I'm used to it.'

'You have a strong mind,' Tosin said. She looked through the window at the water flashing past, to which she directed the sadness of her next words. 'The way we stare at others, at white people, we Nigerians, it makes me ashamed. It's just plain rude.'

'Yes, I agree,' Furo said. 'But don't let that bother you. There's nothing you can do about other people's rudeness.' As the boomeranging meaning of his words struck home, Furo felt a stab of embarrassment, and he said quickly: 'I'm sure people stare at you too.'

'Me? Why?'

'Because you're pretty.'

Tosin threw him a pensive look, and then glanced forwards as Headstrong said, 'What are you ashamed of, ehn, Tosin? What is the bad thing about looking at oyibo people?'

A spasm of annoyance crossed Tosin's face. It was by force of will that her tone remained civil as she addressed Headstrong. 'Look at it this way. How would you feel if you travelled overseas and everyone stared at you just because of your skin colour?'

'Like a superstar!' Headstrong exclaimed.

As Furo fought back his laughter, he heard Tosin say, 'Victor, be serious.'

'OK,' Headstrong said in a serious tone. 'I will tell you what I think. Number one, your question is not correct. Because why? White people are not like us. They treat everybody in their country with respect. In fact, they treat us black people special. A policeman cannot just go and stop a black person on the street and be asking for his ID card. Not like our own police. Yes, listen, let me tell you! Even if oyibo want to deport you from their country, you can tell them that they're fighting

220

in your village and all your family are dead, that you're a refugee and you want asylum. Because of human rights, they can't do you anything. You see what I'm saying? Those are better people.' Out of breath, he fell silent. But the next instant, while Tosin and Furo exchanged glances in mute accord that Headstrong was something other than compos mentis, he spoke again. 'Abi am I lying, Oga Frank?'

Furo looked at the rear-view mirror. This was the first time Headstrong had spoken his name since their falling-out. And yet, though the question was offered in a genial tone, the topic was the same that had started the trouble on Monday. Furo had no desire to go down that route again. And so he said, 'It's not that simple. But no, you're not lying.'

'Aha!' said Headstrong, and raising a finger, he wagged it in triumph.

With a laugh Tosin said, 'I give up.' She turned to Furo. 'Has Headstrong told you of his plans to migrate to Bulgaria?'

'Poland! Poland!' Headstrong corrected, slapping the steering wheel in emphasis.

'Sorry o,' Tosin said in tone that showed that she wasn't, and as Furo said with a grin, 'He has,' she smiled back at him. Furo deepened his voice in imitation of Headstrong:

'My elder brother lives in Poland—'

'And he's married to a white woman,' Tosin completed.

'Two of una no serious,' Headstrong said. But he laughed too.

And then Tosin said, 'And you, Frank,' but her voice trailed off. After some thought, she reached over the seat back and tapped Headstrong's shoulder. 'Before he bites off my head, abeg, Victor, ask him where he's from.'

'Even you?' Headstrong said with amazement. 'He has shown you his bad temper too?'

'Yes o,' Tosin replied. 'And just because I asked him one small question.'

'What of me? He threatened to make MD sack me!'

'You're joking.'

'I'm not, I swear to God. The dude dey vex like full Nigerian.'

The smile Furo maintained during this exchange was beginning to droop at the edges. Tosin and Headstrong's tones had remained good-natured, but the facts they traded pointed to the opposite in Furo. In the pause that followed Headstrong's last statement, Furo felt he had to speak up to defend himself from the guilt his silence signified. 'Come on guys, I'm not that bad,' he said, his tone conciliatory, and then closed his mouth as Tosin whirled on him and demanded, 'What are you saying? So you mean Nigerians are bad?'

Even as Furo was occupied in weighing what was heavier in Tosin's tone, the mock or the serious, Headstrong decided. He gave a grunt of amusement, looked over his shoulder, and then burst out, 'Fire on, Tosin!' For the first time in days, with a pleasure he had never thought he would feel at the sight, Furo saw spittle flying from Headstrong's lips. And then he felt it on his face, sprinkling his cheeks – as it also did Tosin's face. After Headstrong turned back around, Tosin widened her eyes in pretend horror and wrinkled her nose in real disgust. Acting on a feeling that had been building since Tosin entered the car, Furo reached out, took her hand in his, and squeezed. When she looked at him, he mouthed, *I'm sorry.* She returned the pressure of his fingers. Releasing her hand, he settled back in his seat and said in a chatty tone:

'Actually, I think Nigerians are great people—'

'Let me hear better thing abeg,' Headstrong interjected. 'Just tell us where you're from.'

With a glance at Tosin, Furo said, 'I'm American.'

'*Barack Obama!*' Headstrong yelled, and punched the car horn with both hands.

Approaching the Ikoyi end of Awolowo Road, turn into the last street before Falomo Bridge, then take the first right and keep looking left, keep going until you see a shrine. Seventies Lagos in its architecture, the facade of the two-storey building was neo-rustic. Set in the front fence, which was streaked with creeper plants and daubed with protest graffiti, was a wrought-iron pedestrian gate. From the gate a stone-paved walkway cut through a grass patch populated with scrap-metal sculptures, cracked clay pots and wooden wind chimes. More wood inside, from the ceiling beams to the stocky unvarnished armchairs to the slabs of mahogany trunk that served as tables in the restaurant-cum-bar. Hanging from the walls of the dimly lit chamber were pencil drawings of Fela and canvases of Ehikhamenor iconography and framed photos of Lagos street scenes captured in monochrome. A widescreen TV rested on brackets beside the bar, and from a concealed stereo the voice of Fela bemoaned the lot of the common man. The place was packed with dapper folks engaged in one or more of four activities: talking, drinking, dining, and surfing the web on their pricey gadgets. The scent of incense commingled in the air with tobacco smoke.

Furo walked into this scene, the destination for the book delivery, and after halting underneath the entrance archway to take his bearings, he headed towards the barmaid who welcomed him with a gap-toothed smile. He smiled back before saying, 'I'm here to see Mr Kasumu,' and after the barmaid placed a call on the intercom, she told him that Kasumu wasn't in but he'd left a message that his visitor should wait. Picking up a menu from the stack on the bar counter, Furo turned and approached a nearby table. Headstrong was waiting in the vestibule with the delivery package, and now, in response to a hand signal, he came forwards and placed the carton by the table, and then left to fetch Tosin from the car. Furo passed time by reading the menu, and when Tosin arrived with Headstrong, he offered the menu to her, but she shook her head no. Handing the menu to Headstrong, he asked if he wanted a drink, to which Headstrong replied he wouldn't mind a cold Harp. Then Headstrong opened the menu, and his expression darkened until, bending towards Furo, he said in a scandalised whisper, 'Their beer nah four times normal price! I can't drink here o, the beer won't taste sweet in my mouth. If you give me half the money I will go outside and buy something to eat. That one is better than wasting money in this rich man juju house.' Chuckling at the truth of Headstrong's words, Furo reached into his wallet, then passed across five hundred naira, and as Headstrong stood up with a thank you, he said to him, 'Don't go far. We won't be here long.' But now, for the time being, he was alone with Tosin in a setting that lent itself to romance, and since neither had ordered drinks, they soon discovered they had nothing to do but avoid each other's eyes and eavesdrop on the chatter from other tables, some occupied by couples, none of whom seemed as awkward as Tosin looked and Furo felt. A lull in the room's conversation threw into sharp relief a phrase from the song that was playing at low volume. *Bend your yansh like black man,* Fela chanted angrily, and Furo, with a frisson of apprehension at the prophetic force of those words, shifted his buttocks in his chair, and then glanced towards the clomping footsteps on the wooden staircase at the front of the room, from where emerged a heavyset man with skin so pale it looked bluish. He carried a tripod in one hand, a video camera in the other, and he was dressed like a journalist, in khaki shorts, canvas boots, and sun-faded face cap, with a backpack riding his shoulders. His T-shirt gave him away as an old Nigeria hand. It was plain white except for the large green lettering inscribed across the chest, which read, OYIBO PEPE. Marching past the table, he caught the direction of Furo's eye, and winked at him from a deadpan face.

'That's a man who's sure of himself,' Tosin quipped as she watched the man over Furo's shoulder. Her gaze soon changed direction, a guarded look entered her face, and leaning closer to Furo, she spoke in a whisper. 'I think someone knows you. She's coming this way.'

Syreeta, Furo thought with a sinking feeling, but when he raised his eyes to the woman who halted beside him, the stone loosened from around his neck. The first thing he noticed was that she wasn't Syreeta. The second was that on all ten fingers she wore silver rings in designs that ranged from animal motifs to adinkra symbols. She was slender, bosomy, her dark skin glistened with lotion, and her henna-dyed dreadlocks fell to her neck. Her unpainted lips, now curved in a smile of greeting, were cigarette-blackened. On closer inspection, her air of melancholy was an effect of her large, deep-set eyes.

'Hey you,' she said to Furo. She stared at him as if expecting to be recognised.

Her appearance was too striking for him to have forgotten, so he was sure they hadn't, and yet he asked, 'Have we met before?'

'We have,' she said. 'You're Furo.'

At that name, Furo's heart leapt like a flame. He dug his

heels into the ground in an effort to keep his face from breaking into expression. In a controlled voice, a voice that barely shook, he said, 'I think you've made a mistake,' and turned away in a show of indifference.

'I haven't,' the woman said. Her tone was dismissive with confidence. 'We met a few weeks ago at The Palms. I bought you a drink, a chocolate milkshake. It's me, Igoni.'

Furo remembered. He remembered Igoni. He remembered their meeting at The Palms, and their chat in the cafe, and the favour he had asked that Igoni refused. He remembered talking to Syreeta after Igoni left, and then going home with her. He remembered everything about that night, and the next morning, and every day that had passed between then and now. Such as who had bought him a milkshake. And this woman, this Igoni, wasn't that man.

Not any more.

Furo felt like laughing and crying.

It had happened to Igoni, too.

Somewhere, in some way, it was always happening to someone.

'I remember you,' Furo said at last. He stared at Igoni's breasts. 'You look different.'

'I know,' Igoni said with a throaty laugh. And then, glancing at Tosin, she added, 'Let me not keep you. I just wanted to reintroduce myself.' She opened her clutch purse and drew out a complimentary card, which she handed to Furo. 'We should meet up soon. Please call me.'

'Sure,' Furo said. 'Bye.'

As Igoni walked away, Furo listened to her fading footfalls, thinking at the same time about what to tell Tosin, how to explain away that nuisance of a name. He was more worried by what Tosin thought than he was curious about Igoni, though he wondered even now about how she handled her transformation. He felt less threatened by the appearance of Igoni than by Tosin's overhearing of his old name. She and he were in this together, and maybe someday, when he was better settled into his new life, he might call her up just for the sake of finding out what sort of blackassness was hidden under her skirt. But for now, Tosin had to be answered.

When Furo spoke, his tone was affronted. 'Some of these Lagos girls are so bold you won't believe it. That one approached me in the mall and started chatting me up. I had to give her a fake name to get rid of her.' He paused, watched Tosin's face, and saw the dawning of comprehension. 'That's what I use Furo for – to protect myself from people like that Igoni.'

On his late return to find Furo waiting for him, Kasumu accepted the carton of books with profuse apologies – so sorry to have kept you waiting, I had no idea my order would be delivered by a white man, he said, his words slurring between belches – and he offered to make amends by buying dinner for Furo and his girlfriend. Furo corrected him about the nature of his relationship with Tosin, to which Kasumu responded with insinuating laughter. At Furo's refusal of a meal, and then a drink, even one drink, Kasumu raised his hands in surrender before escorting Furo and Tosin to the car with his matchmaking arms draped around their shoulders and his beery hiccups clearing mosquitoes from their path. After Headstrong unlocked the car and Tosin climbed in, Kasumu grabbed Furo's wrist and dragged him away from the open door, then crowded him against an electrical pole and with frantic whispers offered him the directorship of his NGO for motherless children. The salary and perks would be better than whatever Furo got as a delivery boy, assured Kasumu, and, but of course, everything was negotiable based on his success with attracting donations from all those white people who believed anything they were sold by one of their own. 'What do you say?' Kasumu ended, peering into Furo's face.

'No thanks,' and freeing himself from the hand that gripped his elbow, Furo jumped into the car, slammed the door, and told Headstrong, 'Go, go, go!'

Night had fallen during their wait to deliver the books. Good enough reason, Furo told Tosin, to cancel her plan of dropping off in Lekki to catch a taxi the rest of the way to her sister's house in Ajah. And so, despite Tosin's objections that it was too much trouble, Furo instructed Headstrong to drive on past the turning into Oniru Estate. The weekend traffic to Ajah held them up for several hours, and it was almost eleven o'clock when they arrived at their destination in a moonless neighbourhood where the temporary power cut was approaching three months long. After bidding goodnight to Headstrong, Tosin alighted from the car, followed by Furo, who escorted her through the sea-bottom darkness all the way to the front gate before saying:

'Lest I forget, you can book my flight under Furo Wariboko.'

'All right,' Tosin replied in a tone that sounded preoccupied, and Furo was about to ask what she was thinking when she pre-empted him with the question, 'Do you want to come in?'

During their conversation while waiting for Kasumu, Tosin had told him that the house she was going to was her older sister's, who along with her husband and their toddler son had travelled to Dubai on vacation, and so she would be alone. She didn't like being alone, she said, especially in a house without electricity. That was when it crossed Furo's mind that he could, if he wanted, spend the night with Tosin. But did he want to?

'I do,' Furo said.

It was the weekend. Knowing Syreeta, she wouldn't be home, but he would keep to the rules she had enforced on him. He would call her to say he wasn't returning tonight.

There was only Headstrong to get rid of.

Staring at Tosin through the gloom, Furo said, 'What about Headstrong?'

Tosin caught his meaning. 'He can leave. You can stay the night.'

But the First Lady, Arinze's warning, Haba! property. He had forgotten about that. It was getting too complicated. The more he had to strategise, the less he felt like starting this romance. Besides, under and beneath all, he wasn't ready to show his black buttocks to anyone.

Furo said, 'Arinze warned me not to let Headstrong keep the car overnight. I can give him money to take a taxi home, but I can't drive. If he parks here, how do I move it tomorrow?' Tosin was silent long enough for him to make up his mind, and when she said at last, 'Do you really want to stay?' he voiced his decision: 'Of course I do. But maybe not tonight.'

The drive to Lekki was swift. It was minutes to midnight when Headstrong eased the First Lady into its usual parking spot in Oniru Estate. While Furo waited by the roadside for Headstrong to lock up, he looked around to confirm that Syreeta's Honda was missing among those parked. Headstrong approached, and as Furo held out his hand for the car key, the driver said, 'I think you know Tosin likes you.'

229

'Goodnight,' Furo responded, and they parted, back on good terms.

Upon entering the house, Furo headed straight to his bedroom, dumped his laptop bag on the bed, and was shedding his clothes when the lights blinked out. Standing in the dark with his trousers in his hand, the deep silence before the storm of generators stirred in him a bitter loneliness, so he reached for his phone, and suppressing his misgivings about the line he was about to cross, he dialled Syreeta's number. The ringing was cut off by a blast of dancehall music. 'Hello, hello,' he said without getting a response, and then he raised his voice to a shout, '*Syreeta!*'

Her cheerful tones broke through the din. 'Hey sweetie, are you home?'

'Where are you?'

'I can't hear – I'm in a club.'

'With Bola?' Furo announced with the clairvoyance of jealousy, and Syreeta's loud laughter only enraged him further. Her laughter fizzled out as she caught the whiplash of menace in his answering silence, and when she said in a cautious tone, 'You know his name?' Furo swatted aside her question with his own:

'Are you with him?'

A teasing note slithered into her voice as she retorted, 'Are you jealous?'

'Just answer me!'

'No,' she said, and through the percussive music he caught her sniff of derision. 'The weekends are for his wives.' She paused. 'I only see him on Tuesdays.'

'But you go out every weekend.'

'I go clubbing with friends. I thought you knew that.'

'Friends?'

'My friends,' she said sharply. Then she relented. 'Anyway, Baby's here.'

'How come you've never invited me?'

'But I have. Think well. The day rain fell.'

'I don't remember.'

Her sigh retained its force over the distance. 'Why are we discussing this now?'

'You're too busy to talk to me?'

'Come on, Furo.'

'Don't call me Furo!'

He, too, was shocked by his yell.

Syreeta spoke. 'Something's wrong. I'm leaving right now. I'm coming home.'

'No, no, don't. I'm sorry I shouted at you. You can stay.'

'Thank you, lord and master,' Syreeta said with a strained laugh. The bass of a hip-hop tune filled the interlude. 'But I'll come back early, tomorrow morning. I'll take you out. We'll go watch a movie. Would you like that?'

'I guess,' Furo said. 'Sorry again I shouted at you.'

'That's OK. You're just a big baby. My—' Her words got drowned out as a male voice shouted above the partying noises, *Oi, Sy, get off the bleedin' phone*, and then she said hurriedly, 'I have to go now, see you tomorrow,' and ended the call.

The first time Furo's phone rang on Saturday, it was Tosin calling. Syreeta was in the bathroom, she was preparing to take him out to get a pizza and catch a movie, and so, despite Tosin's hints about the freeness of her day, he kept the conversation brief. On the drive to City Mall, his phone rang a second time. 'Aren't you answering?' Syreeta asked, and after he replied that he didn't know the number therefore it must be work so it could wait till Monday, Syreeta turned the radio volume back up. His phone continued to ring in the restaurant, and in the time between departure from La Pizza and arrival at The Galleria, a trip of twenty minutes, it rang four more times, all of the calls from the same number that had pestered him during his meal. While Syreeta bought tickets for a showing of *The Avengers*, Furo stood in line for popcorn and sodas. In the dim theatre, as they walked up the aisle, his phone rang once more. Hurrying down a middle row to the accompaniment of irate shushes from nearby moviegoers, Furo arrived at the velvet-padded wall, sank into a seat and, after thrusting the popcorn buckets at Syreeta, he finally gave in to the caller's doggedness by switching off his phone.

'You should call that person back, it must be important,' Syreeta whispered as the movie started.

On the drive back to Oniru Estate, while waiting at a red light on Ozumba Mbadiwe Avenue, Furo was startled by a pained moan from Syreeta, who, when he looked, was doubled over the steering wheel but straightened up as soon as the amber flashed. After the Honda darted forwards, she responded to his queries by saying it was her period and she had forgotten to buy tampons and so would make a stop at a pharmacy in The Palms. 'I'll be quick, wait here for me,' she told him after she parked, and leaving the engine running and the air conditioning blowing, she set off for the Rubik's Cube building of the mall. When Furo lost track of her pink blouse in the rainbow crowd that swarmed the mall's entrance, he took out his phone and powered it on. The start-up tone was interrupted by the beep of an incoming message and, tapping the keypad with cold sweaty fingers, he saw that the SMS was indeed from the same number that had been SOS-ing him. As he read and reread the words, '*I know who you are & I'll tell everyone the truth soon, just wait and see!*' the suspicion he had been suppressing ever since his pizza breakfast was ruined by the persistent ringing rose from his belly in seafood-smelling waves of nausea.

The message was clear. No doubt about it, someone had found out the truth about him. Thirty green blinks of the dashboard clock were all Furo could bear of the eternity of suspense, and in that time he cursed Obata, he ruled out Tosin, absolved Arinze and dismissed Headstrong, so in the end, with his heart beating in his fingertips, he took up the phone, dialled the malignant number, and was still waiting for it to ring when a female android voice uttered into his ear, '*The number you have dialled is unavailable at the moment. Please try again later. The number you have dialled is unavailable . . .*' He dialled again and again, all the while hoping the automated response was the usual falsehood from network providers to conceal their shoddy service, but at last, on sighting Syreeta in the distance, he gave up trying and accepted that his fate was that of a crying child whose mother couldn't sleep. No rest for him until he cut off all ties with his former life.

Monday night in bed, during a lover's quarrel over nothing, Syreeta said to Furo, 'Why are you such a big dictator?' to which he replied smirking, 'Because you're a small country.'

They laughed together.

Night, Tuesday, alone at home, sprawled on his back in Syreeta's bed, surrounded by the ghosts of her woman smell, a book – *Are You Ready to Succeed?* – clutched in his hands, eyes smarting from the friction of reading, Furo looked up and sighed, 'Igoni.'

He had been thinking of her lately.

On Wednesday morning, Headstrong drove Furo and Arinze to the airport in Arinze's Mercedes jeep, and when they arrived at MMA2, after alighting with his pigskin suitcase, Arinze told Headstrong, 'Head straight back to the office and hand over my key to Tosin.' The sternness in Arinze's voice caught Furo's attention as he lifted out his borrowed carpetbag, and the driver's response, in a grovelling tone, 'Yes, sir – journey mercies, sir,' made him wonder what he was missing in the exchange. Then Arinze led the way into the bustling terminal, where long lines of people waited at the airline counters, and Furo nodded yes at his boss's suggestion that they check in at separate counters to halve the chances of both missing the flight due to encounters with glitchy computers or bungling personnel. Before parting they agreed to meet afterwards in the departure lounge. Furo joined a queue, and after long minutes of watching in fuming silence as cowards in front of him yielded to incursions by bullies from behind, he got his chance at the counter. He handed his passport to the neckscarved ticketing agent, who shot him a searching look and stared down at the passport, but looked up again at his face, and then called over a colleague, a man. Furo's cheek muscles suffered to uphold his mask of unconcern as the two agents consulted in whispers while glancing from the passport to him, and at last the male agent laughed, gave Furo a cheery thumbs-up, and walked away shaking his head. After checking Furo in, the woman passed him his passport and boarding pass before saying by way of apology:

'I've never seen a white man with a Nigerian name before.'

Furo passed through immigration without incident, without so much as a curious glance from the bored-looking female officer who thumbed through his passport, and without the body scanner detecting his metal buckle. A male officer, green-bereted and rubber-gloved, noticed the buckle while conducting a body search of the spread-eagled Furo, and then told him in a listless tone that he should have removed it, but when Furo apologised and dropped his hands to his belt, the man waved him through. Smiling with relief at this casual confirmation that he had passed all the tests, that his passport was authentic and so was he, the passport holder, Furo strode to the conveyor belt, picked up his property, and after putting his shoes back on, he ambled off in search of Arinze, whose waving hand he shortly spotted from a seat row beside their boarding gate.

Their flight was two hours late, and yet Arinze was unbothered by the wait. He reassured Furo by reminding him that the meeting with Yuguda was set for five o'clock, and he disclosed that the only reason they were catching a morning flight for a forty-five minute trip was because he had expected the delay. As he and Furo rose from their seats and joined the surge towards the boarding gate, he said to Furo, 'Trust our airlines too much and you'll be late. Fly them long enough and you'll be dead.'

After the plane landed, as Furo followed the press of bodies down the aisle towards the exit, he passed by a first-class-seated woman in Bob Marley braids who clasped a mixed-race toddler in her arms. The child, on catching sight of Furo, stretched her toy arms in welcome and cried out in a tone of rapture, 'Dah-dah!' Furo was startled, but the mother more so. 'Jeez!' she exclaimed with a shamed expression, and tightened her grasp on the squirming child.

Even a baby, when surrounded by people of identical skin colour, is prone to the error that one slight difference constitutes an individual.

This was Furo's first visit to Abuja. Arinze, though, was a recurrent visitor, a frequent flyer to Nnamdi Azikiwe International Airport. This showed in the confidence with which he navigated the domestic terminal and ignored its patches of happy-green synthetic turf scattered with gold-painted stones and forested with mirrored pillars. Holding his gaze away from the funhouse glitz, Furo walked beside Arinze with mimicked poise. Arinze's regular driver was waiting for them outside the terminal building. On the long drive to their hotel, he indulged the man's talkativeness, while Furo, alone in the back seat, stared out the taxi's windows at the broad avenues of the Federal Capital Territory, the brutalist architecture of the government buildings, the unfamiliar Sahel skyline, the swathes of greenery awash in sizzling sunlight, the roadside cameras which the driver pointed out as the latest effort against the machinations of those fanatic murderers who hated books. After the driver ran out of Boko Haram bombings to report, Arinze craned his neck over the seat back and asked Furo what he thought of Abuja.

'I don't know,' Furo responded. 'It's different from Lagos.'

'That's true,' Arinze said. 'Lagos was built from blood and sweat and raw ambition. Abuja was designed as a playground for the rich. I'm sure some will argue that there's nothing wrong with that, but when the rest of your country is popu-lated with desperate people, your dream city hasn't much chance of retaining its character. Some of the worst slums in Nigeria can be found on Abuja's outskirts.'

'Just like where I live!' the driver exclaimed. 'I've done taxi business in Port Harcourt and Lagos, and I've driven buses in Ghana, in Liberia, but Daki Biu is the worst place I've ever lived. They don't have water anywhere.'

On that topic the taxi driver took off again, as he described his experiences in the fantastical shanty towns of the West African coast – Makoko in Lagos, Rainbow Town in Port Harcourt, Old Fadama in Accra, and West Point in Monrovia, all of which existed by waterways, unlike the dustbowl of Daki Biu – and he didn't exhaust his nostalgia or empty his windbag of stories until the car drew to a stop at their destination, a multi-storey hotel in the upmarket district of Wuse II. There was no time to dawdle as their meeting at Yuguda's residence was drawing near, and so Furo and Arinze dropped off their luggage in their rooms, then sat down to a quick lunch with the driver in the hotel restaurant. In Furo's hurry to finish his outsized meal, he spilled banga soup on his pearl-grey necktie, his favourite, the only one he had brought along on the trip, but Arinze said in response to his muttered apologies, 'Don't worry, I'll wait for you.' They left the restaurant, Arinze and the driver heading for the car, while Furo ran to the elevator and rode up to his sixth-floor quarters. His equilibrium restored by the wet patch on his tie, he joined them in the car, and they set off for Asokoro just after four. All through the drive Furo faced the open window so the car's draught would dry his tie.

Yuguda's residence, from outside the towering fence with its gate of armoured steel, looked like a wartime castle. But once the gate opened, the property took on the splendour of a summer palace frozen in time. Royal palms lined a driveway the length of a small-town main street, and shimmering beyond the trees were landscaped gardens. The terrain climbed from the gate in a natural slope, at the crest of which stood a two-storey Greek-columned house. It was built of marble blocks, floored with marble-chip, and a marble frieze of Arabic script circled the salon that Furo and Arinze were led into by a liveried old man – who told them to wait standing up. An instant after the double doors closed behind him, a lady emerged through a gauzy portière on the far side of the room and padded towards them, her sari swishing. Halting in front of Furo, she exchanged glances with him in mutual appraisal, and his eyes locked on her thin lips as she said, 'How do you do?' Her Ivy League accent bore the faintest trace of a Hausa intonation.

'I'm fine, thank you,' Furo replied. He waited for her to greet Arinze in turn, but she again addressed her words to him. 'My father will join you soon. Do you want your assistant to be present at the meeting?'

Furo reddened in embarrassed silence, which he finally broke with the stammered words, 'He's not – this – Mr Arinze is my boss.'

'I see,' the woman said, her tone unruffled. 'Please have a seat, both of you.'

The two men sat down, and then Yuguda's daughter, with no sign of her thoughts on her haughty face, rang an electric bell. It was answered by a boy-child who was clad in the house colours, and after she gave some instructions in Hausa, he left and soon returned carrying a tray bearing two glasses, a bottle of orange juice, and a jug of iced water. Yuguda's daughter waited till the guests had been served drinks before taking her leave, and as the portière fluttered into place, Furo whirled to face Arinze and started to apologise for the lady's slight, but Arinze cut him short. 'Forget about it. We came here for a reason. Let's focus on that.'

The meeting with Yuguda lasted half an hour; the agenda was hammer-on-nail straightforward. Upon Yuguda's arrival, he exchanged quick greetings with both men before shooting Furo some questions about his accent and where in Nigeria he was from, and then he switched his attention to Arinze and asked for twenty titles on how to start a business. At a nod from Arinze, Furo pulled out the prepared booklet Arinze had given him the previous day, and holding it steady on his knees, he read out the information in a loud clear voice. The instant he finished, Yuguda said: 'There are no Nigerian books on that list.' The truth of this observation startled Furo into uncertainty, but Arinze's tone was assured as he replied, 'You're quite correct. We only sell world-class books. None of the Nigerian titles were good enough to make this list.' Yuguda riposted with: 'How are my people supposed to run businesses in this country when all the books you're putting forward are based on foreign models?' The combative phrasing of Yuguda's question convinced Furo the deal was lost, déjà vu Umukoro all over again, and yet his disappointment took nothing away from his admiration for the fighting spirit displayed by Arinze's answer. 'I strongly believe, sir, that the best business practices, like the best books, are universal. I have nothing against business books by Nigerians. But until they measure up, my company will never sell them.' Yuguda's comeback was swift: 'Measure up to what – whose standards?' 'Yours,' Arinze said. 'The Yuguda Group deserves only the best.'

When Furo and Arinze stood up to leave, Haba! Nigeria Limited was nine million naira richer. Yuguda approached and shook their hands for the first time, first Arinze's then Furo's, and while holding Furo's hand, he asked for his business card. Furo handed it over with an apology for forgetting to do so earlier, and after Yuguda glanced at it, he rang for an attendant to show them out.

On arrival at the hotel, before Arinze dismissed the driver for the night, he instructed him to pick them up at six o'clock the following morning for the drive to the airport. Entering the hotel lobby, Arinze invited Furo for a drink at the lounge bar, and though he ordered soda water for himself, he gave Furo leave to drink the bar dry of alcohol if he so wanted. 'You've earned it,' he said. 'You did a fantastic job today. We both did.' Furo thanked him for the compliment, and then told the barman he wanted soda water, too. The drinks came, Arinze rushed his down, and after spending a few more minutes chitchatting with Furo, he retired at five minutes to eight. He had to tuck in his four-year-old daughter by telephone, he told Furo.

Alone at the bar, Furo wondered what to do with the rest of the night. With Syreeta in faraway Lagos, he realised this was the freest he had felt in a long time. The vestiges of his old life still haunted the old city so different from this one where no one knew him, where everything was new, even the mistakes a man could make. Abuja was pioneer land, a frontier city, though the founding fathers were all rich folk and politicians. The bandits here rode Bentleys and settled fights with money blazing. Returning to the thought of what to do, Furo checked his wallet and saw that he had only three thousand naira left from the ten thousand he'd borrowed from Syreeta the previous week. Without money he couldn't afford the freedom Abuja offered, he admitted to himself as he put away the wallet. He couldn't even afford the only leisure that came to mind.

In Abuja after dark, the ladies of the night were everywhere. Or so it had seemed to Furo on the return journey from Yuguda's residence. He kept catching glimpses from the car window. Flashes of colour under lightless streetlamps, flickering shadows in the shades of trees, the glow of cigarettes at the mouths of lonely streets, and gathered in fearless packs by the gates of noisy nightspots: the shapes slouching, prancing, gesturing, the painted faces turned to passing cars with a longing that tugged the purse strings. Even at the hotel, as the taxi slowed in front of the gate, Furo saw the women staring at him.

Furo struggled awake to the ringing of his mobile phone, and reaching across to the bedside table, he answered it blind.

It was Yuguda.

'Hello, sir,' Furo stuttered, and sat up in bed, wiping the sleep from his eyes.

Yuguda was waiting at the Piano Bar in the Transcorp Hilton. 'Come alone,' he said before hanging up.

Furo checked the time. 11:43. Night.

He dressed and dashed from his room. Six floors down, the hotel lobby was empty except for the concierge, who Furo asked for a taxi, only to be informed that he would find many in the car park. Crossing the lobby, he remembered with dismay that he had only three thousand naira on him, besides having no idea where the Transcorp Hilton was or how much it would cost to get there. The one thing he was certain of was that the taxi drivers would charge outrageous fares, especially from a white person at midnight in a city as expensive as Abuja. He arrived in the car park without yet having found a way out of this quandary. After identifying the oldest taxi, a Mitsubishi Galant with a new paint job, he drew up to the car and saw that the driver was asleep on the bonnet. He roused the man with a soft tap on the knee, stated his destination, and, bracing himself for the haggling to come, asked what the fare was. 'Maitama, abi?' the driver said, rubbing his eyes with both hands. 'Your money is five hundred.' Without a change of expression or the slightest pause to give the man the chance to regain his senses, Furo said, 'Let's go, I'm in hurry,' and climbed into the front seat. The driver slipped in and told Furo to wear his seatbelt, then started the engine. As the car nosed through the gate, several streetwalkers straggled into view. One of them whistled at Furo, and on impulse, he whistled back.

He was beginning to like this city.

Arriving at the Transcorp Hilton, Furo entered the lobby to find it as crowded as a crocodile watering hole in drought season. Jostling in the electric atmosphere were Senegalese kaftans, gold-braided military dress, European designer rags, and the people who wore these at midnight. Lights poured from the vaulted ceiling, and the mirror-bright floor turned the world upside down. A black automobile, polished to a gloss, was on display near the lobby's centre. The banner beside it announced to onlookers that they were ogling a BMW Gran Turismo. (The tyre rims clearly impressed more than the zeros on the price tag.) But Furo only had eyes for the Piano Bar, which he found in a recessed wing to the left of the lobby. Walking down the short flight of steps, he looked round at the gathered drinkers, and spotted Yuguda. He was in Furo's line of sight, seated in one of the tub chairs arranged in *ménages à trois* around the lounge, and the cocktail table in front of him held a bottle of Irish cream and a martini glass. A woman lounged behind him. Curvaceous in a sleek sequined gown, her crimson lips opened and closed over the microphone in her hand, and her other hand stroked Yuguda's shoulder as she serenaded him to the plonk of piano music. Yuguda seemed less austere in the jeans and tucked-in T-shirt that had replaced the brocade babariga he'd been wearing at his house. He was almost a different person, this one beaming with catlike

242

pleasure as the chanteuse planted a kiss on his shaven scalp.

During their meeting earlier, Yuguda hadn't once smiled. Not even when he joked that whenever Furo spoke he had to look at him to confirm he was a white man. His smile now faded as he saw Furo approaching and, raising an imperial hand, he waved the woman away, and then motioned Furo towards a chair. His first words, 'Do you like the Irish?' threw Furo into a tizzy of misapprehension until he kenned it was a drink he was being offered. At Furo's perforced assent, Yuguda crooked a finger, and an eager waitress arrived the same moment the chanteuse ended her song. The waitress had finished pouring Furo's drink and was refilling Yuguda's from the Baileys bottle when the chanteuse, purse in hand and high heels clicking, swept past their table with a goodnight aimed at Yuguda. He didn't respond or glance at her, and neither did he speak to Furo until the waitress curtsied away, whereupon, reaching for his glass and raising it in a toast, he announced in a solemn tone, 'To the future.'

One thing was unchanged about Yuguda: he got straight down to business. 'I have a job for you,' he began and took a sip of his drink. The glass left a line of cream on his upper lip, and after he licked it clean with a flick of his tongue, he balanced the glass on his chair's armrest, his fingers gripping the stem to hold it in place. 'My GELD project is a CSR investment that has the potential to become a PR disaster.' Furo nodded with rapt attention. 'On paper I have the team to execute the project, but this is Nigeria.' Yuguda paused for several seconds. 'I need someone at the helm to keep everyone on their toes,' he said at last. 'I need a leader who can command respect and inspire fear. That person is you.'

Inspire fear, command respect – me? Furo thought with a

mental burp of surprise, but he remained silent out of a stronger feeling of sacramental reverence. After all, any place where the highest is sought is a holy ground – and what was higher than the pursuit of happiness? Here was Yuguda preaching salvation, happiness on earth, thus he was worthy to be Messiah. Besides, the whole truth was, Furo was thoroughly tired of stewing in perpetual brokedom.

Yuguda took another drink from his glass, and bending forwards, he set it on the table before continuing. 'You'll get respect because you're white. They'll fear you because you're Nigerian. You know the tricks, you understand the thinking, you speak the language. You can figure out their schemes, and you'll know how to block them. Catch me some scapegoats and I'll deal with them, then you just watch the others fall into line. You'll get some training, of course. We'll send you for management workshops, leadership seminars, all of that. But fear and respect – and power – those are your real tools. Your power is half a million naira per month. You'll also get a car and a furnished apartment in Asokoro.'

While Yuguda was speaking, Furo picked up his glass and raised it to his dry lips, and he only stopped sipping when Yuguda finished. In the silence that followed Yuguda's words, Furo replaced his glass on the table, and after burping into his cupped hands, he said:

'I don't have a degree.'

'That's not important,' Yuguda replied. He stared at Furo from under his heavy eyelids. 'But you attended university, didn't you?'

'I did.'

'In Nigeria?'

'Yes.'

Yuguda's nostrils flared with pleasure. 'I knew it. You are the right man.'

Furo spoke again. 'I don't have a Nigerian passport.'

Yuguda's surprise showed in the length of his pause. 'Why is that important?' he asked.

'I just want you to know that I can't prove that I'm Nigerian.'

'I see,' Yuguda said, and seemed to weigh his words before asking, 'Do you want a Nigerian passport?'

'Yes.'

'That can be arranged,' Yuguda said in a firm voice. And then, glancing down at the face of his platinum wristwatch, he asked, 'Anything else?'

'When do you want me to start?'

'Next Monday – the sixteenth. The GELD office opens then.'

Furo bowed his head in calculation. Unlike the other offers he'd received since joining Arinze, this one was impossible to ignore. This was what he had dreamed of since graduating from university, what he had worked so hard for all those long years of submitting job applications. This was the better he deserved: a job that gave him a chance at independence. Yuguda's offer came with real money, a new car no doubt, and a house of his own in Abuja. There was no question in his mind about the meaning of this opening: it was the road to a final break with his past. He had no choice but to take it. And since he could find no doubts about embarking down this path, then better to take it running, grab it by the horns, and ride it bucking into the future. At this decision, Furo raised his head and spoke.

'Thank you for your offer. But there's one thing. I want seven hundred thousand a month.'

'That's too much,' Yuguda said. He stared Furo down before adding, 'There's free accommodation. Few of my employees get that.' Furo remained with his eyes lowered and his thoughts guarded, and so Yuguda pressed on. 'Your car is a brand-new Kia Cerato. It also comes with a driver.' At Furo's stubborn silence, Yuguda spoke again in gruff tones: 'I'll give you six hundred thousand. That's my best offer. You should take it.'

'I'll take it,' Furo said. 'But there are some things I need to settle in Lagos before moving down here. I'll need some cash. Can I collect an advance on my salary?'

'Of course,' Yuguda said. 'I'll send instructions to the Lagos office. You can go there on Friday. *Shikena?*' As Furo nodded in agreement that that was all, Yuguda checked his watch, and then rose from his seat. Furo leapt up to accept his handshake. 'Welcome on board, Mr Whyte.'

When Furo and Arinze landed in Lagos on Thursday morning, Kayode, the second driver, was waiting for them. After they entered the Mercedes, Arinze asked, 'Where's Victor?'

'He has travelled,' Kayode said.

'Travelled where? I wasn't told he was going on leave.'

'Not leave, sir. Victor has travelled to Poland. Tosin said that he called her last night from inside the aeroplane.'

'That's a surprise,' Arinze said and sank back in his seat.

Furo was likewise taken aback by the news of Headstrong's departure. He hadn't suspected that his driver was so far gone in his scattershot schemes. But he had done it, he had turned his silly notions into dogged action, he had walked his talk, and for all his efforts, for all the laughter he had endured and the mockery he had ignored, he was right this moment arriving in his Polish dream. *So that's how it is*, Furo thought.

One day a man was a talkative dreamer stuck in a dead-end rut, a laughing butt who spat defiance at his country and yet grovelled before his bosses, and the next day he was living his dream. If a moral existed in Headstrong's story, then it was loud, clear, and staring Furo in the face.

Coincidences are messages to the blind.

Furo now understood that. His twinges of guilt at his own impending exit were eclipsed by the realisation that the news of Headstrong's departure, the fact that it was coming as he was going, had deeper meaning. It was yet another lesson in letting go, in moving forwards.

Arinze stirred in the comfort of the jeep's leather seats. 'Furo,' he said, 'we'll have to find you a new driver. I'll put Obata on it this morning. Hopefully we'll get a replacement by Monday. I can—' He fell silent as Furo's phone started ringing. Furo pulled the phone from his pocket, saw it was Syreeta calling, and after rejecting the call, he said to Arinze:

'Please continue. I'll call the person back.'

'I was going to say I can drop you off tonight. Oniru Estate is not far from where I live.'

'Thank you, but you don't have to.'

'No, no, it's nothing.' Arinze fell silent, and Furo hoped he was finished, but he spoke again. 'Look at Victor, he's worked for me for almost two years, and yet he left without even saying goodbye.' He paused in reflection, then exhaled a long sigh before saying, 'One of the reasons I will never leave Nigeria is because, in this country, anything can happen.' Cocking his head at Furo, he smiled into his eyes. 'And you, Mr Whyte, are a perfect example of that.'

They arrived at the office, and while Kayode parked the Mercedes alongside the unwashed First Lady, Arinze told Furo to come for a meeting after lunch so they could discuss the delivery of Yuguda's books. They alighted from the car, walked together into the building, and Arinze mounted the stairs while Furo stopped in the reception to talk to Tosin. Headstrong was sly and Yuguda was a godsend, he agreed with her, and he'd missed her too but couldn't do lunch today because he had a meeting with Arinze. By the way, he needed to discuss something with her. Could she come up to his office as soon as she was free?

In the upstairs hallway, by the door of the lavatory, Furo came upon Obata talking in low tones with Iquo, who watched his mouth with paralysed raptness. Obata hushed as Furo drew close, and he swept past them without speaking, then changed his mind and returned to where they stood. They met his gaze with mirrored expressions of enmity. It was all he could do to stop himself from laughing in their faces. He felt so far beyond their small-minded intrigues that he almost pitied them for the putrid pleasure they got from thinking that he cared. And yet, despite not caring, he couldn't help wondering how long it would take Obata to go running to Arinze with the news. Maybe today, probably tomorrow, but whatever, he would be long gone by then. And so, staring hard at Obata's face, Furo spoke:

'I know it was you who sent me that text message.'

'What message?' Obata's voice and face, insouciant and deadpan, gave nothing away. Furo hadn't expected anything else, nothing better than cowardice and denial from a man who bullied those in his power, who only raised his voice to those who couldn't fight back, and who gossiped with underlings in the open. Furo was sure it was Obata who had sent the message, for who else could it be; and he didn't doubt this conjecture enough to waste his time proving it. Besides, it didn't matter any more. 'You can deny it all you want,' Furo now responded. 'But I just wanted to tell you that you're right. I'm not Furo Wariboko.' At this confession, Obata and Iquo locked wide-eyed glances, and Furo turned away to leave them to their chewing of that bone.

Entering his office, Furo found nothing changed, yet everything appeared different. Lifeless, drab: like the soul had flown from the place. In the light of new ambition, the cosy office was exposed as a dingy jail. Furo set about clearing all traces of his sojourn in the first office he'd called his own. He gathered the printed documents that strewed his desk and ripped them up, tore out the notepad sheets he had jotted on and crumpled them up, emptied the trash can into a plastic bag and stuffed that in his travelling bag, replaced the books he had taken down from the bookshelf to read, and all through this methodical cleanup he brooked no nostalgia, allowed no regret, he felt nothing but excitement about his resolution to spend his last days in Lagos in Tosin's bed. By the time she knocked on the door, he had made up his mind against confiding his plans to her. Instead, he said, after taking her hand and drawing her inside:

'I want to kiss you.'

'What?'

'I said—'

'I heard you the first time.'

'Can I?'

'No.'

'Tosin—'

'No.'

'What are you afraid of?'

'I'm not afraid.'

249

'No one will enter. I'll lock the door.'

'I said no.'

'Don't you like me any more?'

'I'm not answering that.'

'Please, just one kiss.'

'Stop it. This isn't the time for that.'

'What about tonight? We can go to your sister's house. I'll spend the weekend.'

'You're being insulting.'

For a man accustomed to getting his way, a woman's refusal is a flapping flag on the ramparts of a besieged fortress. Thus Tosin's resistance only made her more desirable to Furo. Each time she puckered her lips in no, it took all of his control to obey her. He wanted to close the gap between them. He wanted to crush her mouth beneath his, to suck the pureness from her lips, to thrust his tongue into her goodness, her decency, her refusal to be corrupted.

Tosin took a step backwards and crossed her arms over her chest, this movement forcing Furo back from the brink. When she spoke, the sharpness of her tone punctured the fabric of his parachuting illusions. 'I have to go back to work. What was it you wanted to tell me?'

That he was going to give her the gift of his final days in Lagos. It was straightforward. It should have been. She liked him, she had told him so. He didn't understand what was wrong. 'I don't understand,' he said. 'What's wrong, Tosin?'

The flash he caught in her eyes cleared his confusion. It was a simmering blend of disappointment and distress. No one had ever looked at him that way before. Not since he changed.

Tosin was dangerous.

She saw through his whiteness to the man he was.

For a kiss, a weekend fling, she wanted a better person than he was willing to be.

It was time to leave.

'I'm sorry,' Furo said. 'I got carried away.' He spun around, walked to the desk, picked up the laptop bag, then returned to her side and held it out to her. 'I wanted to return this. I don't need it any more.' Tosin reached for the empty bag, and the tension between them grew, but it was the wrong kind. Furo knew this was the end of him and her. There was nothing else he owed her, nothing he wanted from her. Except that he had no money for the journey back to Syreeta.

'I also wanted to borrow some money,' he said. 'Two thousand naira, if you can spare it. I have to go out to get something and I don't have enough on me.'

'My purse is downstairs,' Tosin said. She moved towards the door, placed her hand on the knob, and then turned to face him. 'You just want what you want. It's only about you.' When Furo said nothing, she walked out and closed the door.

Minutes later, he left the building.

In his office, arranged on the desk, a Zinox laptop, a Toyota key, a Haba! ID card, a pack of business cards, and a note that said: *Thank you for everything.*

It was late evening when Syreeta walked through the front door with a load of shopping bags. She kicked the door shut, dumped the bags on the kitchen floor, flicked the light switch, and then spun around as Furo said from the darkened parlour, 'There's no light.' A relieved sigh rushed out the kitchen doorway ahead of her. 'You frightened me!' she said as she reached the settee, and then she bent down, brushed Furo's forehead with her cold lips, and sank down beside him. 'Why are you home early? I didn't see your car outside. And I called you this morning but you didn't pick up. I have some news to tell you. Why are you home early?'

Furo said, 'I also have some good news for you.'

'You first,' Syreeta said.

'I have a new job. It's in Abuja. They'll pay me six hundred thousand!'

In the darkness, Furo couldn't see the expression on Syreeta's face, but he heard her sharp intake of air. And then she said in a small voice, 'In Abuja?'

Furo leaned closer. 'What's wrong? Aren't you happy for me?'

'I am. Of course I am. You should earn what you're worth.' She seemed to swallow the rest of her words. 'When are you leaving?' she said at last.

'Sunday,' Furo replied. 'I start work on Monday.'

Silence stretched rubber band-like between them. With a sudden movement, Syreeta broke it. 'Congrats,' she said. She started to rise from the settee, but Furo flung out his arm and found her wrist. She fell back into the seat.

'You haven't told me your own news,' he said.

'I'm pregnant.'

A drum began to beat in Furo's head. *Oh no*, it said, *not now*. The same words over and over, diastole and systole in the pumping rhythm of life.

'And yes, it's yours,' Syreeta said.

Oh no.

'I want to keep it.'

Not now.

'I'm keeping it.' She stood up from the settee and whisked into the bedroom.

And now? Furo asked himself, looking around in the darkness.

Syreeta had him trapped. She might have planned this, or maybe she didn't and the pregnancy just happened, but either way, she had him where she wanted him. Rooted in her life. Implanted in her womb. Sprouting a life he would have no control over. A child was a mistake he couldn't make. For many reasons, but above all for the same reason he had left his family behind. Suffer alone and die alone. Strike a path through life without worrying who stands in the way of your blind blows. On this island of existence, the survivor is the man who understands he is trapped. Syreeta, for all her uses, was another trap.

Furo knew the reason Syreeta had picked him up on that second day of his awakening. Perhaps he had always known. Lagos big girl, with her sugar daddy and her snazzy jeep and her apartment in Lekki, but missing the white man to give her entry into the mixed-race babies club. Why else had she fed him, fucked him, pampered him, if not for the reason she now carried in her womb? She was a grasper who had stretched out her hand in help, so how could he expect there to be no catch to her giving? Despite her slips into compassion, Syreeta was successful at her lifestyle exactly because she focused on what she got out of it. In spite of the fondness she bore him, she was tough enough to endure the moral itches and emotional blows of her fancy prostitution, her Tuesdays-only concubinage. Regardless of his complicity in her condition, the Syreetas of this world could withstand its knocks without changing themselves into something else. The hardness of intention was stuck deep within them, within her. And so she knew what she wanted all along. Same as he had always known what he wanted from her. A roof over

253

his head, food to hold in his belly, human comfort to ease his loneliness, and some money to borrow. Nothing he couldn't pay back. Nothing she couldn't give. But what she wanted in return, what she was demanding, this pound of baby flesh, he couldn't, no, wouldn't give.

Furo resolved to stop Syreeta. He wouldn't allow her to bring a baby into the world he was building for himself. It was a risk he couldn't take. His black behind was trouble enough to live with, impossible to be rid of, but a black baby would destroy any chance of a new life. Of that he was certain, the baby would be black. Furo's baby. Not Frank's. Not his.

Because he was, frankly, white.

That question answered, he turned his attention to the problem. As he saw it he had two choices. To go to Syreeta this instant and confess the truth, show his buttocks as proof, and try to convince her that the child she was carrying was not the one she was expecting.

But the truth was not his way.

And so he stood up from the settee and went into the bedroom and told Syreeta she couldn't keep the baby. *Why not?* I want us to do this properly. *What do you mean?* Come with me to Abuja. Give me time to save some money. Then we'll get married. *What did you say?* I'm asking you to put your past behind you. I want you to be my future. I want to marry you.

Moments later, during lovemaking, she accepted his proposal, though without words, her body moving beneath him like a wave of yeses.

In the morning, after Syreeta left for the clinic, Frank rose from her bed, strolled over to the fridge and took out a carton of lychee juice. Holding the carton in his right hand as he drank, he scratched with his left a stubborn itch on his buttocks, then turned around and stared over his shoulder into the mirror. His buttocks had healed, the scabs had fallen off, and the effects of the bleaching creams – the lightening, the reddening – had worn off.

His ass was robustly black.

He turned away from the mirror and strode off to the bathroom. Afterwards he got dressed in his blue T.M. Lewin shirt, his black trousers, his brown shoes, and after pocketing his wallet and his white handkerchief, he stuck his plastic folder under his arm. Picking up the phone that Syreeta had lent him, he switched it on and ignored the *beep-beep* of text messages tumbling in as he copied out Yuguda's number, before deleting it from the phone along with every number he had saved. And then he walked out the front door with nothing, and left nothing behind except, in Syreeta's bedroom, arranged on the bed, a phone, a house key, a ripped-up passport, a folded pile of clothes, and a note that ended with: *I'll pay back what I owe.*

METAMORPHOSES

'Everything changes, nothing perishes.'

—Ovid, *Metamorphoses*

Friday, 13 July, I got the call from Frank. (The first thing he said was, 'It's me. I've changed my name. I'm Frank.') He was about to leave Lagos for ever, but he had two nights that he could spend with me, if I wanted to talk. I gave him directions to my house in Surulere and he arrived in the afternoon. At the knock, I opened my door, and there he was, dressed the same as the first time I saw him, the only difference being that he carried a new travelling bag instead of his old folder. As we exchanged greetings, there was some awkwardness about if we should shake hands or buss cheeks, but that was settled in favour of cheeks. He came in, I led him to the sitting room, and after we sat facing each other in the sofa, he said, 'I still can't get over how good you look.'

I found Frank attractive. He was slim, straight-backed, with a self-assured posture. The contrast between his soft red hair and his hard green eyes was striking. His nose seemed long when he was facing me, but with his face in profile, it fitted his features. His skin changed with his moods. When he was calm, it was porcelain smooth; when he was agitated, it grew patchy; and when he laughed, it became a healthy red. The first time we kissed, I thought it felt different because it was the first for me, but later I saw that his lips were thin, barely there, different from mine. Before kissing, we talked. He asked the usual questions men have about women's bodies, and also those other questions, the same ones I had for him. How did it feel to be different from what I had always been?

Did I have any regrets about my transformation? How did my family receive it? Whenever I batted his questions back at him, he found ways to evade them. *I'm asking you*, he said. *Before I answer that, I have another question.* And then, when I asked him if he ever thought of seeing his family again, he said:

'Can I see your breasts?'

I felt no shame with Frank. Even more, I wanted him to see me for what I was, same as I needed to see through him. He was the hero of a story that had set me free, and knowing him felt no different from knowing me. Which was why I stood up and removed my blouse, then shed my bra, and when I sat back down, after he drew closer, he looked and touched, we kissed and told. I found out about Syreeta, Tosin, Arinze, Yuguda, Headstrong, Obata, all the lives that had shaped his own in the twenty-five days since I first saw him. He entrusted me with his story, and as his confessor, I made no judgements, I only listened to absolve. No one's path is laid out from birth, we must all choose our own through life, and what greater gift is given a person than the chance to see the destinations where the roads not taken might have led you. I will admit that Frank had hurt some people. He had used them and moved on. Same way he was using me as a spittoon, a receptacle for all the emotions he had bottled up during an ordeal that few could understand as well as me, his fellow traveller down this path of self-awareness.

By this time we had moved to my bedroom and were side-by-side in bed. It was late at night, the city had gone to sleep, and the silence skulking outside the windows had forced our voices into intimacy. I had most of my story, but Frank wanted something else. His caresses had grown bolder over the course of our conversation, for hours I'd stopped his hands from reaching under my skirt, and with each peak of excited groping he had shed more of his clothing until all he wore were his boxer shorts. I wasn't ready to let him go all the way, though he tried until sleep came.

At sunrise, I discovered his black ass. And when he awoke, after he called me back to bed and slipped his hand between my legs, he, too, found my secret.

It is easier to be than to become. Frank should have known that. His shocked reaction to my penis proved that he didn't. Which was why, after he hurried into the bathroom, I phoned his sister. Yet I felt like a fraud, a woman playing God. Of all the flaws his story had exposed about his character, his most tragic was trusting in me. His lack of understanding for our shared fate, his black ass and my woman's penis, and his unchanging selfishness towards me and everyone else, those weren't enough reason to excuse my own meanness of spirit. I had got my story, and he, too, deserved to get what he wanted. For my own redemption as much as his, I had to give him the choice of ending his story as he wanted. And so, when he returned from the bathroom and began putting on his clothes with his buttocks turned away from me, I confessed:

'I went to Egbeda.'

He lifted his head and saw the guilt in my face as clearly as I saw the fright in his.

'I met your mother, your sister – everyone.'

As he stared at me with eyes darkened by comprehension, a small part of my mind couldn't help noting that the expression on his face was just right for describing how Syreeta must have looked when she returned from the clinic to find an empty apartment.

'I called them. They're coming here.'

Frank had never answered me about seeing his family

again. He didn't need to, because the choice he made when given a second chance was more telling than anything he could have said. After I shared the news of his family's coming, he finished dressing in silence, then picked up his travelling bag, walked to my front door, and stood beside it for one hour and six minutes until the knocking started and his mother called out, 'Furo – are you there? Come and open the door.'